i

MAELSTROM
PART II

iii

Rip Converse

MAELSTROM
PART II

The characters and events in this book are fictitious. Any similarity to real persons, living or dead, is coincidental and unintended by the author.

1st eBook edition: November 2019

Maelstrom Part I: ISBN 978-1-64669-248-4
Maelstrom Part II: ISBN 978-1-64669-249-1
Maelstrom Part III: ISBN 978-1-64669-250-7
Maelstrom (the whole): ISBN 978-1-64669-251-4

*To my father Courtland who died far too young and my mother Joey
who lived on; both wonderful people whom I admire greatly.*

Many thanks to my wife Louise for cover design, social media, encouragement and emotional support in this my first work, to MH Syin for her help with editing and proofreading and to a small group of beta readers, whose careful reading along the way helped me to complete this work. Thank you all.

Table of Contents

Prologue

In Part I of Maelstrom Ryan Cunningham decides to leave
Sippican; the small, New England, coastal town that he grew up in.
One day he simply realizes that the dreams and values that he'd
pursued and attempted to emulate for 37 years, were those of his
parents and grandparents. There was nothing wrong with them, they
simply weren't his. His plan was to set off on a voyage of self-
discovery aboard his classic wooden sailboat Parthenia heading first
for the Caribbean via Bermuda and then on to wherever and whatever
felt right. He'd planned on taking this trip alone.

Six weeks prior to his departure he meets 27-year-old Tory McCane
and her two children Jan and Willy, 12 and 5 years old respectively.
Tory is a single mother in recovery from drug addiction who is trying
to rebuild her life and re-acquire the trust of her children. She asks if
the three of them can sail South with him. He agrees, and in the weeks
leading up to their departure, she works side by side with Ryan to
prepare the boat for sea. They become close but not intimate.

On the first leg of the trip from Massachusetts to Bermuda they
endure a two day long, offshore storm with hurricane force winds.
Ryan goes overboard at the height of the storm due to an equipment
failure and ends up dragging through the water underneath the stern
from his safety harness. Tory is ultimately able to recover him, and
they make it safely to Bermuda.

Their closeness blossoms into a relationship that is both intimate and special for both of them. Several weeks later, Tory's Grandfather passes away. Tory leaves the children with Ryan in Bermuda while she returns to the U.S. to offer support and consolation to her estranged Grandmother and to bury her Grandfather with whom she enjoyed a very supportive and close relationship with.

The day she is to return to Bermuda an amoral, international, drug smuggler named Edward enters St. Georges Harbor on his mega-yacht, White Lady. Edward and his crew of maritime misfits are carrying 180 kilos of premium Peruvian cocaine in a false bottomed water tank. Ryan, who has encountered Edward once before, vocalizes his suspicions about the White Lady to a customs inspector. Edward is then subjected to an intense customs search. Despite the thorough search, Bermuda Customs does not find the cocaine. Edward saw Ryan talking to the customs inspector prior to the search, however, and decides to make Ryan's life a misery.

Tory returns to Bermuda. Edward has her followed and discovers that she's a recovering drug addict. He briefly kidnaps her, injects her with drugs and before releasing her stuffs a bag of coke into her shorts and tells her that if she says anything to anyone, he will slaughter Ryan her and the children. Edward expects that re-awakening Tory's addiction will ultimately destroy their family unit.

Chapter 1

As soon as she was below, Tory peeled off her top and examined her nipple. She gently gathered it between two fingers and bent it downwards in the direction of the cut and started to shudder and sob. Edward's actions had been very calculated and scared her on a primal level. Her nipple would heal without stitches, but she knew she would go to her grave remembering the moment he'd pinched it between the shiny scalpel blade and his thumb. She sat there for several minutes sobbing quietly, confused not just by the whole incident, but also from the effects of the cocaine. Eventually she pulled herself together enough to realize that if Ryan ever found her like this, he would be uncontrollable and demand to know what'd happened. For the time being, she couldn't let that happen. She believed absolutely what the animal on the yacht had said about slaughtering all of them and for the moment her maternal instincts overrode her anger and fear. She quickly gathered her blood-stained top off the floor and buried it at the bottom of the galley trash and then ran into the head where she showered carefully and then applied two Band-Aids across the nipple to stabilize it. She prayed the separated area would reattach itself with time and not become infected. As she dressed in clean clothes and brushed her hair, she felt the first effects of the drug wearing off and sat down, overwhelmed at the atrocity committed on her.

'I have to pull myself together!' she thought and reached down to pick her shorts off the floor to throw in the hamper. As she did so she remembered the bag of coke. She sat down again at the salon table and took the baggy out. Inside there was more coke than she'd ever seen in one place at one time and she absently fondled the rocks through the plastic. She wanted things to be as they'd been several hours ago, but the addict in her had other plans and suggested that it was probably a good idea, 'just in case', to hide the cocaine instead of flushing it. Although she didn't at this point plan on using any of it, better safe than sorry and she put it behind one of the bulkheads in the head. The significance of her keeping the coke instead of throwing it out was not lost on her.

Clifton had been laying in the cockpit with his head at the top of the ladder since she'd returned and whined softly in empathy at the sound of her crying. Tory looked up at the sound and climbed the ladder bringing her head level with his. She desperately needed a hug from someone and reached out to the big dog. Clifton seemed to see right into her soul, and he licked the tears off her face with unusual gentleness.

"Oh Clifton, I'm not a bad person. Why is this happening to me?" She began crying again. Clifton lay there as she hugged him. The sound of Ryan and the children broke the spell only moments later. Clifton heard them first and lifted his head at the sound of their voices. Following his lead, she peeked around the corner of the cabin house and could see them at the float getting into the dinghy and knew she only had a few more minutes to pull herself together and retreated to the head to wash her face again. The shot that Edward had administered earlier was giving way to the crashing depression that always followed the coke high and she was certain that Edward or one of his men was watching the boat. She knew if she went on deck feeling as she did, she would fall apart. With almost no conscious thought of the consequences she grabbed a Bic pen off the salon table and rushed back into the head. Once inside, she opened the cabinet behind the toilet, reached behind

2

the bulkhead and withdrew the coke. Then with a deft skill borne of years of experience, quickly crushed one of the smaller rocks on the countertop with a deodorant can, pulled the ink cartridge out of the pen and then using the empty barrel as a tube, inhaled a large line of the crushed cocaine into each nostril. It was as if only hours instead of years had passed since her last snort and she rocked her head back with the pleasure of the pure coke smacking into the sensitive tissue in the back of her nose. Almost immediately her fear and depression were replaced by the artificial courage and elation of the coke. Now she could face the three of them. She quickly ran a brush through her hair again before facing Ryan and her kids.

"So how did it go?" She asked from the companionway hatch as they pulled alongside. She tried her best to sound nonchalant and normal.

Willy was first to reply. "Oh mom, you should have seen that thing. After we rigged it, Mike took us for a sail, and we raced against one of the other ones at the Dinghy Club. There must have been a million square feet of sail on that thing."

"Yeah mom, it was pretty cool. You should have been there," Jan added as if everything Willy said needed to be verified and played down.

Ryan was still tying up the dinghy with his back to her and Tory waited expectantly for him to turn around. If she could just hold it together when their eyes met for the first time, she was sure she'd be all right. Ryan turned. "Hi babe."

Tory looked up at him with the beginnings of a smile on her face, and then her lip started to tremble, and she turned away.

Ryan came over, sat down next to her, and put his arm around her. "Are you OK?"

"Yeah. Why?" she replied keeping her face averted.

He reached over and gently turned her head towards him. "You look sad. Is everything alright?"

'Christ, how could he have noticed so quickly?' she thought to herself. She knew her eyes were still puffy and he was so tuned into her he must know that something is wrong.

"I guess I've just been having kind of a delayed reaction to the whole week in Massachusetts. You know, thinking about Pops. I've been a little sad is all."

Ryan hugged her and pulled her head onto his shoulder. "I know, it's tough. You'll probably have rough days for a while yet. Anything I can do?"

Tory felt a tremendous guilt for the lie she'd just told him. It was her first one and a way of being that she thought she'd left behind forever. "I don't think so, I think I just have to go with it. Thanks for asking though."

"Do we have anything special planned tonight?"

"Not that I can remember." she replied. "I think I'd just like to hang out though, I don't feel like doing much of anything."

"No problem. Just let me know if there's anything I can do."

"I will."

As the dinner hour approached the cocaine wore off again and Tory found it increasingly difficult to sit still. The high she'd experienced earlier had not provided the same good feelings as her highs of the old days, but the depression and paranoia that followed were everything she remembered, and more. As the afternoon wore on the boat seemed to get smaller and smaller and she started to feel as though everyone was watching her. She couldn't read for more than a few moments at a time, didn't feel like cooking, and whenever one of them engaged her in conversation she'd cut it short because she was sure they'd somehow know that she'd been using. She knew her body language was jumpy, and she had trouble looking anyone in the eye. Jan had always been able to tell when she was high and until she figured out what to do, she couldn't bear the thought of any of them knowing that she'd fallen off

4

the wagon. Edward may have introduced the drug into her system, but when she'd gone into the head and had those few lines after, there had been no one standing over her. She could rationalize all she wanted, but bottom line, she blamed herself for the subsequent use.

"Are you cooking tonight, or am I?" Ryan finally asked.

"Would you mind? I really don't feel that well."

"Sure, no problem. Do you want anything in particular?"

Tory felt like she was going to explode from the tension of even this simple conversation and tried to think of some way of escaping. "I don't think so. My stomach's been bothering me all afternoon and I feel kind of punk."

"You want something for your stomach?" Ryan asked.

"Yeah, that's a good idea, but I'll get it. Maybe I just need to sit on the toilet for a while." Tory hurried for the head knowing that the moment she was alone that she would use again to relieve the anxiety. She crossed the cabin quickly and shut the door, grateful for the respite from everyone's imagined scrutiny, quickly reached behind the bulkhead and removed the coke. Then she sat down on the closed toilet and just stared at the bag for almost a full minute. 'After these lines, the rest goes down the toilet,' she told herself firmly. 'I still don't know what I'm going to do, but this shit sure as hell isn't helping.' She took a rock out of the bag and when she heard Ryan getting out the pots and pans in the galley for dinner took advantage of the background noise and crushed the rock and quickly snorted it.

As Ryan cooked, he thought about Tory's behavior all afternoon. She'd seemed sad about something, but she also seemed unusually nervous and distracted as if something else were troubling her. He was trying to give her the space she obviously wanted to work something out, but when she hurt, he hurt, and decided to bring it up with her later. Whatever it was, there wasn't any reason she should have to go through it alone.

5

In the head, Tory snorted several more lines and after carefully cleaning up the coke residue off the counter she brushed her hair and returned to the salon, her thoughts of throwing out the coke forgotten. She felt like she could deal again. Anxious to cover her earlier withdrawn behavior she came up behind Ryan and put her arms around him. "I feel a little better now. It must have been something I ate."

Ryan continued to chop vegetables as she spoke, grateful for her touch. "I'm glad you're back. I know you've been kind of distracted all afternoon and I didn't know how much I'd missed you till now. You're touch feels good."

"I'm sorry I've been so distant. You know how important you are to me right?"

"Yeah, I know."

"And that I'd never intentionally hurt you," she continued.

Ryan turned. "Of course, I know that. What do you mean?"

"Nothing. I just wanted to say that." She kissed him warmly.

Tory hardly touched her food but kept it together for the next two hours as the others ate and then got ready for bed. Ryan climbed into Willy's bunk to read him a story and Jan lay in her own bunk, also reading. Tory went up on deck to try and think the whole situation through. She sat in the dark in the cockpit and looked across the water at the White Lady. Although the darkness made her feel less visible to the boat across the harbor, she knew they'd be watching for any signs of movement and the blackness seemed to heighten her increasing sense of isolation and panic. The lines she'd had several hours before had worn off again and she knew she had to think of something to break the cycle that Edward had so cleverly instigated. Her physical compulsion for the drug was like a sleeping giant that had been reawakened. She'd been an addict long enough to know that her use would go on and on until she either ran out of drugs, or something disastrous happened to

MAELSTROM

the four of them. Neither alternative was acceptable. She sat for almost an hour going round and round trying to think of some way out, becoming more depressed as the drug gradually wore off. Finally, with depression overwhelming her she peered down into the main cabin. The only light still on was the one in Willy's bunk where Ryan had fallen asleep reading. Jan's light was out, and Tory assumed that she'd also fallen asleep. As quietly as possible she climbed down the companionway ladder. Clifton was at the bottom and groaned softly as she gained the foot, looked up at her and yawned once before putting his head back down and closing his eyes. Tory knew where all the worst creaks in the floorboards were and continued to creep across the cabin, avoiding those areas until she got to the head door. She surveyed the cabin once more and, satisfied that everyone was still asleep, eased the door open, entered and closed it softly behind her. The door was only three quarters of an inch thick, so she kept her movements as quiet as possible, wishing that there was some background noise in the main cabin as there had been earlier, to cover the sounds as she got high again.

Jan was not asleep as Tory had assumed and watched through half closed eyes as Tory crept across the cabin and into the head. Because of her normally quiet nature no one seemed to notice that she too had been quiet all afternoon and she'd just stuffed her suspicions like the old days, afraid to speak and confront, feeling somehow responsible as children often do when bad things happen to their parents. Jan felt like someone was crushing her chest or choking her, because she had suspected, just minutes after returning to the boat, that Tory was high again. She'd spent too many years terrified of Tory's next binge not to be hypersensitive to the slightest change in her mother's behavior and although she wasn't sure what she was high on, she knew there was some poison cursing through her. She felt totally powerless in addition to feeling responsible. What had they all done wrong for Tory to want to use again? In what way had she failed her mom?

7

She listened intently for the next several minutes hearing occasional movement in the head, and then after a pause, the distinct sound of Tory snorting the lines. It was a sound she knew well, and she hugged herself as a tear rolled down her cheek. 'I don't know if I can go through this again,' she thought to herself. 'No matter how I am, how I act, how much I try to help she goes back to it. Maybe she'd be better off if she didn't have the responsibility of me and Willy and maybe she could finally get sober and find some peace.' That's all she thought her mother wanted, peace, from whatever demons drove her. Jan knew she wasn't a bad person and knew that Tory loved them very much, but she also knew how much pain Tory had been in over the last few years and she just wanted her to have some happiness. "Yes, maybe she'd be better off without me."

Assuming everyone to still be asleep Tory decided to stay in the head a few minutes longer and have several more lines and didn't hear Jan as she quietly slipped out of her bunk and up onto deck.

Jan stood in the stern for several minutes quietly crying to herself, wishing life weren't so unfair and afraid she would lose her nerve if she waited too long. Finally, she climbed over the stern rail, hung from it, and dropped as quietly as possible into the still, black water.

Below, Tory leaned back against the toilet seat with her head back, reveling in the rush of the almost pure cocaine. Totally into the high she heard nothing as Jan swam slowly off into the dark.

Jan didn't really know how she'd do it but assumed if she swam long enough, eventually she would tire and slip under the water; out of her own pain and able to take some away from Tory. She continued to swim towards the darkest area of the harbor.

MAELSTROM

Clifton did not stir when Jan crept past him and up the ladder, but when she slipped into the water, the sound registered in his mind for what it was, and he pulled himself to his feet. As their self-appointed guardian he took his responsibility for the two children very seriously. Anything out of the norm got his special attention and the sound of the little girl climbing the stairs into the dark of night and going into the water, was wrong. Jan made very little noise as she swam away from the boat, but he continued to concentrate on the diminishing sounds. Following his instinct that something was wrong, he tentatively put his front paws on the ladder. Normally Ryan or one of the others would have lifted his hind section at this point to help him the rest of the way up the ladder and he looked expectantly back into the cabin, but no one was there to help. He hesitated a moment more, desperately wanting to get on deck to check on Jan but scared of falling down the stairs. He whined once softly and looked back over the cabin again and realized that he'd have to do it on his own and raised himself as high as possible on his hind legs. His front paws were only two steps from the top of the ladder. He knew he would only have to jump once if he did it just right. He hesitated again for just a second, squatted down several inches on his hind quarters for maximum thrust and jumped, hoping his hind legs would find purchase on the second step that he would need to push him up and over the lip and into the cockpit.

Only one of his hind legs found the step and he almost tumbled back down; the wind knocked out of him from smashing onto the top stair. After a brief struggle he was able to locate the step with his other rear leg and bounded the rest of the way and into the cockpit.

When Clifton stumbled and scrambled up the remaining steps, Ryan woke immediately. He opened his eyes and rubbed the sleep out of them before looking over the cabin. Where were Tory and Jan? He eased himself over the edge of the bunk trying not to wake Willy and walked to the ladder and climbed up, expecting to see Jan and Tory in the

9

cockpit. When he gained the deck his eyes slowly adjusted to the dark and instead of finding Tory and Jan, he saw only Clifton looking intently into the dark night.

"What's wrong boy?" Clifton looked back at him and then back at the water and barked sharply several times. Ryan walked to Clifton's side in the stern and strained his eyes into the night to see if he couldn't see what had upset him so. He noted that their Zodiac and Mike and Jill's dinghy were both still securely tied off their stern. "Clifton, shush! You're going to wake everyone up."

Below, Tory was also startled out of her drug-induced state at the sound of Clifton bounding up the stairs. Expecting the sound would also wake everyone else, she hurried to hide the cocaine and pen shaft behind the bulkhead before heading out into the cabin. Ryan and Jan were no longer in the cabin and she could hear Clifton barking on deck. As she started up the stairs to see what was going on, she met Ryan on his way down.

"Oh, there you are. I heard Clifton and went up on deck and didn't see you or Jan when I got up here. I couldn't figure out where you were,"

"What do you mean me or Jan?" Tory looked back into the cabin towards Jan's empty bunk. "She's not up here with you?" A sick feeling started in her stomach.

"No, check the foc'sle bunk."

Tory ran quickly to the bow. "Oh God Ryan, she's not here!" She immediately assumed Edward or one of his crew had somehow taken her.

Clifton barked a few more times, whined, and then jumped over the side. He immediately started swimming towards the area where he'd last heard Jan.

"Christ, what's going on?" Ryan asked in alarm after hearing Clifton land in the water.

"They must have taken her!" Tory screamed.

"Who? What? You're talking crazy Tory?"

"The men, the men on the boat!"

Ryan was perplexed by what she was saying but knew he had to get Clifton back and grabbed the cockpit flashlight and jumped down into the dinghy. As he untied it Tory ran on deck.

"Oh Ryan, it's all my fault. They must have her."

"Tory, get a grip! What men? What boat?"

Tory just pointed towards the White Lady.

Ryan still couldn't figure out what she was talking about but knew he had to hurry before Clifton became lost in the night. "Wait here, I'll talk with you as soon as I get back. I've got to get Clifton."

"No Ryan. They'll kill you!"

"Look I don't know what's wrong with you, but I have to go now or I'll lose him." He started to row away from Parthenia.

"No Ryan!" she cried after him.

Jan had a two-minute head start on Clifton, but he was a good swimmer and caught up with her about 100 yards from the boat. Jan had heard him earlier when he'd started barking and lost some of her earlier resolve at the sound of his bark. It was so dark and lonely in the water and all at once she was scared and not at all sure she wanted to die. She heard Clifton paddling up behind her just as she was starting to panic and turned as he swam alongside. Years before, when Clifton had been a puppy, he'd scratched Ryan on the back when the two of them were swimming. Ryan had since taught him not to swim up on top of people and when Clifton reached Jan, he started swimming a tight circle around her as he'd been trained. The sight of the big friendly dog was all it took for Jan to end her earlier thoughts of suicide and she gratefully grabbed onto his collar with one hand. Clifton immediately turned back towards the boat dragging Jan behind him.

Ryan turned the dinghy in the direction he'd seen Clifton head and turned on the small flashlight hoping he hadn't gotten far. 'Christ what a crazy night!' he thought to himself. 'And what the hell was Tory raving about men off the boat taking Jan?' As he rowed, he started to wonder if Clifton's jumping over the side had something to do with Jan's disappearance. He himself had once sleepwalked over the side of a boat as a child and started becoming more concerned wondering if the same thing might have happened to Jan. 'But she would have woken up when she hit the water,' he thought to himself. 'unless she hit her head. Shit!'

Ryan only had to row about 50 yards before picking up their forms in the beam of the flashlight. They were about 25 yards off his starboard side. He angled the dinghy towards them. Jan raised her free arm as his light swept over them and he quickly rowed the remaining distance. He grabbed Jan and lifted her into the dinghy first and then the two of them reached back over the side and hauled Clifton in. As soon as Clifton was safely aboard Ryan reached around and hugged Jan tightly to his chest. "Are you alright sweetie?" Jan just looked up with teary eyes, nodded yes, and hugged him back.

Tory was almost hysterical with relief as they pulled back alongside Parthenia. Ryan passed Jan up and Tory gathered her in her arms. "Are you OK baby? They didn't hurt you, did they?"

Jan looked at her mother confused. "Who, Mom? What're you talking about?"

"The men. The men off that boat." She pointed again towards the White Lady.

Ryan had lifted Clifton through the safety lines and was himself climbing over the lifelines as Tory pointed to the White Lady across the harbor.

"Tory, she was all alone out there. Why don't we all just go below and see if we can't figure out what in the hell is going on."

Once they got below Tory helped Jan out of her wet T-shirt and bundled her up in a large beach towel and then again hugged her. She'd been convinced that Jan had been taken by the men on the White Lady and swore to herself she would not let either child out of her sight again until all of those men were either in prison or dead. She felt doubly responsible, however, because when Jan had ended up in the water, she should have been there for her, but had instead been in the head getting high.

Ryan sat down on the bunk across the table from the two of them and looked pointedly at Tory. "Somebody please explain to me what's going on?"

Tory still wasn't sure what to say. So much hinged on her next few words and she did not want to lose their love and trust. For the moment she remained mute and just stared back at Ryan not really knowing how to begin. Ryan waited a few moments and then turned to Jan. "What about you. What are you doing out swimming alone at 11:30 at night?"

Like Tory, Jan was afraid to speak. She didn't want to add to Tory's problems or stand between her and Ryan. She too remained silent.

"For Christ's sake! What's going on? You, you're ranting on about men off a boat across the harbor kidnapping Jan, and she's out taking midnight swims, alone in the dark! Somebody talk to me," Ryan demanded.

Tory had shared many of her darkest secrets while in the treatment center, but nothing she'd ever confided before had the implications and possible immediate effects on her and her family, than what she was about to tell. She searched her mind for the right words to begin, and just couldn't find them. Instead, all the built-up strain and pressure of the last 12 hours spilled out and she burst into sobbing tears.

"I was kidnapped, threatened, shot full of fucking drugs, sexually molested and threatened with all of your deaths if I said a word! That's what's going on."

Ryan didn't know what to say at first. At this point about the only the thing he did believe for sure was that somehow Tory had gotten her hands on some drugs and was in some sort of delirium.

"Tory, why do you think these men would want to hurt you? The whole story seems crazy, I mean we're in Bermuda. If any of what you just said is true these men will be put away for the rest of their lives! You're not making any sense."

"I know it doesn't make any sense. That's what I'm trying to tell you! That's the scariest part of it all. No one in their right mind would do what these men did. That's the kind of people we're dealing with, they're insane!"

"But what could their motivation be? It's crazy!"

"I know it's crazy, I'm the one who was assaulted and threatened. What Edward said didn't make any sense. When I asked him why, he told me it was because of you, that you had somehow insulted or annoyed him as if that were justification to assault me, drug me and threaten the lives of all of you. You tell me, what did you do to this man?"

Ryan thought back to his only direct contact with Edward at the restaurant. It didn't make sense. The only part of the story that rang at all true was that Tory had in fact gotten some type of drugs from the men on the boat. He thought back over her erratic behavior all afternoon and what she was claiming. He knew she was committed to sobriety and for another moment tried to give her the benefit of the doubt. "All right, why don't you start at the beginning."

Tory knew he didn't believe her. "Ryan, I can tell you don't believe me. You've known me for months now, been around me day and night, seen me up, and seen me down. I finally have my kids back and I'm in love with you. Why would I endanger all of that to get high again? I have my life back for Christ's sake!"

Ryan hung his head and muttered, "I don't know Tory. That's what addicts do. They fuck up their lives and everyone else's."

Tory was deeply hurt and enraged at the same time. "Ryan, how do you explain this?" She roughly pulled her shirt up over her head, reached behind, unfastened her bra, and held her injured breast out for him and Jan to see. Then she carefully peeled off the Band-Aids and tenderly pressed down the nipple so that the two of them could see where it started to separate from the breast. "He did that! He put a fucking scalpel to my breast and threatened to cut my tits off if I said anything to anyone! Do you think I'd do that to myself?"

Tory's indignation and anger were undeniably genuine to both Ryan and Jan. He knew right away that no woman would ever do something like that to herself and that she was telling the truth. A black fury started to build in him as he tried to comprehend what type of person would do this to Tory and without another word he got up, climbed the ladder into the cockpit and started throwing life-preservers and sails aside as he dug his way down to the box beneath in which his pistol and shotgun were stored.

Tory was too startled to move for several seconds when he rushed on deck. 'How could he just leave without saying anything?' When she heard him starting to throw things around in the cockpit she got up off the settee and climbed the ladder far enough to see what he was doing.
"What are you doing Ryan?"
"I'm getting my gun! I'm going to kill him!"

"No, no, no, no! You can't! Please stop. We have to talk! You have no idea what he's like, and there are at least five men on that boat! Please Ryan, stop. We have to talk first. No one is angrier than I am about this whole thing but please don't rush off and do anything stupid. There's too much at stake!"

"Tory, this is unbelievable. We can't let someone get away with something like this."

"I know, but please Ryan just come back below so we can talk and figure this thing out."

Ryan stood there seething for several more seconds and then reluctantly went below and listened to the whole incredible series of events that had befallen Tory that afternoon.

Chapter 2

R yan was disbelieving at first, then angry and ultimately silent as he became convinced of Edward's sociopathic nature. His first inclination was to commit a simple, impetuous act of vengeance, but Tory's fear was legitimate and he soon realized that he was dealing with something very different than a simple schoolyard bully as he got the details of what had happened and what was said to Tory. There were obviously no rules or limits to what this man might do, or how far his power extended. Any action he took would ultimately expose both Tory and the children to further danger, especially if he were unsuccessful. This was underscored to him as he watched Jan's face as she listened to Tory. She was clearly frightened to death of the men on White Lady. Jan's reaction as much as anything else reminded him that this was not just about Tory and him, more importantly, it was also about Willy and Jan.

"Jan, I'm so sorry you had to hear this, but I want you to know that Ryan and I will not let anything happen to you or Willy, no matter what."

Jan spoke with a voice older than her years. "It's not your fault mom and in a way I'm almost glad this happened."

Ryan and Tory looked at each other.

"I thought you'd gone back to the drugs on your own. This way it's not your fault."

"Thanks Jan, that means a lot to me."

Ryan interrupted. "Jan, there's one thing I don't understand that sort of got lost in all of this. What you were doing in the water?"

Jan hung her head. "I don't want to talk about that right now. It's not important anyway." At another time both Ryan and Tory would have pursued the subject further but considering their current situation they didn't press.

"So, what're we going to do?" Ryan asked again.

"We've decided that you're *not* going to motor over there with a gun and shoot the prick. There are too many of them and where would that leave us even if you were successful? You'd be arrested by the Bermudians for murder and spend the next 25 years in prison and that would still leave his men for us to deal with. And we can't go to the authorities. This whole thing would be too hard to prove and with my past record of addiction I would have credibility problems. Also, we'd still be vulnerable to retribution. Can we just run?"

Ryan thought for a few seconds before responding. "I suppose we can, but what's to keep him from following us and attacking us. I think it's even more likely once we leave Bermudian waters. Something tells me that getting you hooked on drugs was not the end of his plan. From what you've told me about him he'll want to somehow know that he's hurt me specifically. To do that he has to be close to us. I think he'll definitely follow us if we try and run."

"Is there anything we could do to his boat to keep that from happening, you know, so that at least we could get a head start?" Tory asked.

Ryan thought hard about it for several minutes. "I think have an idea."

***

18

MAELSTROM

Paulo was bored and tired of watching the Parthenia. Edward didn't seem to have a specific plan. If it were left up to him, he'd simply rape the two women, kill everyone and steam off into the horizon. Or, just steam off into the horizon. It didn't really matter to him nor did he understand Edward's obsession with the American. He preferred they leave as soon as possible for a city so that he might avail himself of all-night barrooms, child whores and all the other good things available in a decent-sized metropolis. He picked up the binoculars and scanned the Parthenia. Although the night was overcast, the ambient lights from the shore made it possible to see Parthenia a half mile off. He was looking at them when their interior cabin lights winked off. He looked at his watch noting that it was 1:05 a.m., sat back down in the plush captain's chair behind him, assumed they'd finally gone to sleep, and quickly followed suit.

***

Ryan turned out the last light in the salon and waited for several minutes before creeping out into the cockpit. He wanted to give his night vision an opportunity to acclimate and stayed as low as possible in case they had night vision glasses. Tory followed, also staying low in the bottom of the cockpit. They spent several minutes looking over towards White Lady with critical eyes as to their distance, orientation, ambient light and the lights still burning aboard her.

"Our swing is better than I'd thought." Ryan commented, referring to the direction Parthenia trailed from her anchor relative to the White Lady.

"There's also no moon, so you shouldn't have to worry about being seen in the water until you get right up to them," Tory said.

19

Ryan opened the lazarette and pulled out his mask, fins, diving knife, underwater light, scuba tank, BC and lastly a coil of polypropylene line that he'd saved years before. Polypropylene is seldom used on sailboats due to its high stretching coefficient and poor coiling characteristics, but he hated throwing anything away. The cheap line would be perfect for his current use. Then he climbed down into the Zodiak floating alongside.

"Do you really think this will work?"

"Yeah, I do. The question is, how much of a head start it will give us. That's what's tough to figure. All right, pass all the equipment down to me and then help me get the tank on."

Tory did as he asked. Ryan slid over the side of the Zodiak into the water as Tory steadied it. He had her pass the coil of line to him in the water along with the underwater light.

"Turn on my tank, would you?"

Tory reached over the side and turned the large black knob on top of the tank. Ryan took several test breathes through his regulator.

"And pass me that coil of yellow line."

"I guess I don't have to tell you to be careful?" she said.

Ryan laughed. "No, you don't, but I will. Remember, keep the glasses on them and if you suddenly see a lot of lights and movement on board get yourself and the kids into the Zodiac as fast as possible, wake up Mike and Paula, and all four of you get to a police station, pronto. And remember to be careful leaving their place also. From what you told me he's had someone watching us from the shore and for all we know they're on Mike's property right now. As a matter of fact, if you do have to run for it take my pistol with you. Do you know how to use it?"

Tory shook her head.

"It's the kind that all you have to do is point and pull the trigger. Be careful with it. I put it in the second drawer in the chart table. Hopefully you won't need it. Be back shortly."

MAELSTROM

After checking his regulator and wrist compass Ryan dove beneath the surface and started the long swim to White Lady. He surfaced twice on the way to check his bearings and distance and came up under the huge hull about 15 minutes later. He had approximately 45 minutes in his tank at the start and figured he could safely spend about 10 of them under the White Lady before starting back. He didn't need the underwater light he'd brought with him as White Lady had under-hull lighting in the stern. Ryan supposed it might have something to do with boarding passengers or swimmers off the stern, but to his way of thinking it looked an awful lot like the purple undercarriage lights favored by pimps and kids driving shit-box *Hondas* with loud mufflers. He wasn't complaining tonight though because it provided brilliant light underwater near the propellers. It was this area that he intended to sabotage.

Before beginning he used the buoyancy compensator on his BC to adjust his float rate to slightly negative so that if he were to hold motionless in the water, he would tend to sink rather than float. He wanted to avoid banging the hull in any way as he worked. He was certain that the sound of his metal tank hitting the steel hull would be heard throughout the ship. Ryan swam to the first of the four large propellers. He started with the outboard port one and tightly wound several feet of polypropylene line around the shaft between the prop and the bushing the shaft went through. He planned on using the boat's own power to wind and bind the four massive propellers and counted on the fact that as the polypropylene was wound tight, it would stretch and eventually melt, making it all the more difficult to un-foul. He worked quickly, mindful of the time and wound all four shafts with lengths of the plastic line. He made off the bitter end of each piece of line right to the propeller blade it was wrapped around so that as soon as each screw started to turn it would stretch and pull the rope tight, around, and hopefully into the cutlass bearing of each shaft. He finished up within

21

his self-imposed time limit and after checking his compass he re-oriented himself in the direction of the Parthenia and began swimming back. It was too late to change anything anyway with his tank down to the last third.

Tory stayed crouched in the cockpit with the glasses trained on White Lady looking for any signs of alarm or movement. The coke was starting to wear off again, but she resisted the impulse to go below. She knew that if anything happened while she was below, she would never forgive herself and was determined to tough it out and just get through the withdrawal process. She knew it would probably only take a day or two for the drugs to leave her system and she believed she could make it.

Jan stuck her head into the cockpit from below. "Mom do you want me to wake Willy?"

"No, sweetie, let him sleep as long as possible. There's really nothing he can do to help anyway and it's just one more thing we'll have to worry about if he's up. Remember, we can't use any lights until after we clear the harbor and I think we'd just scare him more if we woke him up then made him sit alone in the dark below."

Jan continued to stand in the companionway. "Do you think Ryan's OK?"

"I hope so. I haven't seen any signs of life over there yet." The two of them were silent for the next few minutes. "Jan, I really meant what I said before about it being important to me that you believe it wasn't me that started using again. I never would have chosen this, and your trust means a great deal to me. I really think I'll be able to get back to the way things were if we can get out of this situation."

"We will Mom. I know we will," Jan replied.

Ryan surfaced a few minutes later and Tory crawled over to the side of the boat where the Zodiak was tied and lowered herself into it. "How did it go?"

MAELSTROM

"Well enough, although we won't know for sure until it's too late to do anything else. We'll just have to pray." Ryan slipped out of his tank so that it was floating next to him. "Hold this while I climb aboard."

Tory did as he asked and after he pulled himself into the Zodiak, he reached back into the water, grabbed the tank, and pulled it in after him.

"Let's just leave all the equipment in the bottom of the Zodiak. We're not going to have time to deflate and store it anyway. We'll leave Mike and Jill's dinghy attached to the mooring ball when we drop it."

They both climbed back aboard and after tying the inflatable off to the stern went below. "We have about four hours of darkness left and we have to get as far out to sea as possible before they come after us. Tory, as soon as we clear the harbor, I want you to get out the No. 3 jib and hank it on the forestay. I think it's blowing about 25 out there right now so we'll also need two reefs in the main. That's something we can do as we steam out of the harbor and up the channel. Jan, I want you to start stowing everything loose below. It's going to be rough out there and I don't want things flying all over the cabin. And don't worry about making it neat, you can throw things in the bunks if you have to as long as the lee cloths are up."

***

Paulo shifted in his seat trying to find a comfortable angle but no matter how he sat, his ass was sore, and he finally decided he might just as well head down to the galley and get a cup of coffee. He had to take a piss anyway. As he got up out of the chair, he looked over in the direction where Parthenia had been anchored. Even as he turned towards the stairway down to the galley a sick feeling arose in his stomach and he quickly turned back.

23

'No, the wind must have changed and we're just laying differently,' he silently wished to himself. He grabbed for the binoculars and started scanning the harbor, but he knew; they were gone. In a panic he rushed out on the wing of the bridge to look aft towards the harbor entrance in time to see the vague silhouette of Parthenia passing through the cut, out towards the open sea. He picked up the inter-ship telephone next to the helm. Edward answered sleepily after three rings.

"What?"

"Senor Edward, they … they've left the mooring."

Edward was instantly awake. "Where are they now?"

"They're just clearing the cut, headed for the open sea."

"Wake up the captain and all the crew, now! We're going after them!" He shouted into the phone. Edward swung his legs over the side of his bunk, turned on the light, and snorted two fat lines before doing anything else. "Now I'll teach that prick a lesson!" he said out loud and hurriedly dressed and then rushed up onto the bridge. As he came onto the bridge the captain was just coming out of his cabin.

"Fire 'em up Hank. Our little friends are flying the coop and I want us underway and out of here in five minutes!"

"But Senor Edward, we must clear out with customs first!" He replied.

"Fuck customs!"

"But it's against the law. We're sure to arouse their suspicions and they in turn will alert the U.S. authorities and possibly even come after us."

"Hank, are you deaf? Get this fucking boat underway!"

Hank knew it was foolish but did as he was told and. using the hand-held radio ordered the crew to begin weighing anchor. He fired up all four diesels and the two radars as the windlass in the bow slowly wound in the chain. When word came back over the radio that the anchor was secure and in the chalk, he checked the oil pressure and rpms and moved all four throttle levers to slow ahead. He heard the familiar whoosh of air as the pneumatic controls were engaged and looked down at his instrument panel in time to see all four rpm indicators increase, hesitate, then fall to zero one at a time. Not one or two but all four engines had stalled.

Edward turned to him anxiously. "What's going on?"

"I don't know. I'll try and restart them." He put all four in neutral and engaged the starters again. All four fired immediately and he was relieved to see the rpm's rise. "I don't know what happened Senor, they seem fine now. I'll try them in forward again." They all immediately stalled again.

Edward hit him on the back of the head, furious. "What is wrong with this piece of shit boat. Fix it now!"

"I have no idea! Something is binding the shafts!"

"Goddamn it." And even though Edward was almost blind with rage he realized that they'd have to fix whatever was broken before they could go after the sailboat. "All right, well whatever it is, fix it. He must not get away!"

"Si Senor I will try, but we must re-anchor to avoid drifting up on shore," the captain replied.

"Just do whatever you have to but do it quickly!"

***

Ryan kept the Parthenia close to shore and out of the main channel as he made his way out of the 150-foot wide cut that separated St. Georges harbor from the sea, watching anxiously for any signs of movement or alarm aboard White Lady. Just before they cleared the cut, his heart sank as he saw all their deck lights go on and crew hurrying forward to the bows. They'd seen them leaving and would no doubt come after them as quickly as they could! He had really hoped for the extra hours underway they would have gotten if their departure had gone unnoticed till morning. Now everything relied on his sabotage and he doubted that would stall them for more than a couple of hours. "Shit!" He said out loud as Tory dragged the bag containing their No. 3 jib up through the companionway hatch and onto deck.

"What is it?" she asked.

"I'm pretty sure they saw us just before we cleared the cut. I saw their lights go on."

Tory was already crashing off the coke and this news made everything even blacker. "Ryan I'm so scared. If that animal catches up with us, I don't know what I'll do."

"Don't give up yet. I'm pretty sure we have a good head start on him. With luck, we'll never see him again,"

"Ryan, he can't get his hands on the children! I saw his eyes when he threatened us. He meant it when he said he would sexually mutilate them and slaughter all of us."

"Calm down Tory, I believe you. If by some chance he does catch up to us I promise you that I'll do whatever's necessary to protect the kids. I mean that. Anything! Get that sail hanked on to the forestay so we can get as much speed as possible."

"I'm sorry I yelled; I'm just scared!"

"I know, I am too." Ryan was having serious second thoughts over their decision to run rather than report them to the authorities. But he knew that they had virtually no proof of Edward's abduction. It would just be Tory's word against him and his men. A charge of introducing drugs into her system would be even harder to prove given Tory's criminal record for possession. They just had to play out their decision and hope for the best. His biggest concern was Willy and Jan.

Ryan and Tory raised the main and the jib and after he got the sails trimmed, he had Tory take the wheel and went below to plan a strategy and plot a course away from the island. He needed to first guess the likely course White Lady would take as they attempted to catch them.

Edward would suspect that they were headed south to the Caribbean. He knew they had left from New England and Bermuda was the normal stopping place for boats headed to the Caribbean offshore. He also knew from his conversations with customs that White Lady was enroute from Nassau to somewhere on the New England coast. Going due south was out of the question. He was reasonably certain that would be the direction Edward would search first for them. West would turn them around back towards Bermuda and all the reefs, and east towards Europe would take them on a route they really weren't supplied for. Ryan put his head in his hands and tried to think, "What direction will he expect us to go?" There were so many scenarios and it was difficult to predict how an unknown entity thinks. He finally settled on a southeasterly course that was not quite in the direction of the Caribbean, rather more towards the northern coast of Brazil and planned that they'd alter their course to a southerly one after several days if they were successful in eluding him. He put his foul weather gear back on and went back up on deck.

"You can go below and get some rest if you want. I don't mind taking it."

"Did you decide what direction makes the most sense?" Tory asked.

"I hope so. I've got us heading for Brazil right now."

Tory looked surprised.

"No, it's not as bad as it sounds. It's only about 35 degrees off the course we'd normally take to The Lesser Antilles. I just hope it's enough different from where he'll expect us to head."

"Ryan, even though I didn't do anything to this Edward guy I still feel like all this is my fault somehow."

"That's ridiculous."

Tory hung her head. "I didn't tell you quite everything earlier."

He waited.

"Before he let me go, he gave me a bag of coke and I used several more times this afternoon. No one forced me."

Ryan was a little shocked but put his arm around her. "The drugs told you it was OK. The question now is what can we do to get you clean again so that you have that choice back?"

Tory was amazed at his understanding. She was so grateful for this that without even thinking the next thing that came out of her mouth was a lie. "When we were leaving the harbor I flushed the rest down the toilet." She wanted to show that his faith in her wasn't misplaced. It was a harmless lie anyway because as soon as she went below, she would flush it.

"We'll get out of this somehow. You go below and get some rest. I'll wake you in a couple of hours."

Tory stopped at both Willy and Jan's bunks and kissed them both softly as she passed through the cabin on her way to the head and made a silent promise to each of them that somehow they'd all get out of this situation and return things to the way they were before.

She continued into the head and immediately reached behind the bulkhead. She didn't want to spend a lot of time thinking about what she was about to do and knew the sight of the pure coke would tempt her. She just wanted to do it before she started obsessing about it. She quickly unzipped the baggy and started pouring it into the toilet. It went against every instinct in her to pour perfectly good cocaine down the toilet. She remembered nights in the old days when she would lick the inside of a baggy just for the faint powdery residue that clung to the inside, before throwing it out. After pouring about half of it out, she stopped.

The drug started speaking to her; reasonable, rational, soft and seductive. "What's once more?" it asked. "Who's to know? The damage is already done and you deserve it, especially after what you've been through. You know you'll feel better after."

Tory had heard it all before and tilted the bag again, but even as she did so she knew, absolutely knew, that all of it would not make its way into the toilet. At that moment she loathed herself and her lack of will.

MAELSTROM

The voice became more insistent. "You need this, and you need it now. No one will ever know, and besides you'll be absolutely no good to anyone if you're in withdrawal."

She stopped pouring again, her heart pounding with the conflict going on inside her and sat down on the toilet quietly sobbing. Then in a series of simple movements fished one of the remaining rocks out of the bag, crushed it on the counter and inhaled the contents. 'There, done!' she said to herself. 'Discussion over, end of story.'

She sat back and waited for the promised relief to start flowing through her bloodstream again. Immediately she felt better physically but the guilt, fear, and sense of total failure were only heightened. She pounded her knees in frustration and the tears started anew. 'Oh God, why have you left me?' she sobbed. Not even the drugs worked anymore. She defeatedly tucked the baggy containing the last of the coke into her shorts pocket.

Rip Converse

Chapter 3

The crewman sent under White Lady quickly resurfaced and confirmed the captain's and the engineer's suspicion that their props were fouled. As Ryan had hoped, on two of the four shafts the synthetic polypropylene had been drawn in so tightly that it had actually fused to itself making it extremely difficult to unwrap from the screws. "It's gonna take a while," he warned.

"Just get it done. What do you need for tools?" Hank asked.

"Just a big knife, vice grips, and time," Jorge answered back.

"Well we've two out of three anyway," the captain replied and passed him down the knife and vice grips.

Jorge pulled the last of the rope free at 4:10 a.m. and surfaced at the stern to the anxious faces of Paulo, Manuel and Hank.

"That's the last of it," he handed some of the scrap line up onto the platform along with the tools.

Hank turned to Paulo and Manuel. "Help him out of the water and then the three of you stand-by to weigh anchor. I'm going to start the engines and try them in gear." He hurried up the outside stairway to the bridge and started all four engines. After waiting for the oil pressure to rise he put all of them briefly in gear. All props spun freely when

31

engaged. He immediately picked up the phone to let Edward know they were ready to get underway.

"Get moving. I'll be up in a minute."

Edward was reasonably certain they wouldn't head north. That course would force them to circumnavigate the northerly reefs that surrounded Bermuda and would not afford them a horizon to get over in the two short hours it had taken for them to clear their props. As he looked at Ryan's other options, he quickly realized it was foolish to commit to one course in his search and smiled smugly as he realized they didn't really have to. The American's boat could at best be making 8 to 10 knots. The White Lady would do over three times that. Edward simply took the protractor off the chart table, set it to thirty miles, and drew an arc using Bermuda as the center. He started the partial circle to the northeast of the island and carried it all the around to the area of sea to the southwest. He was certain that Ryan was somewhere in that quadrant and all he had to do was make speed all the way out to the edge of his arc and follow it around using the island as his pivot point. Radar would do the rest.

Chapter 4

The wind veered to the northeast as they sailed away from Bermuda, and Ryan was forced to sheet the sails in tight and turn the engine back on so that they could maintain their southeasterly course. The engine added no more than a half a knot to the speed the sails were generating, but he was grateful for anything he could get. He did a quick calculation in his mind and figured that they'd made about 16 miles in the last two hours which was enough to put them over the horizon and out of sight of the naked eye. He could only hope that Edward went in any other direction than the one in which they were headed. Suddenly a cold feeling washed over him as he remembered the radar on White Lady. He looked aloft to the small plastic buoy-shaped object affixed about half-way up Parthenia's mast.

"Shit!" He'd forgotten about the radar reflector. Quickly he yelled below for Tory to come on deck and then turned back to the port side sail locker and started pulling out lines and life preservers as he looked for the bosun's chair.

"What is it Ryan?" Tory asked fearfully from the companionway.

"I forgot our radar reflector! We have to get it down immediately. I can't believe I didn't think of that!"

Tory was amped from the coke she'd snorted and had lain below in her bunk for the past hour, paranoid and wide-awake. She was still edgy and self-conscious and had hoped to avoid any contact with Ryan until the coke had worn off some more. "What do you want me to do?"

"I need you to haul me up the mast so I can get it down. The problem is that it's permanently affixed to the mast so I'm going to have to unscrew it."

Tory looked out over the large ocean swells and then up the mast. Every inch the mast swayed at deck level translated to several feet two thirds of the way up the mast. "Ryan, you can't go up there in these waves. It's too rough."

"I have to. That reflector will make us visible to radar from 25 miles away."

"Ryan, I don't know if I can haul you all the way up, and what if you fall?"

"We can't worry about that now. We don't have a choice."

Tory stood there frozen, not wanting to deal anymore and watched as Ryan stepped into and then secured himself in the canvas bosun chair. All she wanted to do was crawl back into her bunk below and escape from everything.

Ryan looked over at her sensing that something was wrong. "What is it?"

"I just don't know if I can cope anymore."

"Tory listen. I can't do this alone." She continued to stare ahead with a blank look on her face.

"Tory!" Ryan shook her. He could see the panic in her eyes. And then suddenly it made sense to him. "I thought you flushed the rest of that shit down the toilet?"

Tory kept her gaze down and said nothing. Her lack of denial confirmed his suspicions. He shook her again. "Tory, forget me, forget yourself if you have to, but don't cop out on the kids. Please help me to do this."

"I don't think I can."

"This isn't a case of doing things we want to do. We have a responsibility to those two kids sleeping down below. I'm not thrilled about going up the mast on a night like tonight, but I'm more scared of that maniac catching up to us and what he'll do to you and the kids. Please!"

She knew he was right. "I'll try."

"All right good. Now get some foul weather gear on. The waves are coming over the bow pretty good. While you're below get me a Phillips-head screwdriver and a small pair of vice grips while I go rig the halyard."

Ryan set the recently repaired Aries self-steering vane then grabbed the flashlight from the cockpit and made his way forward, hanging onto the combing rail as he went, stopping twice to brace himself against waves that swept down the deck. Although going up the mast was always a challenge at sea, tonight would be particularly so with the current wind and sea state. He wished they had some other choice, especially with the condition Tory was in. She came back on deck a few minutes later and he shone the light down the deck to help light her way and waited for her to make her way forward. "I've already got the halyard rigged so all you have to do is grind me up. I'll try and pull myself up as much as possible to take some of the strain off the halyard. Remember, when it's time to lower me, keep a couple of wraps around the winch, it's a long way back down."

Tory kept her back to the wind and spray coming over the bow and just nodded her head, as talking was difficult. Ryan put four wraps around the winch, pulled in the slack, ran the tail over the self-tailer, and put the winch handle into the socket. "Ready when you are," he yelled.

She nodded her head again and bent to the task of grinding him up the 65-foot mast with the two-speed winch. Ryan helped as much as he was able by hugging the mast with one arm and pulling himself up by the inner shroud, but it was a long grind and Tory had to stop twice to rest just getting him as far as the first set of spreaders. When he reached them, he swung a leg over one and rested. Tory looked anxiously up the mast. She could just barely make out his form in the darkness and could tell it was a struggle for him to stay on his precarious perch. What would it be like for him nearer the top with no spreaders to support himself on?

"Take her up," he yelled after he was rested. Tory started grinding again. She was now on the lower speed of the winch which meant it took less effort to turn the handle, but it also meant she had to turn the handle twice as many times to lift him the same distance. Again, she had to stop several times as she hoisted him the rest of the way.

"OK. Hold it there!"

Tory made the halyard fast to the cleat. She couldn't even see him anymore until he was suddenly illuminated by the flashlight he was using to see his work. As far as she could tell from the deck, he would have to use both arms just to keep himself attached to the mast and couldn't see how he could possibly hang on, hold the flashlight and work at the same time, but somehow he did and she could see that he'd wrapped both legs and one arm around the mast and was holding the flashlight in his mouth which left him one arm free to unfasten the radar reflector. With each wave that roared under Parthenia she could see that the mast was swinging as much as 10 to 15 feet aloft as he hung onto the mast and she wondered how much stamina he had. Suddenly it was quiet on deck. Tory turned and faced forward as Parthenia descended into the trough of a particularly large swell. The swell was so large that it blocked the wind as they surfed down into the trench. Then, the stillness was replaced by the unmistakable sound of the wave behind it curling into a break. Tory braced herself instinctively as half of the huge swell slapped into the side of Parthenia and the rest crashed over the deck. She was hit by a wall of water and almost swept off the cabin house. She hung on though and looked up in time to see Ryan lose his hold and swing into the outer shrouds 45 feet aloft. He held out one of his arms to break the impact against the wire rigging, but as he hit, the flashlight was jarred from his mouth and it fell tumbling into the water on their leeward side. Now she couldn't see him and had no way of knowing if he was injured. Tory crouched, frozen, not knowing what to do next.

Soaked through, she rode out the next series of waves feeling helpless and overwhelmed. The only source of light on deck was the dim glow of phosphorous agitated by the breaking waves and Parthenia's passage through them. They were 'running dark' without running lights so even that familiar glow was absent. Eventually her paralysis was broken by the sound of Jan's voice screaming at her from the cockpit.

"Mom! Mom! Are you all right?"

She kept her grip on the mast and turned just enough to see Jan coming up the deck on the leeward side crouched low and gripping the grab rail. The sight scared her into movement and she immediately let go of her hold and crabbed down the deck towards her.

"Get back in the cockpit," she yelled without replying to her question. She met her halfway down the deck and got her turned around. After reaching the safety of the cockpit she hugged her.

"What were you thinking? You don't have a life preserver or a safety harness on. You could have been washed right over!"

"I was scared! I came up into the cockpit and neither one of you was there and then, when I looked forward, all I could see was you holding onto the mast."

"I know, I'm helping Ryan ..." And Tory remembered. "Jan, Ryan is still up the mast and I have no idea if he's all right. There isn't enough light to see. Can you go below and bring up one of the other flashlights? Ryan dropped the one he was using. I've got to get back forward to let him down."

"I know where one is. I'll be right back." Jan scurried down the ladder and went immediately to the drawer in the Nav station where it was kept. Before coming back up she tested it to make sure it was working then climbed back up the ladder and handed it to Tory. She took the light from her. "Don't leave the cockpit again! OK?" Jan nodded her head. "I'll be back as soon as I can."

As soon as she regained the foot of the mast Tory shone the light aloft.

Ryan had managed to swing back to the mast, and using touch alone, was trying to unscrew the last of the screws that held the reflector in place. He waved down to Tory to acknowledge her presence and then turned back to the reflector hoping his strength would last. "Shit!" he said to himself. The last screw was particularly corroded. He'd inadvertently stripped the head in his haste to unscrew it. Frustrated and tired he realized the only chance now he'd of getting it off now was to try and break the bracket or the screw holding it and started to bend the reflector back and forth. Finally, it broke free and he took the whole unit and threw it off to leeward where it quickly disappeared into their wake. Tory still had the light on him and he signaled to her to start lowering him back to the deck.

When Ryan had swung free into the rigging, he'd broken the thumb in his right hand trying to stop his motion. He couldn't grip anything with it. He realized, as Tory started to lower him, that it would be impossible for him to use that hand to help control his descent. If Tory lost control of the halyard while lowering him, he would have no way of stopping his fall to the deck. First light was just arriving on the eastern horizon and he looked down anxiously as Tory untied the halyard from the cleat and began easing it over the winch drum. He could tell from the jerky motion as she paid out the line over the winch that she'd kept several wraps on it providing the necessary friction to lower him in a controlled way. This made him more comfortable and he relaxed the grip he had around the mast with his good arm and took a few moments to scan the horizon for lights or any other signs of boats as she lowered him. There were none.

MAELSTROM

Tory slowly let the halyard line slide over the winch drum as Ryan had showed her, holding the tail of the line in one hand, the other alternately easing and squeezing the wraps on the drum for maximum control. Although this method made for a slower, less smooth descent, it was the safest way to bring a man down. Tory focused her attention on the task ensuring that the tail was led onto the winch at the proper angle thereby lessening the chance that it might ride-off the end of the drum taking the rest of the wraps with it as she lowered. If that were to happen, she wouldn't be able to hold the line and it would run free as Ryan fell to the deck.

Sailors and surfers often talk about sets of waves, each with a different opinion as to the order of magnitude. Both, however, acknowledge the rogue wave and its unpredictability. Rogues are frequently large, but not always so. What distinguishes them from other waves is the fact that they are often out of sync. As sailboats move through the water, they adopt a certain rhythm that enables them to move smoothly through it, like a good dancer in a room full of other good dancers, everyone ebbing and flowing in time with the music. Rogue waves have the same effect on boats as the introduction of a drunken man into a room full of skilled dancers. Tory's attention was completely focused on two things as she lowered Ryan, his descending form and the manner in which she paid out the halyard over the winch drum to the total exclusion of all else. As a result, she didn't feel the first ripples of change that presaged the approach of the rogue that hit them. It was not a particularly large wave, but it was out of sync and from a slightly different angle.

Ryan, however, did feel it approaching and was aware enough to look windward in the instant before Parthenia stumbled. He tightened his grip around the mast with his good arm and called out a warning to Tory below. She looked up, instead of out, just as their bow dipped. Her leg muscles tightened unconsciously to account for the increased bow down angle, but instead of rising in rhythm onto the crest of the next wave that her body expected, Parthenia fell, precipitously into the trough of the rogue wave that twisted their bow in an unexpected and uncharacteristic way. Tory lost the rhythm her body had been subconsciously following and she lost her balance and subsequently her hold on the halyard.

Ryan watched the whole thing from 40 feet above, helpless. The most he could manage was a last second, one armed attempt to hug himself to the mast, but the skewing of the bow that threw Tory off balance below was exaggerated by a factor of five at his position high in the rigging, and he lost his grip.

Tory looked up in disbelief as the rope ran through her hand. She tried to hold on, but it instantly burned her palm and the insides of her fingers as it ran through them. She looked aloft long enough to see him lose his grip and begin to fall. He fell awkwardly and she turned her head not wanting to watch him hit the deck.

The thump of his body never came, however, and she looked back up the mast. The spreaders had checked Ryan's fall. He was sprawled and barely hanging on, but it looked as though he was all right. She quickly grabbed the halyard where it came out of the mast, took up the slack and got four wraps on the winch again. At least he wouldn't fall any further.

Ryan landed on the shin of his right leg when he hit the spreaders and heard the unmistakable crack of bone when he hit. He scrambled to get a solid hold on the spreader, got his good leg over the top and looked down at the injured leg that was hanging below. His fear was confirmed. At least one of the two bones in his lower leg was broken and evidenced by a jagged piece of bone that protruded through his skin.

***

MAELSTROM

Edward didn't leave the bridge in the hours immediately following their departure and instead stood hunched over their long-range radar screen with only short breaks to demand distance and speed information from Hank. He was obsessed with finding them to the exclusion of all care and reason. Departing Bermuda without clearing customs and immigration had been foolhardy. The Bermudians would now alert the U.S. Coast Guard of their illegal departure. White Lady would show up on everyone's hot sheets. Edward knew this in the back of his mind and also knew it might be the last straw in his employers' minds for continued employment by them. God help him if he lost the shipment as a result of his personal vendetta. He blamed the American. If it hadn't been for him, he wouldn't have been forced into the untimely departure. They would pay dearly when he caught up.

***

Tory watched as Ryan swung his good leg over the spreader and she raised him several inches using the winch handle to help take some of the strain off him. There was enough light now so that she could see him grimace as he hauled himself onto the spreader. "Ryan, are you all right?" she yelled.

Ryan took several deep breaths before replying, "My leg's broken. Give me a minute."

Tory was relieved that he hadn't fallen to the deck, but she began to cry again. This was all her fault. She was fucking up. Once again, the drugs were robbing her of everything. No rationalizations, no justification; she was certain that this would not have happened if she'd been straight and she had no one to blame at that moment but herself.

"Tory. Tory!"

41

She looked aloft.

"I'm going to slide off the spreader and I want you to start lowering me again. Can you do that?" Ryan knew she was at some kind of breaking point from her body language and the sobbing he could hear from below. "Tory, please, you need to get it together."

She carefully cupped the wraps around the winch drum with her left hand and started to feed the slack end of the halyard with her other. It was slow going and painful as her hand was swollen and raw where the line had run through it earlier, but she got him down to within several feet of the deck before he spoke again and stopped her.

"Tory, my leg's broken, and we're going to have to splint it somehow. Tie off the halyard here where I'm hanging and then go below and get some Ace bandages and a piece of scrap wood out of the forepeak about this long." He indicated a length with his arm pointing first to his ankle and then to his mid-thigh.

Ryan's leg was hanging right in front of her now and she put her hand to her mouth at the sight of the bone pushing through his chin. "Oh Christ, Ryan, I'm so sorry. I tried to hold on but that wave hit and I just couldn't!" She held out her raw and bleeding hand for him to see.

"I know. I saw the whole thing. Don't worry about it now. Just get the stuff and let's see if we can set it. I'll be fine, just go get the stuff." Ryan had his good arm wrapped around the mast and now that he was close to the deck, the arc of the mast swing was short enough that he could easily hold on. "I'm OK, really."

Willy and Jan greeted her with anxious expressions as she came below. Jan had only told Willy that there were some men after them and had left out everything else that had gone on during the previous afternoon and evening.

"What's going on Mom?" Jan asked.

"Ryan hurt his leg." Tory started to rummage through the medicine chest and then the forepeak.

"Is he going to be all right?"

"I don't know. I hope so. It's broken and we can't move him off the deck till we put a splint on it." Tory stuffed the various supplies she'd collected into her pockets and picked up the makeshift splint she'd found before starting up the ladder again.

She rushed forward to the base of the mast. "How're you doing?"

"I'm OK. It doesn't seem to be bleeding too much but we're going to have to pull the bone back into place before we put on the splint. You're going to have to lower me the rest of the way with one hand on the halyard and use your other to help support my lower leg."

Tory looked at him askance.

"It'll be all right. Just use two wraps on the winch so it slides over the drum easier. Can you do it?"

"I'll try." Tory knelt to untie the halyard again from the cleat, took two wraps off the winch as Ryan had instructed and held tension on it with her left hand.

"Good, now cradle my lower leg in the crook of your right arm."

She did as instructed and Ryan leaned back in the bosun's chair so that he was horizontal to the deck. She looked closely at his leg as she did so. "Jesus, Ryan, this looks bad."

"Just get me down the rest of the way down." He grimaced as she started to lower him the last few feet to the deck. He was now horizontal, laying on the cabin roof. Once stable Ryan unclipped the end of the halyard from the chair and clipped it to an eye in the deck next to him.

"OK, here's what you've got to do. Take your left hand and put it right on my kneecap. Then take your right hand and grab my ankle and pull it away from the knee until the bone goes back beneath the skin. Hopefully we can get both ends to set against one another. Ready?"

"There's no way I can do this."

"Tory, you have to. I can't do it myself!"

She continued to shake her head in a "no" direction but finally said, "OK, I'll try."

43

"Good, now don't be shy. You'll have to pull it hard to make this work. My leg muscles are strong and contracted right now."

Tory started to reduce the break but seeing Ryan's face twisted in pain, she stopped.

"Tory, don't look at me, just fucking do it!"

She took another deep breath and pulled again, harder. Ryan's whole leg was shaking with pain, but she continued to pull on his ankle until the bone disappeared reluctantly back beneath the skin. Then she changed the angle of the lower leg slightly and allowed the muscles to contract it back into place. Her instincts told her that it had re-set correctly.

"I think I got it. You still here?"

"Oh, you bet. I wouldn't have slept through that," he smiled at her. "How's the bleeding down there?"

"It looks OK, I mean it's not pouring out or anything."

"Good. Now, just put a bandage over the wound and then strap the wood tightly to the leg both above and below the break."

She worked for the next few minutes with Jan looking on anxiously from the cockpit.

***

They had been underway for three hours when a bright crimson sun inched its way above the cloud line that filled the horizon. Edward remained on the bridge and traced his finger over the arc that he'd drawn on the chart. They were still steaming outwards from Bermuda to the northeast. Once they reached his imaginary line, if they hadn't yet sighted Parthenia they'd turn in a southerly direction. He was almost certain they hadn't headed West due to the reefs off Bermuda and doubted they would head to the North, but he wanted to rule that out first. His best guess was that they'd head due South or some variant in that general direction. Once he ruled out the Northern possibility, they would quickly steam South if they hadn't yet intercepted the sailboat. With his 30 plus miles of radar visibility he was confident they would find them within the next few hours. Visibility was over 10 miles as he looked out the windows on the bridge, and although the sea was running about six feet, he didn't expect that it would substantially impact their ability to overtake the American. Hank had the high seas forecast on the radio. There was a low rushing towards them from the West which might impair their search, but it wasn't scheduled to come through till late in the afternoon. Edward was confident that they would find them and that he'd be through with the meddling American before the low-pressure area reached them. Hank stole a nervous glance over at Edward as he turned his attention back to the radar screen.

***

"Is that tight enough?" Tory asked, wrapping the last of the gauze around the splint and his leg.

"It feels secure. Now, if we can just get back to the cockpit. I'll pull myself along with one arm and skid on my butt. You stay at my leg end and try and block any waves coming down the deck."

Tory crouched down low and held onto the cabin-top rail with one hand and kept her other protectively on Ryan's bad ankle as he pulled himself down the deck. Luckily no large waves came aboard, and they were able to get to the safety of the cockpit in a short amount of time. After a brief struggle to get him over the cockpit combing Tory propped him up so that he was facing aft with his back against the cabin house.

"Are we still holding steady on southeast?" he asked

Tory looked over at the compass and nodded her head.

Jan slid over next to him. "Does it hurt Ryan?"

45

He reached over and touched her hand. "Only when I laugh, so no jokes. We just have to keep moving. Do you think you can help your mom? I can't move very well."

Jan nodded.

"OK, here's where things are at. I know it's still too early to count our chickens, but it's a good sign that he hasn't caught up to us yet. If he'd guessed our course and come straight after us, he would have overtaken us by now because his boat's a lot faster. I guess our sabotage worked. But I won't be comfortable until we get through another night and have that much more distance between him and us. I think I can still do a watch as a helmsman, but obviously I can't move around like before, so if we have to make sail changes and do other things that require mobility, the two of you are going to have to do them."

Willy had awakened and stuck his head through the hatch.

"Willy, I know that what's going on is probably confusing. It is for us too. The biggest help you can be right now is to stay below with Clifton and do as your mom and sister tell you. Can you do that?"

Willy nodded.

"Good. Jan, will you make us all a couple of sandwiches? Peanut butter's fine, and would you also get me a couple of aspirin? Actually, make that a handful, and Tory, would you take the first watch? I'd like to rest for a while and try and figure out how far we've gotten. The only thing is I hate to go below because I know it will take me forever to get up and down those stairs." Ryan realized all at once how he must be sounding and was suddenly depressed with the responsibility that his unilateral decisions implied.

"I'm sorry. I've been sitting here telling you what we should all be doing. Do you guys have any ideas? The reality is I don't know anything for sure. I don't know how or why we're in the position we're in and I don't mean to give the impression that I know what will work best. I'm just guessing. I'd be bullshitting you if I said any different. Do any of you have any suggestions?"

Tory and Jan shook their heads.

46

"You owe me fifty cents," Willy offered.

Ryan looked at him with a confused look. "What?"

"You owe me fifty cents," He repeated. "You said, 'bullshit."

The other three started laughing, breaking the desperate mood of their makeshift meeting. Ryan finally reached out and ruffled his hair.

"Willy you are un-fucking believable and if we get the shit out of this Goddamn situation, I'll pay you double."

Willy was obviously confused by the math of Ryan's outburst and the good fortune it represented.

"Don't even try to figure that one out, I'm sure it's worth at least 10 bucks." They all started laughing again. "Tory would you get me the local chart from below and write down our position off the GPS in the corner of it? I want to see how far we've gotten."

As the morning wore on, each of them became more and more hopeful that they'd successfully escaped. Their course was such that the Aries was able to steer most of the time and, though he was in a fair amount of pain, Ryan eventually fell asleep in the cockpit for several hours. Jan and Willy also lay down around 11 a.m. leaving Tory with little to do as she stood watch. She was jumpy and moved back and forth several times between the cockpit and the salon not knowing what to do with herself, but the whole time very aware of the few grams of coke that remained in her pocket.

At times it burned her leg with its presence. If you'd asked her if she'd use again, especially after Ryan's accident, her answer would have been a firm and definitive no. Now was the time to throw the rest overboard. She was well into the withdrawal again and all she had to do was get through the rest of that day and night. Yet the addict in her continued to engage her in conversation as if there were some way to safely use, as if she had choice. The debate went on for almost 10 minutes before she finally went below into the head and snorted more shit into her nostrils.

47

***

At 8:30 they reached the Northern edge of Edward's arc on the chart without sighting Parthenia. He had Hank alter their course.

"Turn South now Hank and make as much speed as you can. I didn't really expect them to head North, but we had to rule that out. We should intercept them in the next couple of hours."

By 10:00 that morning Edward was feeling the effects of his self-imposed abstinence and decided to go below to "freshen up". He summoned Manuel to the bridge to take his place. Manuel arrived and noted Edward's red, rheumy eyes and shaking hands. That reinforced the decision he'd made in the previous hours to leave Edward and the ship at the earliest opportunity. Although he was still fearful of him, things seemed to be spiraling totally out of control. Also, he no longer felt he could turn a blind eye to the drug trade and all the people it touched. It was the first time they'd spoken since Edward had raged at him for failing to divulge everything about Tory and he approached him with some trepidation.

"Manuel, I don't think I have to tell you how important it is to me that we catch up to these people."

"No, senor."

"Good. I'm going below to rest for a while, and I trust that you and Hank will be vigilant in my absence. This is your last chance. Fuck this up and I swear I will cut your fucking eyes out and then skull fuck you while I eat them!" His rage was genuine, and Manuel nodded back.

"Good. Hank, the same goes for you. I'm depending on you. Call me if you see anything."

Hank also nodded and Edward left the bridge.

"He's getting worse isn't he?" Manuel asked quietly.

"I don't want to talk about it," Hank replied.

"We have to talk about it. He's completely off the rails, endangering all of us and harming innocent people. When did we sign up for that?" Hank stayed mute but Manuel continued on as the first faint return appeared on their radar screen eleven miles off their starboard bow, both of them oblivious to it.

"Hank, there comes a time in all of our lives when we must take some responsibility for our actions and I can tell you I am disgusted with myself and this shit we're involved in."

"Manuel, I told you, I don't want to discuss this. I just want to be done with this foolish trip. What are you suggesting anyway, that we tell Edward to fuck off? And then what? What are we going to do with $8 million worth of cocaine, sell it ourselves? Oh no wait, I get it, you think maybe we should just chuck it over the side. And then what, spend the rest of our very short lives running from the people that own it? I don't think so. Just do as he told you and hopefully, we can get out of this with our skins intact."

Manuel stood staring at him for several seconds realizing that much of what he'd had said was true. He couldn't refute his logic and turned back to the radar screen and noticed a faint echo on the screen. It was not a solid return, but it was there occasionally and appeared to be just 9 miles away. Ryan's removal of the radar reflector had markedly reduced their long-range visibility on radar, but it didn't make them invisible at shorter distances.

***

Tory's earlier despondency was displaced immediately by a cold determination of sorts as the drug entered her system. 'I may be a totally worthless human being,' she thought to herself, 'but I'll be damned if I'll let that narco piece of shit hurt us.

Buoyed by false confidence from the cocaine, she reached into the drawer in the chart table to get the handgun that Ryan had left with her during the night when he'd gone to sabotage White Lady. She wasn't really sure what she would do with it, but the weight of it in her pocket left her feeling less powerless. Ryan was still snoozing as she came on deck and she looked anxiously out over the water ahead, and then slowly turned her head aft. Right away she noticed the dark front line coming up behind them, and although faint, she could also see something else. She strained her eyes but could only see that whatever it was, it was white. If there hadn't been the stark contrast between it and the black clouds, she never would have noticed it. Tory felt sick to her stomach as she reached for the binoculars hanging from the binnacle.

"Oh, please God, don't let that be them!"

***

Manuel continued to stare at the screen for a few more seconds noting the position of the radar return, relative to their heading and then casually brought his head up and looked out the windshield to the corresponding vector on the horizon. It was very faint, but he could see the top of a sail and knew that it wouldn't be long before Hank also noticed it. He made a big decision.

"Hank, you've been up here a while now. Do you need to take a leak or anything?"

"Yeah. Thanks Manuel, I do. Will you take her for a while? I won't be long."

"Sure, no problem, take your time." Manuel slid in behind the wheel as Hank walked the short distance to his cabin just off the bridge. He figured he had two to three minutes max to make up his mind what to do next.

Rip Converse

Chapter 5

Tory raised the binoculars to her eyes and tried to steady herself against Parthenia's movement. Her heart was pounding as the image came into focus. Along with it, came a feeling of utter despair. "Oh, no!"

Ryan came instantly awake at her cry and followed her line of sight. He knew before he'd even finished rotating his head what he would find. White Lady's form and speed were unmistakable.

"Tory, let me have the glasses."

She didn't move.

"Tory, let me have the glasses," he repeated louder. He could tell she was nearly catatonic with fear and painfully slid his bad leg off the bench seat, turned and moved aft a few feet so he could touch her.

"Tory please, it's very important. I have to see if they've spotted us yet." He reached out and gently took the glasses from her then spent several seconds digesting the information that came to him through the glasses. It did not appear to him that they had been spotted yet, as White Lady was not on an intercepting course. They would, however, pass within about two miles of each other if they both held their present courses. All Ryan could think to do was drop their sails to reduce their visibility and to alter their own course away from White Lady. He took in the approaching front line at the same time and figured that the rising seas would also help to hide them. They had to get the sails down immediately.

"Tory, listen to me. We've got to get the sails down right away."

Tory was somewhere else. Between the 36 sleepless hours, the cocaine and fear for the children and herself, she had gone inwards to a safer place. Ryan knew it would be pointless to continue to ask her. He turned back quickly to the hatch area and stuck his head inside.

"Jan. Jan! I need you up here on deck right away." She quickly came awake, crossed the cabin and climbed the ladder.

"What is it Ryan?"

"Listen, things aren't looking too good up here and I need your help. We can see the boat off on the horizon, but they haven't seen us yet. We have to get the sails down immediately. Do you think you can do it like I showed you?"

Jan noticed Tory sitting mutely in the stern with her head hung. "What's wrong with mom?"

"She can't help right now Jan. She's too scared. I know it's a lot to ask but I really need you to do this. Can you?"

Jan nodded once.

"Get a harness on, clip into the lifeline and do it as fast as you can."

Jan climbed out into the cockpit 30 seconds later, clipped onto the lifeline, climbed over the cockpit combing and made her way to the mast without once looking back. Once she gained the foot of the mast, she put her hand on the mainsheet halyard and looked back towards Ryan for confirmation. He nodded and she quickly un-cleated it and let some of the pressure off, then let the halyard run free. The main quickly came down draping itself over the boom and the cabin top. She turned immediately to the other side of the mast, pointed to the jib winch and again Ryan nodded. As the jib fell to the deck Ryan restarted the engine so they could keep steerage and altered Parthenia's course to the right, away from White Lady.

***

Manuel altered their course slightly to port while Hank was in the head. He knew Hank would feel it if he made any major course changes and would be sure to notice once he came back on the bridge. He heard the toilet cycle, then the closing of the head door. He kept his body between Hank and the compass as Hank came up behind him and asked as casually as possible, "Hank, I sure could use a cup of coffee, how about you?"

"Yeah, good idea, do you mind taking her for a few more minutes?"

"Not at all. Grab us something to eat while you're down there too."

"I'll see what's lying around but I don't want to hang around down there too long in case Edward comes back on deck."

"Yeah, you got that," Manuel nervously agreed.

Manuel returned his attention to the area of ocean where he'd last seen Parthenia as soon as Hank left the bridge again. He couldn't find her at first and looked again in the radar to see if she still showed up there. Yes, she was still there, but had dropped her sails. With her low freeboard and darker color, she presented an almost non-existent profile to the naked eye from this distance.

Hank returned slightly quicker than anticipated with a small tray containing two coffees and several sandwiches. "There were already some made," he answered noting Manuel's surprised expression.

Manuel slid out of the helmsman's seat and Hank passed him a coffee and pack of crackers before sliding back into his chair. He noted their compass heading as he sat.

"Hey, where're you going?" He altered their course back to their previous heading.

"Oh sorry, I guess I wasn't paying attention."

"Well it's a good thing it's just me. No telling what might have happened if Edward had found you off course and me below getting coffee."

Manuel turned his attention back to the radar screen. They were still approaching at an angle that would bring them within several miles of Parthenia. He could only hope that he was able to keep Hank's attention elsewhere and that Edward stayed below for the next 15 to 20 minutes.

***

"Jan, help your Mother below. I don't think they've spotted us yet but if they do, I don't want any of you on deck. And before you go, reach into the port sail locker and hand me the shotgun that's in there."

Jan handed him the shotgun and then slid over next to Tory and put an arm around her. "It's going to be OK Mom; they haven't seen us yet. Just come below with me; I'll take care of you."

Jan's words got through Tory's fog and she moved to the companionway ladder without looking towards Ryan. Inside she was riddled with guilt and self-loathing and promised herself that if they all got out of this alive, she would do everyone a favor and kill herself. Enough was enough and she was confident that the contempt that she felt for herself at that moment would ultimately give her the strength to end it all.

***

Edward snorted almost a gram of coke and alternately gulped at a glass of straight scotch as he sat below. Even though the potent drug sang through his system, he couldn't put the American and his family out of his mind and instead lay on the bunk in his cabin fantasizing what he would do to whom when he caught up with them. The owner's cabin was equipped with a set of instrument repeaters that enabled him to monitor various functions aboard the ship including course and speed, and as chance would have it, he'd been staring at them when Manuel altered their course to port. Edward thought nothing of it at first. It was a large ocean they were searching, and helmsmen never keep an exact course, but after several minutes he became suspicious and decided he'd best make a trip back to the bridge. He was having one of his feelings and before leaving the cabin, tucked a short, ugly, serrated sheath knife into the small of his back behind his belt. He'd nicknamed the knife OJ.

Manuel didn't hear him as he came up behind them and started at the sound of his voice.

"Anything?" Edward asked abruptly of the two and peered over Hanks shoulder at their course.

"No, senor," they both answered at once.

"Well I noticed from the instruments in my cabin that we'd gotten off course and I wondered what the fuck the two of you rim jobs were doing up here! I told you I wanted you to keep a sharp eye, you two can't even steer a straight course!"

Manuel knew that next Edward would most likely push him aside to take a look at the radar screen. If he did, he would see Parthenia, and suddenly, no matter the personal cost to him, it was important to Manuel, that this did not happen. His right hand was still on the radar panel, and maintaining his look into Edward's eyes, he used his sense of touch to count up three adjustment knobs from the bottom of the control panel and turned that knob a quarter turn to the right. The setting he changed was for sea clutter and it dampened the sensitivity of the set. It was normally used in bad weather to prevent ocean swells from showing up on the screen as targets. He'd noted that Parthenia was wood when he'd had her under surveillance and was counting on the fact that the majority of her mass was so close to the water that she wouldn't reflect back a signal on the dampened setting.

Edward missed very little, however, and Manuel's simple act of holding his stare when being yelled at made him suspicious. He looked down in time to see Manuel's fingertips move off the sea clutter knob.

"Is the radar out of tune Manuel?" he asked with a sneer.

"I, I don't know what you mean senor," he stuttered back.

Edward pushed him aside and still keeping one eye on him peered into the screen and readjusted the sea clutter knob. Parthenia's return immediately glowed back at him. Edward raised his head and looked out the window in the quadrant that the return had showed up in. He immediately saw the boat.

"Manuel, do you remember the crazy football player who butchered his wife and her lover and then went for a drive around LA with about 100 police cars behind him?"

"Si, senor." He replied back confused as to why Edward would bring up such a thing at that moment.

"Good, that's very good."

Manuel was confused.

"I'd like you to meet OJ." Edward paused, casually reached behind his back, and then with remarkable speed, drew OJ out of the sheath, spun around and swung the knife at Manuel's belly, his intention to totally eviscerate him and empty the contents of his belly onto the floor of the wheelhouse.

Manuel was anticipating a reaction of some kind from Edward and stepped back quickly as he started his swing. Instead of slicing deeply and across his whole belly-front as Edward had intended, it caught only his side. Manuel did not have Edward's speed or rage, but he was a powerful man and a street fighter at heart. When Edward backed him up against the bulkhead for a second and final strike, he kicked out instinctively and caught Edward squarely in the groin. Edward fell to the floor in agony and Manuel stumbled from the wheelhouse holding his side. Almost immediately he regretted not having finished him off while he'd had the chance. His only chance now was to get one of the firearms from below and hope that he didn't run into Paulo or one of the other crew while doing so. There were two weapons lockers on board and he immediately headed for the one in the engine room as there was less chance that he'd run into one of the other crew there.

Hank leaned down to help Edward up off the floor.

"Forget me!" He screamed. "Arm the rest of the crew and corner him. And make sure he's alive! I'll take the helm. Go!" Still hunched over in pain, Edward took the wheel from Hank and altered their course to a converging one with Parthenia.

***

Ryan's heart sank as White Lady changed course towards them. What could he possibly do against such a large ship with so many men, especially in the condition he was in? He was scared for himself, but more so for Tory and the children. He only had the shotgun and the pistol, both of which were only effective at short ranges against a human target. To fire either at the ship was pointless and would only serve to anger to them. The only other thing he could think of doing in the few

58

minutes remaining was to try talking with them, although he'd little hope for that. Ryan leaned in through the hatch. Jan and Willy were sitting on either side of a crying Tory, trying to soothe her.

"Jan, pass me the radio mike."

All three looked up at him, Tory grasping immediately the significance of his request. "They've seen us. I knew they would. I've brought this on all of us." Tory babbled.

"Jan," Ryan asked again. "Pass me the mike. I've got to try and talk to them and see if there isn't some kind of deal I can make."

Jan got up off the settee, crossed to the radio panel and then handed the VHF radio mike up to Ryan.

"Is it on 16?"

Jan looked at the display and nodded her head. White Lady had closed to less than a mile when Ryan put the mike to his lips.

"M/V White Lady this is S/V Parthenia, do you read me over?"

The call came over the radio in White Lady's wheelhouse immediately and while Edward's normal inclination would have been to respond and toy with them it only served to remind him how foolish his own actions were. With a mast as tall as Parthenia's their radio signal would carry for at least 50 or 60 miles and the American had just broadcast White Lady's name over the open airwaves. There was no telling what he might say next.

"I know you're listening." Ryan paused, trying to think of what might sound rational to a clearly irrational man. "Obviously I've wronged you in some way. Whatever that was, I apologize, but please, you need to let things end here, now, before they go any further. Nothing will be said; you have my word. I have two small children aboard who have done nothing and are terrified. Let it go."

Edward reached up to his own radio set and pressed the low power setting that reduced their transmission area to several miles and in almost a whisper transmitted back.

"I'm going to fuck your children and cut them to pieces and then I'm going to do the same to you."

***

59

All four of them on Parthenia heard the brief transmission and Tory started mumbling un-intelligibly. Jan and Willy started crying, as much in response to their mother as Edward's words. Ryan realized that further discussion was pointless.

In a last-minute Hail Mary, Ryan continued to transmit on channel 16. His set was on high power and he hoped Bermuda Harbor was able to hear his transmission. "Bermuda Harbor Radio, Bermuda Harbor Radio this is sailing vessel Parthenia. Mayday, Mayday, Mayday! We departed your harbor early this morning without clearance in fear for our lives. We're currently 60 miles southeast of you and are about to be boarded or rammed by crewmembers of the White Lady, I repeat, White Lady. Any assistance you can render would be greatly appreciated."

White Lady was now just several hundred yards away her bow cleaving tons of water to either side as she bore down on Parthenia amidships.

***

After fleeing the wheelhouse, Manuel made his way to the engine room avoiding contact with any of the other crew until he stopped in the machine space where the lower weapons locker was located. Jorge the engineer was checking a bank of gauges as he opened the watertight door and gave him only his partial attention.

"Hey Manuel, que pasa?" he casually asked over his shoulder unaware of the events that had just taken place in the wheelhouse.

Manuel had always liked Jorge and had no desire to hurt him but also knew he feared Edward. He did not expect that Jorge would willingly join him. He quickly looked over the worktables in front of him and picked up the most menacing looking wrench.

"Jorge, listen to me." Jorge turned and noticed first Manuel's bloody side and then the wrench in his hand.

"Manuel what happened to you?"

"That's not important and there's no need for you to get involved so I will give you a choice my friend. You can lie down on the floor and let me tie you up, or I can strike you on the head with this rather large, heavy wrench and then tie you up. An easy choice I would think." As Jorge made up his mind Manuel turned back to the watertight door and slid a piece of pipe into the wheel that sealed the door, keeping an eye on Jorge.

"You know what you're doing?" Jorge asked with some concern.

"Probably not, but it is done, nevertheless. Quick, make your decision, I don't have much time."

Jorge shrugged and immediately lay flat on the floor with his hands behind his back. "Like you said, an easy decision."

Manuel could hear Hank, Paulo and one of the other crew outside the bulkhead door trying to force their way in as he tied up Jorge.

"Good luck my friend," Jorge offered as Manuel turned to the weapons locker.

"Thanks, I'll need it," Manuel replied. He selected a 9 mm and four full clips of ammunition and made his way into the engine room as far forward as possible and took refuge behind one of the main engines. This would afford him good cover if Paulo and the rest of the crew were able to breach the steel door and get into the engine room. Despite his wound and the resolve that he was probably going to die, a peaceful calm had come over him and he tried to think of some way that he could make his death mean something. He pulled up the edge of his shirt and looked down at the ugly wound Edward had inflicted. 'Shit, he stuck me good,' he said to himself and realized he wouldn't be conscious long if he didn't stop some of the bleeding. There was an oily rag hanging in front of him and gritting his teeth against the pain he stuffed as much of it as possible into the gaping hole. As he waited for the wave of pain to subside, he looked around at the machinery that surrounded him and tried to think of the quickest way he could stop White Lady before they came alongside the sailboat. He knew he only had a few seconds left and was startled by a bullet that whined off the engine block next to him surprised that they'd been able to force the outer door so quickly. He snapped off several answering shots in the general direction of the doorway. "Think!" he said to himself as he ducked behind the engine.

61

Then he saw the throttle linkage for the engine he was behind, right in front of him.

***

Ryan keyed the mike and started broadcasting again, "Mayday, Mayday, Mayday, this is S/V Parthenia. We are currently 60 miles southeast of Bermuda and are under attack, I repeat, under attack. There are two adults, two children and a dog aboard our vessel. I repeat we are under attack, by a ship named White Lady and require immediate assistance from any vessels in the area."

Edward pounded the dash with his fist at the sound of Ryan's transmission and turned to Hank as he rushed back into the wheelhouse with a fully automatic M-4 and several clips.

"We have Manuel pinned down in the engine room, but it may take a while to get him. He's behind one of the engines and has a gun of his own."

"Fuck him for now. That prick on the sailboat is broadcasting a Mayday that everyone and their mother will hear with that tall mast. Turn our radio to high power on 16 and hold down the mike button. It might override his transmissions. I'm going to ram him and try and take his mast down!"

"Senor Edward, I'm not sure that's a good idea. We may sink ourselves in the process."

"Don't argue with me!"

"Senor please, perhaps we could just shoulder him amidships near his shrouds. That will bring down his mast."

"What do you mean shoulder him?" Edward asked.

"Just turn, right before you strike him so that the overhang of our bow strikes his rigging but so that our bow avoids striking him. His is not so small a boat and I would hate to see us put a hole in White Lady."

Edward thought for a second. What Hank said made sense. "Very well, here, you take it and give me that rifle. I'm going to soften him up some." As they shifted places their speed started to drop, and an unfamiliar vibration came through their feet.

Hank looked down at the instruments. "I just lost all my rpms on one of my engines!"

"Just keep going, you're almost on him."

Edward wheeled out of the doorway onto the wing of the bridge with the M-4 just as Manuel disconnected the second of the four throttle linkages below. White Lady slowed further and started veering to Port. The two he'd disconnected were both on the port side and the increased drag of the dead props on that side was causing White Lady to turn to port. They were only 500 feet from Parthenia. As Hank turned the wheel to compensate, Edward squeezed off his first burst towards the cockpit of Parthenia.

Ryan watched, helpless as White Lady closed on them and frantically repeated his distress call one last time. Just when it seemed certain that they'd be run down, White Lady started slowing and veering to Port. Suddenly the wood next to his head splintered and the air around him was filled with the sound of angry insects. He looked up as Edward tried to get his range and rolled onto the floor of the cockpit as Edward let go his second burst of automatic weapon's fire. Holes appeared all around him from the high velocity slugs and he curled into a fetal position.

Manuel disconnected the third and fourth throttle linkages and White Lady sat back on her haunches as she deaccelerated causing Edward's last few shots to go high. Hank fought the wheel the whole time, however, and using her remaining momentum successfully completed his skidding turn and shouldered into the side of Parthenia as he'd planned, their bow combing taking out Parthenia's port shrouds. White Lady quickly lost the last of her momentum and for the time being was dead in the water.

Ryan was completely exposed to Edward's fire in the open cockpit and helpless to scramble below with his broken leg. He fully expected to die in the next few moments and was surprised to hear the second burst go over his head. When he did finally risk a look, it was in time to see White Lady's bow loom over them. For the moment it gave him cover from Edward's fire, but at a price, as White Lady raked down their side with the curved overhang of their bow taking out the standing rigging on Parthenia's port side. Ryan looked anxiously aloft at the mast. He shifted his focus to the bridge of White Lady and looked at the man responsible for turning his whole world upside down; disheveled and beside himself with rage, Edward feverishly worked the bolt on the M-4, not realizing he'd gone through an entire 30 round clip with his two bursts. The afternoon sun backlit flecks of spittle as they flew from his mouth. He was screaming for someone to bring him another clip of ammunition and reminded Ryan of a vicious, spoiled child in the middle of tantrum. Ryan had not seen him since the evening in the restaurant and ran their confrontation through his mind again. None of it made any sense. He racked a round into the shotgun, threw it to his shoulder and fired five rounds, one after another towards Edward and White Lady's bridge. Edward simply withdrew into the steel wheelhouse after Ryan's first shot. When the shotgun was empty Ryan quickly reloaded another five rounds from the bandolier on the stock.

Parthenia was still under power and in forward gear and started to separate from White Lady leaving her astern. Both ships began rolling steeply in the seas that were increasing with the approach of the front. While Parthenia's mast might have stayed up despite the loss of rigging on her port side, she kept rolling into the side of White Lady as she pulled away and some of the loose rigging wire caught on the White Lady's anchor where it hung in the bow chock. Parthenia was still making 7 knots through the water and as the entangled wire came taught, her own forward speed dismasted her as the rigging pulled tight. The last thing Ryan remembered was the sight of the main boom falling towards him where he lay in the cockpit.

Below in the engine room Manuel was smiling to himself despite his pain and tried to ration his ammunition as he traded occasional shots with Paulo and the other crewmembers. They were at a standoff. Around him all four diesels were still running, but only at idle, the control cables detached from all of them and he tried to think of ways that he might save himself. Unless he was somehow able to kill Edward and the rest of the crew his only hope lay in getting off White Lady, but what would that accomplish?

After the rigging came tight and dismasted Parthenia, she continued to make way through the water dragging loose rigging wire behind her. Half of their mast was on the deck and the other half was dragging in the water. Ryan lay unconscious in the bottom of the cockpit with the boom and mainsail on top of him and unaware when one of the trailing cables fouled Parthenia's propeller and her engine stalled. Both boats were now dead in the water, rolling in the large seas several hundred yards from one another. Throughout the collision and dismasting Tory and both children were hysterical below. They couldn't see what was happening on deck but heard Edward's gunfire and Ryan's answering rounds. There was a thudding crash as White Lady impacted into their side, then the subsequent sounds of breaking wood and the mast crashing to the deck. All three were knocked to the floor during the impact and when their engine finally fell silent it took several moments for them to realize that they were still alive. The onslaught seemed over.

Jan was the first up off the floor and poked her head out into the cockpit. Ryan lay there amidst the tangled rigging, bleeding from the head and unconscious. She started up into the cockpit to see if she could help him, but Edward opened up on Parthenia again with a fresh clip. When several of the rounds hit the cockpit combing, she ducked back below. Tory and Willy were hysterical and all three of them scrambled to the upper bunk on the side of the boat farthest from the incoming fire. Initially Edward focused his fire towards the cockpit area where he'd last seen Ryan, but Parthenia had drifted far enough away so that he could no longer see down into the cockpit. He shifted his fire more generally into the hull of the whole boat. He'd totally lost it and maniacally screamed out for more and more clips, firing a total of eight into the helpless boat before the weapon finally jammed from overheating. The high velocity shells easily penetrated the 1-inch mahogany planked hull and randomly tore up the inside of the main cabin sending bits of upholstery and sharp shards of wood everywhere, the bullets slapping into galley cabinets, the salon table and even the brass clock and barometer. Clifton was the first to be hit and whined out in a pitiful yelp as one of the slugs ripped into his hip.

Willy was next. His tiny chest exploded from the impact of the high-speed military ordinance. Both Tory and Jan were showered in his blood. When Edward's gun jammed, the silence was complete and total within the cabin. Jan opened her eyes first and was momentarily confused by the light coming from the other side of the cabin. Slowly she realized it was daylight coming in through the multitude of holes that the gunfire had opened up in their side. Then she looked over at her mother who was cradling Willy's head against her chest alternately sobbing and screaming. Her face was covered with gore and blood. Then Jan noticed that she too was also covered in blood.

"Mom! Oh God, I think I've been shot!" She frantically ran her hands over her own body and then started to do the same thing on Tory. Tory opened her eyes at the touch of her daughter and seeing the blood covering them both cried out again and started to brush frantically at the front of her own shirt as if she were brushing off swarming bees. She quickly realized she hadn't been hit and turned back to Jan and then in sudden knowing anguish, to Willy. It was his blood that covered them both. She slowly turned his limp body onto his back. When she did so, the devastating wound in his chest revealed itself.

A low sound stirred in her and began to gather force at the incomprehensible obscenity of what had just happened. The quiet in the cabin suddenly became boundless and frightening and as Willy's lifeblood seeped out, so did a part of Tory.

The guttural sounds that came next were inhuman, and gave voice to the incredible guilt, shame and loss she felt. The unimaginable had just happened. Tory screamed in horror and anguish, knowing she would likely hear the echoes for eternity.

***

The distance between the two boats increased as the rising wind blew them farther apart. Edward was frantic to know that all aboard the sailboat were dead and stormed off the bridge towards the engine room. When he reached the anterior room off it where Paulo and the crewmen were trading shots with Manuel, he quickly assessed the situation and ordered them to launch White Lady's Zodiac.

"Forget Manuel for now and launch the rubber boat! I want to know that all of them are dead on the sailboat. Manuel can't go anywhere wounded as he is. Just leave him. We'll take care of him later if he's still alive." Edward turned towards the doorway and shouted through it. "Manuel! This is your employer speaking, I'm afraid I am going to have to terminate you for cause, so enjoy your last few breaths while you can. If you're still alive later, we'll have a 'sit down' and discuss my disappointment in you. In the meantime, I'm going to have Paulo take a little trip over to your new friend's boat and pay them a visit. Understand?"

Manuel understood only too well and fired a shot towards the doorway. Edward quickly pulled back inside. "Paulo, when you get back, I want you to skin that prick alive. Alive! Do you hear me?"

Paulo smiled back. "Si, senor, it will be my pleasure."

"Yes, I'm sure it will, but right now I want you and Juan to head over to the sailboat before they get any further away and make sure they're all dead. And you," Edward pointed to the engineer. "I want you to make sure Manuel doesn't move from where he is, got it?"

Jorge nodded his head, and as soon as the rest of them had moved onto deck he yelled into Manuel.

"Manuel, are you all right?"

He recognized Jorge's voice and figured he wouldn't have asked if Edward was still there.

"I'm still here amigo, but I have to get off this boat if I want to stay alive."

"Where will you go?"

"Is the gringo's boat still afloat?"

"Yes, but Edward just sent Paulo and Juan over there to finish them," Jorge replied.

"Anything's better than here. If I stay here, I'll just bleed to death or he'll kill me."

"Yes, I think you can count on that."

"Will you help me get off?"

Jorge had to think for a few moments. As he did so the idling engines started to change pitch one by one, and then the generators started to also run rough. Both of them noticed it right away. All the engines were exhibiting the same symptoms as they had when they had lain sideways to the seas in the Bahamas, the unnatural motion sloshing the fuel about in their tanks, refloating the gum wrapper until, once again, it was sucked into the main fuel line screen restricting the fuel flow to the whole system. One by one the engines stopped until the ship was silent and dark.

"It seems that our mysterious ghost is back," Manuel offered.

"Yes, I think so."

"So, will you help me? I'm a walking dead man if I stay aboard."

"I guess I must old friend, or I'll never sleep nights again. But you must make it look as though you overpowered me. Also, I'm going to take a few shots in your direction as soon as you are in the water. If Edward has any suspicion that I helped you he will do to me what he'd planned for you and I do not think I will like that very much."

As soon as Paulo and Juan got the dinghy launched, they motored towards Parthenia making way as best they could without swamping in the six-foot seas. Edward had returned to the wings on the bridge to watch their progress. They approached Parthenia warily and circled around her several times before finally pulling alongside. They could tell she was mortally wounded from the plethora of gunshot holes. Additionally, a larger hole had opened up in her side from the broken mast banging into her hull each time she rolled. Neither suspected she would be afloat for long.

Paulo grabbed onto the rail with one hand and using his other to hold a pistol, peered cautiously into the cockpit. Ryan still lay unconscious and bleeding beneath the boom and tangled rigging. He appeared dead or close to it to Paulo. Above the howling wind, however, he was gratified to hear weeping sounds from below.

'Good, the women are still alive,' he thought to himself.

"Juan, you stay here and mind the dinghy doesn't get smashed up against the side and that we don't get to far from White Lady. I'll go below and take care of business there."

Juan looked anxiously around at the black clouds and massive waves that were now occasionally rolling right over the deck of Parthenia as she took on water and settled lower.

"OK, but hurry. This storm is getting worse and the sailboat doesn't look as though it will be afloat much longer."

Paulo crawled through the still standing lifelines and over the combing until he could look down inside the cabin. Both women were on one of the upper bunks crying. The mother was rocking back and forth clinging to the small boy's bloody body and the little girl was trying to comfort her. While most people would have been deeply saddened by such a scene, Paulo found their wounded, vulnerable state erotic. Anything that hurt or damaged women excited him and over the years many women had received unwanted attentions from him that really should have been visited upon his mother. His father had gotten there ahead of him, however, and had beaten her to death in a drunken rage necessitating that he find surrogates to repay her for her years of abuse. The more frightened his victims were the better.

"Buenos tardes ladies," he said in almost a whisper. Tory and Jan both looked up at once, startled by his voice. Paulo's lips pulled back over his rotten, stained teeth in a sneer-like smile and he giggled as he began to climb down the ladder.

Tory had not been able to conceive that anything worse could happen to them. As far as she was concerned, Ryan and her son were dead, the boat was rapidly filling with water and she and Jan would simply drown in the next few minutes. Her earlier fears of the man now standing before her reignited. Paulo shifted his attention to Jan as he reached the bottom of the ladder. The way he ran his eyes over her body was terrifying to Jan. He put the pistol down on the lower bunk on the other side of the cabin and reached behind his back for his stiletto. Paulo loved the effect his knife had on women and made sure that they were both watching as he depressed the button and the long thin blade shot out of the hilt. Both started at the sound. Then he turned to the chart table area and pulled out the first three drawers until he found a roll of duct tape. With the stiletto in his other hand, he turned to Tory.

"Roll over on your stomach right now or I will cut the girl." Tory hesitated and he immediately put the knife against Jan's throat. Tori still had the pistol in her foul weather gear pocket but there was no way she'd be able to get to it and shoot the man before he cut Jan's throat.

"Right now, this second, or she dies. Do it!" he yelled.

Tory saw no other choice and did as she was told. Paulo quickly wrapped several layers around her crossed wrists, and then did the same to her ankles.

"We told you what we would do to your family if you didn't do as we said." With his other hand he reached down and unzipped his trousers. "I also told you I would fuck your children first, although the boy looks a little worse for wear right now. But the pequita hermosa will still do quite nicely, and best of all, you can watch."

Paulo wrenched Jan out of the upper bunk and onto the lower one and then after propping her up into a sitting position held the knife to her throat with one hand and with the other forced her to look at him.

"Look at it my little lover. Ever seen one of these before?"

Jan screamed out in abject terror, Tory in self-righteous rage. She could not allow this final atrocity and tried to lunge her way out of the bunk, teeth bared. If she could only get near his neck, she would tear it out. Before she could get close enough Paulo simply moved the knife away from Jan's neck to hers. If she moved any closer, she would effectively cut her own throat.

"Tsk, tsk mommy. I know you're anxious to join us but you're just going to have to wait your turn." Paulo was straddling Jan's chest and reached behind him for the duct tape again. He pulled the end out several feet and tore off a piece with his teeth and then roughly wrapped it around Tory's head and mouth. "That's better, I wouldn't want you to disturb the mood for me and the young one." Then he turned back to Jan and ripped her cotton top down the middle. He was fully erect, and Jan started screaming again hysterically.

Across the cabin, Clifton stirred. Paulo had not noticed him when he came below as he was lying behind the lee cloth on the upper rear bunk. After his initial yelps of pain when the bullet ripped into his hip, he'd lain down to take the pressure off the leg, and until that moment had lain there stoically, uncomplaining, as he slowly bled to death. Jan's screams stirred some powerful, primal instinct deep within him and he raised his large jowled head far enough to see over the lee cloth. Jan's panic and the smell of blood spoke volumes to him, and he shifted his body quietly so that it was oriented more in the direction of the intruder who was clearly harming his little charge. Silently, his lips pulled back revealing his shining, curved canines. The thick, short hair on the back of his neck stood up, and his eyes, normally soft and warm, turned cold with fury. Big lovable Clifton, who'd never had an aggressive thought towards man or beast gathered his remaining strength and prepared to launch himself from the berth. He sensed the limitations that his wound and position behind the lee cloth imposed on his ability to achieve total surprise, but that was of no concern to him at that moment. All that mattered was that he cross the short distance and get his jaws around any part of the man's body. The pain from his wound and Jan's terror provided all the incentive he needed to overcome any fight the man might put up.

"Paulo! Paulo! We have to leave man. This boat is going down any second and we're drifting too far from White Lady. Let's go!" Juan yelled from above.

"Yeah, I'm coming. I'm almost done down here," he yelled back.

Back aboard White Lady Edward was distracted as gunfire erupted off his stern. He quickly turned and could see Jorge firing at something in the water. He swung the binoculars he'd been using to watch Parthenia towards the area of water where Jorge seemed to be shooting. At first, he saw nothing and then Manuel's floating form rose up on the crest of one of the waves. He was wearing a life preserver but didn't seem to be moving at all. He could also see blood on his head. He was pissed that he wouldn't now have the chance to personally attend to his treachery, but also knew that if he weren't already dead from Jorge's

71

shots or his knife wound then the ocean would take him anyway. He turned his attention back to Parthenia.

"Hank, what the fuck are those two idiots doing over there? Give them a couple of blasts on the horn and get them back here before we're totally separated. Then get down below and give Jorge a hand getting these mother-fucking engines going again." He turned and left the bridge.

Hank just stood there for several seconds before sounding a series of recall blasts on the ship's horn, amazed at Edward's behavior. It was as if the incidents of the previous hours had never even occurred, or that he'd just been responsible for the death of an entire family and one of his crew. More important to Hank; probably every ship in the entire U.S., British, and Bermudian Navies were probably now looking for them as a result of the Mayday call. He sounded the recall again.

Clifton coiled every bit of remaining strength into his three good legs and prepared to launch himself from the bunk. Jan was crying and squirming beneath Paulo hysterically as he fumbled with her clothes. Tory felt the bile rising in her throat. She was the first to notice the slight movement from behind the lee cloth across the cabin and watched as Clifton tried to get himself into a position he could launch from. She could see his bared fangs and the raised hackles on his back and dared to hope for one second that the big lovable beast would be successful.

Paulo turned his head again to look at the expression on Tory's face. That was half the fun of the rape he was about to commit. He sensed her change in focus though, and just as he started to turn his head, Clifton launched off the bunk and across the cabin towards him. He exploded out of the bunk with such fury that under normal circumstances he would have easily cleared the entire distance between them, but his wounded leg caught on the lee cloth and he fell forward onto his chest on the floor just short of Paulo. That gave Paulo the instant he needed to bring the knife around and as Clifton leapt again from the floor towards him, Paulo's knife caught him fully in the chest. It would prove to be a fatal wound, but Clifton's momentum and anger were sufficient to carry his mass squarely onto Paulo's back, knocking him off Jan and onto the cabin sole. On top of his quarry now he started lunging in towards his neck, jaws snapping, eyes crimson with hate and pain. Paulo was punching at his face with one hand and turning the knife in his chest with other but didn't have a chance against the big dog's fury. Clifton's first few lunges inward fell short and he came away with a piece of cheek with one and a lip with the other, but on the third, he reached the soft nape of Paulo's neck and crushed down hard, gratified to feel the rush of breath through his torn trachea. And then, after a brief pause to gauge his timing, he briefly released his pressure, lunged further in to reset his bite and took Paulo's entire throat into his mouth. Then he worked him, crushing, tearing and finally, worrying the entire neck area as if it were that of a rabbit or fox, his fury adequate to finally break the small man's neck as he whipped it back and forth. Paulo was dead before Clifton finally ran out of strength and collapsed on top of him.

He lay atop the torn and broken man taking in huge, wet, gasping breaths. One of his lungs had been torn by Paulo's knife and he turned his head back briefly to look at Jan. In spite of her near nakedness and fear she moved to the other end of the bunk and gently pulled him off Paulo and cradled his big head in her lap. She knew that he'd literally given his life to save hers. He turned his head up towards hers and whined softly. He did this when he was scared or feeling guilty and somehow Jan sensed that he was actually feeling both; scared because he was dying and guilty because he'd been unable to prevent the assault. This just made his death all the more tragic to Jan and she rocked him, back and forth in her lap, much the same way Tory had with Willy as his eyes dimmed and then closed forever.

In the dinghy at Parthenia's side, Juan was screaming to the now dead Paulo that if he didn't get on deck immediately, he'd leave without him. The water below inside Parthenia had risen to the edge of the lower bunks. Tory knew they had to get off the boat immediately or they might be trapped below as she sank. As soon as Jan got the duct tape off her wrists, she drew Ryan's gun from her pocket. They'd have to kill the other man off the White Lady if they were to survive.

73

Before heading up onto deck she looked back over the ruined cabin that had come to mean so much to her in such a short time, now shattered and destroyed. For what? As she turned to the ladder she looked down at Paulo's body. It had floated into a position blocking her way and she kicked at his face and spit on him before ascending the companionway ladder. Behind her, Jan struggled into a T-shirt. Tory was not prepared for what faced her as she poked her head through the hatch and looked out into the cockpit. Ryan lay unconscious, bleeding beneath the fallen rigging. Waves were filling the scuppers of the cockpit and the rising water threatened to drown him if he weren't already dead.

Juan noticed her right away as she poked her head out of the cockpit hatch and he snapped off a quick shot at her that went wide. Tory quickly ducked her head back below and tried to think knowing they had very little time left before Parthenia slipped beneath the waves. Even though she'd only gotten a brief look at him, she sensed that Ryan was still alive. She had to get rid of the remaining crewmember off White Lady or all three of them would certainly drown within the next few minutes. She looked desperately around the cabin, her gaze stopping on the portholes along the port side. She knew the portholes were made from some kind of strong glass designed to withstand the impact of waves crashing against them, but maybe not so strong as to resist the impact of a bullet. She scurried back below and looked out through the small round portholes until she found the right one. Juan was still holding on to the side of the boat, scared enough now to leave without Paulo but not so brave as to return to White Lady without him. His stomach was at the same level as the porthole, and Tory brought the gun up with one hand and with the other partially covered her face. She pulled the trigger on the 9 mm. The loud explosion within the small confines of the cabin startled her but the bullet did penetrate the glass. She opened her eyes and looked out through the hole in time to see Juan double over and then fall over the side of the dinghy into the sea.

She turned back to Jan. "Get the grab bag Jan! I'll get the EPIRB!" Her idea was that they might be able to launch the life raft and survive that way. The grab bag was a small bag of food and essentials they kept near the companionway for a sinking emergency and the EPIRB was a small electronic transmitter that would help searchers find them. Water was starting to come in through the companionway hatch and Tory knew they only had seconds. She looked over the cabin once more trying to remember if there was anything else they should grab and her gaze fell on Willy.

"Jan, get this stuff on deck, I'll be right up."

Jan hurried up the ladder and Tory turned to the bunk where Willy's broken body lay. There was no way was she going to leave him to go to the bottom of the ocean and gathered him up in her arms. As she climbed up through the hatch, the ocean started in. Parthenia's decks were now at the same level as the ocean surface. Once started, it quickly became a flood, and before either of them could make any motions to launch the life raft, Parthenia started to slip below the surface. Tory shouted out to Jan. "She's going down Jan. Grab one of the cushions!" Jan let go of the grab bag as she lunged for one of the cockpit cushions and watched helplessly as Parthenia disappeared, literally beneath her feet. As she struggled to hang onto the cushion in the furious seas, she looked frantically about for Tory. She looked one way, then the other; nothing. And then she felt something bump against her leg and reached down. She felt a shoulder and grabbed the form around the neck and pulled up with all her strength.

"Oh God, please don't let her be dead too!" She thought to herself and hugged the head to her lower body, and then after reaching further down to get better leverage, pulled up again until the head cleared the surface. Willy's lifeless eyes stared back at her. He was all she had left, and she hugged her little brother's limp body to her own and waited for the ocean to take them both.

Rip Converse

Chapter 6

Tory surfaced seconds later near Jan. She was struggling to stay afloat and hold Ryan's head above the surface at the same time. After orienting herself she swam towards her, dragging Ryan in a lifeguard's hold.

"Thank God you're OK!" she cried and quickly closed the short distance separating them. She grabbed onto the same cushion Jan was using for flotation and struggled to continue holding on to Ryan and to catch her breath at the same time. Ryan started to spontaneously breath and cough up seawater. Tory repositioned her grip around his chest so that her arm wasn't choking him. She didn't know till that moment whether or not he was still alive and renewed her efforts to support his upper body above the surface. After coughing several more times he sucked in several huge lung-fulls of air and instinctively started to move his arms in an attempt to tread water on his own. He whipped his head back and forth, disorientated, obviously looking for them and Parthenia. Tory turned him by the shoulders till their eyes met.

Ryan looked at her, then at Jan, and finally, at Willy's lifeless form which Jan still clung to. "What have they done?" Was all he could manage as he put his hand to Willy's head and turned it far enough to look into his face. He knew right away that he was dead from his blue, white color and unresponsive eyes.

Before either one of them could answer, the water around them began to fill with air bubbles. It was as if a submarine was beneath them and blowing ballast.

"What the hell…?" Ryan started. Before he could finish Parthenia's orange life raft popped to the surface no more than 10 feet away. Once on the surface it continued to inflate into a rigid form complete with a canopy for shelter.

"Thank God!" Ryan said out loud.

"I don't understand. How…?" Tory started.

"There's a hydrostatic pressure sensing device on the canister release. If it senses the pressure of seawater surrounding it the life raft inflates automatically. I never really trusted them, but I guess they work," Ryan explained. But even as they spoke the life raft started to drift away from them at an alarming rate due to its windage.

"Tory quick! Do you have the strength to go after it? I can't with my leg."

"I'll try." Tory struck off in a crawl stroke making her best speed in the heavy seas. Ryan watched anxiously, trying to gauge whether she was gaining. He saw within seconds that she wasn't and yelled to her.

"Tory, wait! It's drifting faster than you." He was worried she would quickly exhaust herself and be unable to get back to them. Tory didn't hear him in the wind and waves and continued to struggle towards it.

"Shit!" Ryan said out loud. "Not her too."

Tory started to slow after several minutes and raised her head several times to check on her progress. After one final push she suddenly stopped and looked back towards Ryan and Jan with a sense of failure and frustration written all over her face. She tried to yell back the obvious.

"I can't make it."

Ryan couldn't make out what she was saying but waved her back towards him and Jan. All at once, as he was doing so, he noticed another form in the water that was slightly downwind of the raft.

"Jan, can you see what that is, just behind and to the left of the raft."

Jan strained her eyes as best she could and waited for the object to rise to the top of the next wave.

"I'm not sure. It looks like someone else in the water!"

Tory was treading water between them and the raft still unsure as to what to do and saw that their attention was focused behind her. She turned in time to see Manuel intercept the raft and throw an arm over the side. She immediately assumed that it was the man she'd shot and started swimming back towards Ryan and Jan frantically.

Once Manuel had his arm over the side, he was able to pull himself into the raft through the fabric doorway. He'd watched the whole scene unfold as the life raft had at first inflated and then Tory's failure to catch up to it as the wind blew it away from them. He quickly looked around the raft hoping to find a paddle. He'd lost a great deal of blood and knew he was likely going to die from the wound in his side but was suddenly determined that these people in the water with him would live. A quick look around the tiny interior revealed no paddle, but he did see a sea anchor and after making sure it was attached, he quickly threw the small fabric drone over the side. It would not stop the raft's drift altogether, but it might slow it enough so that the others could overtake it swimming.

As soon as the sea anchor filled with water, he felt the raft slow and started to beckon to Ryan and Jan with his arms to come towards him. Tory had rejoined them by this time and the three of them looked towards their only hope of survival askance.

"What's he doing?" Ryan asked.

"I don't know." Tory quickly explained what had happened while he'd been unconscious. "I think that's the one I shot. Why would he want to help us now?"

"I have no idea, but we won't last much longer in these seas with all three of us holding onto this cushion. It looks like he threw the sea anchor over. Maybe we can make it now. What other choice do we have?" Simultaneously all three of them started kicking and pulling through the water as best they could. Jan was still holding onto Willy and it was quickly obvious that she would not be able to swim and hold onto him at the same time.

"Jan, I'll hold Willy. You just kick as best you can with both feet and keep holding on to the cushion," Tory said.

"Tory, I know this is hard, but you have to leave Willy." Ryan said.

"No!" she shot back vehemently. "We're not leaving him behind, no matter what. You go on if you have to but I'm not leaving him all alone to be eaten by the fish. He's been through enough!"

"Tory, we have to save ourselves."

"No! Fuck you! He is coming with us!"

Ryan knew it was pointless to argue and every second doing so lessened their chances of reaching the raft. He redoubled his efforts with his good leg and free arm. It took them almost a half-hour to reach the raft. Once they were within hailing distance Manuel egged them on from the raft.

"Come on, you've almost made it! Keep swimming," he yelled over and over. And although the voice that pushed them the last few hundred feet was from the enemy's camp, the strength with which he exhorted them to keep struggling made clear that he was on their side. Jan was first to reach the raft and Manuel reached out as far as he could over the side to grab her as she came alongside.

"Come on little one. I have you," Manuel said as he pulled her into the raft. Then he turned back and one by one pulled the other three aboard.

Back aboard White Lady, Hank continued to watch the sinking yacht from the bridge through the binoculars. He watched her as she sank, and he also watched several seconds later as the life raft sprang to the surface. He never saw whether or not the survivors in the water made it to the bright orange raft. As the storm continued to rise the wind eventually carried the raft completely out of sight and he decided not to impart their possible survival to Edward. Enough was enough.

After getting them all aboard the small life raft and giving them a moment to catch their breath, Manuel spoke. He was clutching his side as he did so, trying as best he could to stem the continuing flow of blood from the gaping wound in his side. The man and the small girl were huddled together, and the woman was holding the obviously dead body of her son tightly to her chest.

"I realize this is much too little, too late, but I am so very sorry for what has happened to you," he started.

Tory interrupted him. "I thought I killed you," she hissed, while stroking Willy's head.

"No, it must have been one of the others," Manuel continued. Although I can offer you no excuse for what has happened to your family, I want you to know that I did my best to stop them. That is why I have this." And Manuel opened his hand enough for Ryan to see the tear in his side.

Ryan spoke. "Do you expect us to be grateful? I mean this whole thing is so insane. What did we do to the man you work for that could possibly justify what has happened to us? Her son is dead. Dead! And you've destroyed my home! And what, I ask you, could this little girl have done to justify the terror she's been through, what? I really need to know!"

Manuel cast his eyes downward. "Senor, I cannot answer that except to say that there is no justification. That is why I am here with you now and no longer aboard the White Lady. I hope that in some small way, my act of helping you might help me to atone for some of my past acts before I myself die. I understand if you cannot forgive me, you have lost too much that can never be replaced. What I have done is all I could have, and it is enough for me to know that I was at least in some way able to help you survive. I'm sorry."

All four were suddenly thrown towards the middle of the raft as it surfed down the side of a particularly large wave. Instinctively they all spread their legs and arms and tried to keep their centers of gravity as low as possible in the raft. The sea anchor that trailed to windward had kept them from capsizing, but it had been close and everyone aboard looked anxiously at the others as they waited to see if there would be a second or third larger swell.

Manuel finally moved towards the zip-up door and drew the zipper far enough down to peer out at the raging seas. "It's getting worse. Do you think there's any possibility we might be rescued?"

Ryan had yet to think about their possible rescue. There was very little light in the raft due to the canopy that topped it and he looked around the raft taking a mental inventory of their supplies.

"Tory," he asked softly at first. He'd noticed that she was starting to disappear inwards and tried to be as gentle as possible. "Tory, when you and Jan abandoned ship what happened to the grab bag and the EPIRB?"

She continued to stare straight ahead stroking Willy's head.

"Tory?" he asked again.

Jan responded. "Do you mean the thing that looked like a piece of orange pipe?"

Ryan nodded.

"She had it when she climbed up on deck, and she told me to get the grab bag..." Jan started to cry. "But I lost the bag in the water. I couldn't hold onto it and Willy at the same time."

"It's ok sweetie, don't worry about the bag, but did you see what happened to the EPIRB?"

Jan shook her head in reply and continued to cry softly. It was obvious that the EPIRB was not in the raft with them, so he dropped the subject and hugged her closer in an effort to reassure and soothe her. Suddenly he remembered Clifton.

"Jan?"

"Yes."

"Do you know what happened to Clifton? When the three of us were floating in the water trying to get to the life raft, he wasn't there. Do you know whether he got out?"

Jan looked up at him with sad, teary eyes and took a moment to reply. "He got shot." She started. "But he also saved our lives. When you were knocked out two bad men from the boat came alongside and one of them tied up mom and..." Jan tried to find the words. "And did some bad things to me."

Jan's words brought Ryan's heart up into his throat and tears into his eyes.

"What did he do Jan?" he asked, anger beginning to replace his concern.

"He tore some of my clothes off and, and he made me touch him. I know what he planned to do. I know he was going to rape me, but before he could, Clifton killed him. You should have seen him Ryan. He was so brave, and even though he was hurt already, that didn't stop him, even after the man stabbed him. Clifton never gave up and kept attacking him over and over and finally ripped his throat out. I will never forget him for saving me."

The two of them hugged again and cried together. Ryan felt as though he'd lost a child of his own and thought back fondly of their years together. He was proud of the big, lovable dog and the way in which he'd given his own life to save Jan's. As he reminisced, he suddenly remembered the small back-up EPIRB that was supposed to be in the raft's complement of emergency supplies and quickly reached across to the small rubber bag that was stitched to the inside of the raft. In addition to a knife, fishing hooks, candy bars, medical supplies and sunscreen, the raft was also equipped with a small, personal size EPIRB and he'd forgotten all about it. Not as good as the expensive satellite version that Tory had lost in the water, but it would put out a VHF signal and alert any passing planes of their location if the batteries in it were still good. Ryan held his breath as he flipped the small toggle switch that activated it and stared at the LED on top of it. Nothing! He was about to throw it onto the floor of the raft when the LED blinked, faintly at first, then steady and bright as the capacitor filled with energy from the still charged batteries.

Three more times over the next half hour the life raft surfed wildly down odd size waves and Manuel, Ryan and Jan tensed and braced each time wondering if they'd be capsized. Tory seemed oblivious. Ryan reached out to her several times trying to elicit some response, but she didn't respond to him and instead continued to rock and stroke Willy. The storm continued to rage and build outside their small rubber raft. As nighttime fell Ryan tried several more times to communicate with Tory and get her to give up Willy, but she hung onto him like he was her only reason for living and the one time he reached over and tried to forcibly pry him out of her grasp she spat at him, "Don't touch us! Haven't you done enough?"

Ryan left it at that because he did in fact feel responsible, and instead did his best to comfort Jan.

At 9 p.m. the unthinkable happened. To that point their nylon sea anchor that resembled a small parachute, had performed admirably, checking their forward motion and slowing their decent down the large seas. But it was old, and even though their raft and the contents were opened and inspected every two years, the service people had tended to focus on the raft itself and its airtightness in their examinations. The only inspection carried out on the sea anchor, was to verify that there was in fact one aboard. No one had taken the time to examine it closely. Age and exposure to salt air had weakened the thin nylon thread that held it together along its seam and the constant drag and surges put on it during their hours in the water took their toll. It didn't let go all at once, but it may as well have. As the final few stitches pulled free of their holes, the cone opened into a useless square of nylon, and the raft started to surf wildly down the backside of the waves. They all felt the difference in their speed immediately.

Ryan quickly reached through the canopy to the line that secured it to check that it was still attached. The line was still there trailing out behind them, but without any drag on it. Before he even had time to call out a warning, the next wave took them, and after throwing them down into the trough on their side, the crest of the same wave flipped them over and upside down.

Ryan tumbled inside the raft landing on Jan and Manuel. Tory and Willy in turn fell on top of them, skewing his broken leg and re-breaking it. Ryan cried out in pain as the sharp broken end of the bone tore through the tissue of his already swollen and sensitive shin again. It was pitch black inside the raft making it almost impossible for everyone to orient themselves. They were upside down with the canopy underneath them and the raft on top of them all. The water quickly started to leak in everywhere as the weight of the raft pushed the canopy beneath the water. What air there was inside, leaked out and the canopy suddenly became a death shroud.

Ryan struggled as best he could towards where he thought the doorway zipper was so that they could all get out, but before he reached it, another wave picked them up, righted them momentarily, and then flipped them once again. This time the canopy tore as they were all thrown against it at once and Ryan found himself in the open ocean, the overturned raft next to him. He looked anxiously around in the water for the others, but they were all trapped underneath the raft. He knew they'd surely drown in the next few seconds if he wasn't able to get to them out. The deflated canopy would entangle and smother them all. He was in agony from his leg, but he put the pain aside, took a deep breath and pulled himself under the lip of the raft to try and help them out. He reached Jan first and, keeping one hand above on the gunwale of the raft, pulled her legs free of the canopy and then grabbed her around the chest and surfaced on the outside. She sputtered a few times and coughed up some water but seemed to have a good grip on the outside of the raft.

"Hang on. I'm going back for the others!" he yelled.

Jan nodded and Ryan dove back beneath the surface. He felt first one way and then the other but couldn't feel either of them. He realized they must have been trapped at the other end. Before he could pull himself around to the other side another huge wave swept under them and he braced himself against the possibility that the raft would flip again. It didn't, however, and he pulled himself around to the other side of the raft knowing he had precious little time left. Once on the other side he dove under again and felt first one way, then the other. He felt a leg and although he could tell from its girth that it wasn't Tory's he pulled anyway, and Manuel came choking to the surface next. After helping him to grab on to the side he went back under a third time. Ryan was panicked now and as he kicked out with his good leg to dive beneath, felt it strike something, and turned. Tory was free of the underside of the raft, but she was face down in the water and remarkably, still clinging to Willy. Ryan quickly reached her, but he was unable to tread water with one leg and support all three of them. He started to choke and take water into his lungs. All at once he felt a hand on his shoulder and turned enough to see Manuel.

"I'll get her. You hang onto the raft." Ryan nodded and turned back to the raft that was only a few feet away. He watched as Manuel struggled with Tory's limp body. He pried Willy free of her. Once that was done, he was able to turn her over and drag her back in a lifeguard's hold. Ryan reached out with his good arm as they neared and pulled Tory alongside him. As he looked over her shoulder, he got one final look at Willy before a wave swept the little boy under and carried him out of all of their lives forever.

Together, Ryan and Manuel were able to partially drag Tory up onto the overturned raft long enough for Ryan to give her several mouth-to-mouth breaths. After just three breaths her lungs took over, and she started to vomit seawater. Her first words as she regained consciousness, "Where's Willy?"

"He's gone Tory. We couldn't save both of you." Ryan replied.

Tory tilted her head back and screamed into the black maelstrom that surrounded them; the scream of the forsaken; keening, woeful, and utterly defeated. It was swallowed up by the deaf night and went unnoticed by a God who no longer cared. Tory's pain mirrored his own and at that moment and Ryan swore to himself that the man responsible for all of this would die. This was not something for the legal system. Edward's crimes against them went outside the normal parameters of reason and injustice. The system was too slow, lenient and gentle in its treatment of criminals and Ryan knew it could not be counted on to exact a just and fair punishment. No, that was something that only he alone could do.

Ryan huddled them all together in the next few minutes and explained the process for righting the raft. Although he was weak, Manuel felt that he had sufficient strength left to try it and pulled himself up onto the underside of the raft and grabbed the strap that ran across the bottom for just such an eventuality. He got to his knees and waited for the right moment and then leaned back with all his weight simultaneously pulling on the strap. The upwind edge lifted slightly, and then, with the others pushing up, the wind finally caught the underside. The combination of his weight leaning backwards, and the wind were sufficient to flip the raft back to an upright position. As soon as it settled all four scrambled back aboard.

"I am going to try and jury-rig another sea anchor." Ryan yelled. He pulled in the slack line that had held the old one, and then after looking around the raft for several seconds took his knife out and cut a large square of the torn canopy out of its center. Then he put knots in the four corners of the material and after gathering the four ends together in his fist, wrapped the end of the anchor line around the knots, and cinched the whole mess tightly together.

"Jesus, I hope this works!" He yelled and threw the whole mess over the side.

It did. Their speed was such that the whole package quickly filled with water and slowed the raft immediately. He looked around the raft to take stock of their situation. It wasn't good. The raft was almost completely full of water, they had no food or water and no protection from the elements except for a small piece of the canopy that Manuel had retained. Without looking Ryan also knew that their back-up EPIRB had been washed away when the raft flipped. He knew he should've tied it to something, but it just didn't seem to matter anymore. He was exhausted, in a great deal of pain from his leg and beyond caring. Tory and Jan huddled together on one side of the raft. He grabbed a corner of the torn canopy, pulled it over himself and huddled up against Manuel. For the next few hours he doggedly questioned him for every possible scrap of information he could get as to Edward's background, crimes and habits.

"Who does he run these drugs for? Where does he live when he's not on the boat? Where does the boat move back and forth from? Who else has he killed? How? When? Does he have family? What kind of drugs does he take? What are his strengths? His weaknesses? Where does he keep his money? What does he care about most?"

Manuel did his best to answer all of Ryan's questions but became weaker and weaker from blood loss and finally slipped into unconsciousness around midnight. When Ryan felt for a pulse at 12:30 he realized that Manuel was dead. He said nothing to the others and instead considered the information Manuel had relayed to him and stayed huddled against him until his body heat started to fade.

Something had changed in Ryan, and even though he understood that Manuel had done his best to make amends in his final hours, he could find no forgiveness in his heart. The visage of Tory still hugging Willy's cold broken body to her own and the reality of their situation was too strong for him and in spite of Manuel's help he did not want the reminder that his body presented. After stripping him of his life jacket, Ryan pulled his body up onto the lip of the raft and rolled it over the side. Tory and Jan looked on silently as he did so. He hoped that the man had been able to make peace with himself and his God before he died because Ryan certainly felt none. After he was done, he moved to the other side of the raft and up against Tory and Jan's shivering forms where the three of them remained until just before sunrise when the last of the front blew through.

Chapter 7

The next day dawned uncharacteristically bright and clear for that region of the Atlantic in December. The sky was crisp, blue and cloudless. There was still a 12-foot ocean swell running from the previous night's storm, but only 8 knots of breeze. The three survivors were awakened from their fitful rest by the sound of a long-range Orion submarine hunter out of Bermuda. It overflew their raft at a scant 100-feet altitude, traveling at several hundred miles an hour and shattered the early morning calm as it clattered over. Ryan tried to open his eyes, but had difficulty. They were crusted over with dry salt and lack of sleep and it took him several seconds to awaken to the reality of their situation. As soon as he moved, the pain of his broken leg brought him fully awake and the rest of the horror of their previous day washed over him. Even though the water that filled the raft was tropical in temperature, it had taken its toll during the night and all three of them were hypothermic and incapable of much movement. He turned his head towards Tory and Jan.

Both were blue and shivering from the cold. Jan was able to briefly open her eyes and make a connection with him, but he knew she was in bad shape. Tory also opened her eyes briefly as the plane passed, but just as quickly shut them and returned to the same distant space she'd occupied since Willy's body had been taken from her. None of them exhibited any of the normal excitement that shipwreck survivors normally show at the possibility of rescue. They were instead husbanding the little energy that remained in their exhausted bodies, to fend off the cold. All this went through Ryan's mind and he wondered at the irony of them freezing to death in 72-degree water. He also briefly thought of the flares that still lay tucked in the rafts rubber survival bag, but the idea of moving his arm to grab one seemed impossible. Besides, the plane had damn near hit them as it passed. They must have been seen. His eyes fluttered shut and he did not open them again until he was awakened an hour later by the pain in his leg when two rescue divers off a Bermudian Royal Navy helicopter moved him into the rescue basket.

The next few days were a blur. His leg had become badly infected and required two operations, one to initially clean and reset the break, and a second after the doctors decided to screw a titanium rod along the broken bone for reinforcement. It turned out that he'd broken the leg in two places and although they'd have to go back in again one day to remove the rod, it's reinforcing effect would allow him a faster recovery and shorter time in a cast. Between the normal recovery for hypothermia, pain medications and the two operations that required anesthesia he'd little memory of the events that took place in the days immediately following their rescue.

Jan had been released from the hospital after just two days into the care of their friends Mike and Paula. The entire island was aware of their story and when the helicopter that rescued them landed, Mike and Paula were waiting on the ground when the three were transferred to two ambulances and taken to the hospital. Jan, Mike and Paula had been in several times to check on his progress. They all reassured him that Tory was fine physically, but he knew there was a lot they were holding back from him. Whenever he asked to see her, it always seemed that 'she was asleep,' or 'resting.' And so, it was with some trepidation that he entered Tory's room for the first time on the day of his own release, five days after admission.

Ryan turned to Jan, Mike and Paula in the hallway outside her room. "I'd really like to talk with her alone first if you guys don't mind."

"Sure, whatever you want," Mike replied. "Just don't expect too much," Paula added. "Everybody has their own way of coping with loss. Tory's pretty withdrawn and blames herself for everything that happened. They also have her pretty well sedated."

"I figured as much. But Jan and I can ease her back. Right sweetie?" Ryan could see the hesitation in Jan's eyes, but she nodded back. "OK, in we go. Jan give me a push, I'm not too good with this thing yet." Jan pushed Ryan's wheelchair ahead of her.

The room they entered was filled with bright sunshine and smelled lush and fragrant from the soft breeze blowing in through the open window. This only served to sharply contrast the gaunt figure that lay in the only bed. Ryan knew it was Tory, but the figure before him bore only the most minimal resemblance to the vibrant woman he'd known. She looked 10 years older, was ashen in color, thin as a rail and barely moved her eyes as they entered the room. She emoted nothing. Ryan put on his best face regardless and wheeled himself slowly the last few feet to her bedside and reached out a hand to touch her brow. Tory turned away as he did so and tried to stifle a sob. Ryan's soul ached for her and without a word yet spoken between them, knew everything that was in her head and missing from her heart. Now was not the time for words and he beckoned Jan close so he could whisper to her.

After he spoke with her, Jan moved behind the wheelchair again and held it steady alongside the bed as Ryan carefully eased his casted leg off the wheelchair rest and extended it out ahead of him. Then he eased his bottom out of the seat and up onto the edge of the bed, and finally, pulled the leg up onto the bed and lay down next to Tory. Then he gathered her in his arms and tried to pull her into a hug. She fought at first but once he had his arms around her and began to hug her to his chest, her will to fight dissolved. His touch was like a life-giving transfusion or a jump-start for a dead battery, and after a few tentative sparks their hearts recognized one another and began to speak. His energy and love began to flow into the empty vessel that lay in his arms. An image of her heart flooded into his consciousness and it scared him. What he saw was dark, withered, hard and totally devoid of color and feeling. He also saw his own, and although it was tight, congested, and full of rage, it was also strong, alive and coursing with love. Tory sensed this immediately and clung to him as if her very life depended on him.

He felt nothing but love and sadness for her and a transference from him to her began. Her hunger frightened him at first; he'd never in his life felt such need from another human being. She fed frantically as though she might never feel again and buried her head in his neck and caressed him everywhere and nowhere. She pulled at his hair, rubbed her face against his and even bit him several times. She would have crawled beneath his skin if she could have and he almost pulled away, so strong was her need. But he didn't, and rode with her, and felt her pain, her loss, her guilt and her emptiness. They were vast, and this ethereal transference of life went on for several minutes. Several times she cried out, but Ryan just hugged her harder giving her the strength she needed to go on and live again.

It was as if a great dam let go all at once and she began to cry, softly at first, then she sobbed uncontrollably until she could barely breathe. She had not till that point had the strength and inner resources to even begin grieving for Willy let alone forgive herself. His death was an obscenity of such monstrous proportions that she'd truly been in denial till that point. Ryan almost broke their connection again as he felt the strength of her pain but her absolute need for him and his warmth and forgiveness overpowered that fear and he hugged her even tighter so that she could better take anything she needed from him.

Jan stood mutely by at first, then scared as she witnessed the intensity of her mother's emotions. Eventually she moved to the other side of the bed and climbed up and hugged her mother from the other side, and the three cried together as one until there were no more tears.

Mike and Paula knocked softly several minutes later and getting no response opened the door far enough to peer in. The three of them were all asleep, still clinging tightly together.

Paula put her arm around Mike. "They look like such damaged souls."

"I know. I hope they can come back from it,"

"Remember Cecily and Ben and what happened after they lost their little boy?" Paula asked.

"Yeah, I do," Mike replied. The couple Paula was referring too had lost their four-year-old when Ben backed his car up one morning in a hurry to get to work. Their son had been sitting in the driveway behind the car playing and Ben had never seen him.

"They never could get over the guilt," Paula observed. They softly eased the door closed and turned to find Sergeant Sutton behind them.

"Hello Sergeant, such a terrible thing that's happened. Any word yet on the search for the yacht?" Mike asked.

George took off his cap, nodded to Paula and shook Mikes hand. "No, I'm afraid not. It's quite remarkable actually. I can't remember when there was such an all-out search for a boat except for maybe when that family was lost in the Marion to Bermuda race back in '90. Even the Canadian and Bahamian Coast Guards are looking, and I don't think I've ever seen the American Coast Guard quite so fired up to find anyone."

"How can you hide a vessel of that size?" Mike asked.

"That's just it. You can't. I'm sure we'll turn her up eventually. Whether the perpetrators will still be on board, well, who can say, but it's not such a large world that criminals like these can hide easily anymore, especially when the crime has gotten so much publicity. How are our friends? I'd like to talk with Mr. Cunningham again to see if he has remembered anything else that might help us track this man and I still haven't talked with the woman. Every time I've checked on her the doctors have had her sedated for the shock."

"They're asleep right now, but I think the healing process has begun. They all just had a good cry and my guess is that the woman will be very anxious to provide any information she can. Why don't you just give them a half hour or so." Mike suggested.

"I think I can do that," George replied with a smile.

"Good to see you and good luck. I really hope you can catch these bastards. I suspect that if these three are ever going to have a shot at putting their lives back together these men will have to be brought to justice," Mike said.

"Just so. Just so. I'm sure you're right. If someone killed one of my children and burned down my home, I know I wouldn't sleep till the person was in prison, or better still, in the ground," George nodded to Paula again, put his cap back on and walked stiffly towards the waiting area.

"I don't think I've ever seen old Sergeant Sutton quite so animated about anything." Mike commented to Paula. "If I didn't know him to be the stuffy, old, by-the-book Brit that he is, I'd almost say that he was suggesting that any means would be justified in bringing this man to justice."

"Well, he partly blames himself for what happened. I guess he felt that if he'd done his custom's search and initial inquiry better, he might have turned up something on this man Edward and the whole thing with Ryan and Tory could have been averted," Paula said.

"Too late for that now."

Ryan was the first of the three to awaken some 40 minutes later and he tenderly brushed a strand of hair off Tory's forehead. It felt good to be next to her and to feel her warmth. She opened her eyes several seconds later and held his gaze steadily. The connection was still there between them.

"Ryan, what are we going to do?" she asked.

"I honestly don't know. That's such a huge question. I really don't have any experience dealing with this kind of loss; I guess we just do things one step at a time. What else can we do?"

"I miss my Willy so much. I can't believe I'll never hold him or hear him laugh again."

"I know. I'll never forget his excitement when I taught him to swim and dive or the funny game we played of me paying him for swears. The fact that we'll never see him again or hear him laugh makes me so profoundly sad I can't begin to imagine what you're feeling. Everything we owned went down with Parthenia, most of my money, my home, and I guess my dreams. It's still so overwhelming. I guess one of the first things I'll do is get in touch with my insurance company to make a claim on Parthenia. But even that seems so unimportant now beside Willy. You and Jan are what really matter to me. What do you feel you need to do? I mean we're a team, right?"

Tory stroked him back. "Yeah, we are, and I really don't know what to do next. Right now, I don't feel like I can do anything for a while. I need some time to absorb this whole thing. Whatever it is we do; we have to take Jan into consideration first."

They were interrupted by a short knock on the door and then a nurse entered without bothering to wait for a reply. She bustled busily into the room carrying a tray. She was coal black, about 300 pounds, and had an aura about her which made it clear that she was a 'no nonsense' kind of a caretaker. She brought herself up short when she saw Ryan, and Tory together in the same bed.

"What's all this about then? It looks like the blind, leading the blind. You must be feeling a little better today if you've got your man in there with you."

Jan woke up also and propped her chin under her wrist on Tory's other side. "Hello Mrs. Davidson."

"You too? My gracious, how many people do you folks have in that bed? My God, I'd be hard pressed getting just my own little self into that bitty bed." She shook her head for dramatic effect.

"Now, I can see you folks are having a little hug session, and that's all well and good, but the missy here hasn't eaten enough to keep even a small minnow alive since she got here. I'll make a deal with you. If you can help me to get her to eat something, I'll let you stay. If not, well, out you goes. It's medication time too, deal?"

Tory rolled her eyes in mock disgust then smiled. "Yes, nurse Davidson."

"I think those are the first words you've spoken to me child; I was beginning to think you didn't have a voice. Why don't you just call me Fran, everyone else does."

"All right, Fran. What have you got on that tray?" Tory replied.

"Boy, you are better missy." She lifted the lid off Tory's plate and peered at it. "Looks like Salisbury Steak Belmond, mashed potatoes and carrots. Sound good?"

"Sounds fancy, what is it?" Tory asked.

"Hamburger with gravy." Ryan interjected in a bored voice.

"All right Mr. Cunningham, that's enough out of you. I figure we're all either a part of the problem or a part of the solution and your comment would seem to shade this delicious dinner towards the negative, so out you go. Also, there's no room to put the tray down with all three of you scrunched up together."

95

Ryan sighed and then gave Tory a kiss on the cheek. "Don't worry, I'll hang out for a while, but I better get off this bed before Fran throws me out." He smiled an exaggerated smile at Fran and then carefully swung his bad leg over the side of the bed as she held the chair for him.

Jan also got up and Fran placed the tray over Tory's legs and stood by to see that she took her pills.

"What medication do you have her on?" Ryan asked. Fran looked at the chart. "Well, let's see, Valium for shock and depression, and a multi-vitamin. Not too much. If we can just get her to eat some and gain her strength back, I'm sure the doctor will release her soon." Tory popped the pills into her mouth and Fran handed her the water glass.

Ryan was tempted to say something as Tory swallowed the pills. He knew that Valium was really the equivalent of alcohol in a pill but held his tongue. Tory had been through a lot and maybe it was just as well that she not feel everything yet.

Fran tucked Tory's napkin in front of her hospital jammies and then started for the door. "I'll be back in about 20 minutes. I don't want to see a scrap left on that plate, OK?"

Tory nodded her head, her mouth already full. As Fran opened the door, she almost ran down Sergeant Sutton.

"Sergeant Sutton, what a pleasant surprise." She beamed at the much smaller man.

"Oh, hello Fran," he replied, obviously discomforted by her warm greeting. "I wondered if now might be a good time to speak with Mr. Cunningham and the young lady. I heard she was feeling a little better."

"Don't you dare interrupt the young lady till she's done eating, but you can speak with Mr. Cunningham." Fran replied stiffly. She seemed miffed that he'd so quickly turned the conversation to business matters.

"Good morning Sergeant Sutton," Ryan interjected. "I'd be happy to talk with you. Why don't we head out into the hall so Tory can have a little peace while she eats?"

"That would be fine."

Ryan wheeled himself across the room and through the open door that Sergeant Sutton held open. Once outside he stopped and turned the chair towards him.

"Any word yet," Ryan asked.

"I'm afraid not."

"I don't understand. From what you've told me every ship in both our Navy and Coast Guard is looking for them in addition to the Canadians and Bahamians. How can they just disappear?"

"We're as mystified as you. I suppose we'll have to consider the possibility that they simply scuttled the ship, but to do that they would have had to do it much closer to a coast. I mean they'd need some way off the ship. We think that's unlikely though given the value of such a vessel. Believe me, we haven't given up yet and Interpol is also now involved due to the international nature of the crime. How are you doing?" George asked.

Ryan didn't reply immediately and when he did his tone was bitter. "I'm healing physically I suppose, but things will never be right again, especially if this man isn't caught."

"Believe me, I understand. If such a thing a had ever happened to me, I don't know what I'd do." He paused for a moment. "What's next for you folks?"

"We don't know. Everything we had was wrapped up in our boat. I suppose we'll go back to the States as soon as Tory is able and try and provide some stability for her daughter. From there…? Ryan let the rest of his sentence hang.

"I know that words are inadequate at a time like this, but I want you to know that I'll not let this thing slide. I have children of my own and I would very much like to see this man caught. No matter what happens, if I can ever be of any help, any help at all, just let me know."

"Thank you, George."

George was immediately uncomfortable with the familiarity that had developed in their conversation and again became more formal. "I still have to speak with your missus, do you think she's up to it?"

"I think so, just use your judgment. I know it's just as important to her to catch this man and I suspect it will help her recovery if she can contribute but please don't push her, if she gets too tired or upset just let it go. I doubt she can provide you with any details I haven't," Ryan replied.

"In any case, I have your numbers in the States and your number here in Bermuda. If I don't see you again I promise I'll let you know if we turn up anything. Good luck, and once again, I'm terribly sorry for your loss. It's all so senseless."

"Thank you, George. I'll be in touch." And Ryan reached out and warmly shook his hand.

Chapter 8

Edward turned to Hank. "Blow out that fuel line again if it needs it and fix those cables that that puta Manuel disconnected and then get her back on course for the coast and make all speed. We can't be late for our drop off. Hopefully the gringo's Mayday messages were not heard."

"It'll be slow with this storm," Hank warned.

"Push her Hank. Don't give me excuses. I'll be below. Much as I hate to admit it, I think this little diversion of mine is going to cost us the White Lady. It's quite possible that his Mayday message was picked up and as soon as this storm clears every Coast Guard vessel on the planet is going to be looking for us. I want you to maintain speed no matter what and get us as far away from this location and towards our rendezvous point as quickly as possible. Right after we reach the rendezvous point and offload to the smaller boats, we will scuttle White Lady. Have the crew torch the top off the cocaine tank now to save time and have them familiar and ready to open every thru hull fitting on this boat the moment the coke is offloaded.

***

Tory, Ryan, and Jan boarded a Delta jet and headed back to Sippican, Massachusetts via Logan Airport. Bill and Stephanie had agreed to let them stay at their place until they could find one of their own. The three of them were mostly silent on the flight. The loss of Willy was still very much in the forefront of all their minds. There was also the realization that they had no plans or dreams to pursue and the flight home to where it had all began only served to underscore this. The three were very much the walking wounded.

Before departing Bermuda, they'd decided to have a small memorial service for Willy on one of the small islands that lay at the entrance to St. Georges. Ryan and Tory didn't feel like they wanted to drag Willy's death back to the mainland and to instead close out his life where it had ended. Their plan was to have a local minister say a few words honoring his life. Mike borrowed a small launch from a friend and Mike, Jill, their three children, Tory, Jan, Ryan and the minister traveled out to the uninhabited island. They'd expected to find the island empty, but as they approached Ryan saw that there were dozens of other boats pulled up on the beach and at least 100 people on the shore. Mike was as surprised as Ryan as they drew closer.

"I don't understand, it looks like a large picnic or something. There's never anyone out here except for kids once in a while. Do you want to try one of the other islands or shall we just do this from the boat?" he asked.

"Let's go a little closer," Ryan replied.

As they approached Ryan could see that most of the people were clustered together and all seemed to be dressed in their Sunday best. At the forefront of the group Ryan made out the unmistakable form of Sergeant Sutton, the customs agent. Although they'd only invited Mike and Paula and their children to the makeshift memorial, Ryan suddenly knew that all these others had also come to pay their last respects to the little boy that none of them had ever met. He was touched and leaned down to Tory.

"I think they've all come to say goodbye to Willy. Do you mind sharing this?"

Tory shook her head as the tears started again. "No, it's fine," she replied. They coasted into the beach and as the bow nudged the sand George came forward as the ad-hoc representative of the group.

"Please forgive us if we are intruding Ms. McCane and Mr. Cunningham, but everyone here is very saddened by your terrible loss. Many of us are shamed that such a thing could possibly have happened on our island. If it would be all right with you, we would be grateful if you would allow us to pay our last respects." He shifted his feet uncomfortably. "Of course, we would also understand if you wanted to keep this moment private."

Tory replied before Ryan could. "Sergeant Sutton, thank you for coming. I'm sure it will mean a lot to Willy to know that he has so many friends even if he never met all of you. We'd be honored if you joined us."

"Thank you, Ms. McCane. Here, let me help you down."

"Please, just call me Tory."

"Of course." And George offered his hand and helped her off the bow of the boat and into the sand at the water's edge.

"Ms. McCane," he stopped himself. "I'm sorry, Tory, this is my missus, Virginia and our five children."

Tory held out her hand to the tall, slender woman Sergeant Sutton gestured towards whose only similarity in looks to her husband was her strict and proper bearing. They shook hands tentatively at first and then the older woman took Tory in her arms and embraced her warmly.

"It's a terrible thing that has happened to you dear. I don't know what I'd do if one of mine was taken. Anything I can do, you let me know, even if it's just a shoulder you need to cry on."

Tory looked up into her eyes. "Thank you, Virginia, that means a lot to me. Everyone here does." One by one the rest of group came up and introduced themselves to Tory and Ryan. Tory was overwhelmed by the number and sincerity of them all. They included the pilots and crews of the Orion and the helicopter that had rescued them, employees from Mike's sail loft, crews off other sailboats, and a great many others they had never met but who felt their loss as their own. After everyone had introduced themselves, the minister gathered his new flock together with purpose and led them up the small hill that overlooked the Atlantic, and from there led the group in a short but powerful service in memory of Willy. After reading several Bible passages that Tory had selected, he paused briefly then continued. "I would like to conclude this memorial with a poem by Ralph Waldo Trine," And he looked out over the water and recited it from memory.

"Loving friends! Be wise and dry
Straightway every weeping eye;
What you left upon the bier
Is not worth a single tear;
'Tis a simple sea shell, one
out of which the pearl has gone.
The shell was nothing, leave it there;
The pearl-the soul-was all, is here."

There was absolute silence at first, as he concluded, and then the tears began, tears from the mothers, tears from the fathers and especially tears from the children who for the first time in most of their short lives faced their own mortality in Willy's death. After a suitable pause the minister took a flower that he'd been holding throughout the service and cast it off the hill and into the ocean below. One by one everyone else followed suit, until the water below was littered with small bright bouquets of flowers. And then, clinging to one another for support and courage, they stood by silently and watched as the current scattered and pulled their offering out to sea. The flowers were like the small boy they paid tribute to; colorful, full of life, harmless. One by one the individual blossoms and stems drifted apart and out of sight on the vast expanse of Mid-Atlantic water. The symbolism was not lost on anyone and the weeping began anew as each in his own way envisioned Willy alone on the infinite ocean without the comfort of a parent or loved one to guide and protect him.

***

Six hundred miles to the northwest on the other side of the Gulf Stream Edward was off-loading the last of the cocaine onto a fishing boat that had been subcontracted out of New Bedford, Massachusetts.

Prior to sinking White Lady, he had the crew gather every loose item on board that would float including life preservers, cushions, and life rings, and lock all of it below in the staterooms. He wanted nothing floating to the surface for the Coast Guard to find. The longer he could keep them looking for White Lady the better. Then, after ensuring that all the seacocks were open and personally going below decks to check on the rising water, he jumped onto the fishing boat that had stood by. White Lady was already low in the water but as the sea finally reached the level of the transom where the watertight door to the engine room stood wedged open, she quickly filled the rest of the way and sank beneath the waves and then onto a bottom that lay 2,000 feet below. Once they docked ashore the cocaine would be loaded into the trunks of several cars and delivered to Miami.

Rip Converse

Chapter 9

As they flew back to New England each was lost in his and her own thoughts. Jan had withdrawn back to the person she'd been prior to Tory's recovery. Ryan's thoughts had turned to what they'd do next on returning to Sippican. Tory continued to dwell in her memories of Willy and a multitude of 'what ifs.' What if she'd gone to Ryan immediately after the kidnapping? What if she'd never taken them on the trip at all? What if she'd had the strength to stop using drugs earlier? That was the question that haunted her most. What if she weren't an addict and had been able to throw the damn stuff away before their final confrontation with White Lady? Would she have better been able to protect Willy on that last day?

Ryan was seated in the aisle seat so that he could stretch his casted leg straight out. Jan and Tory sat beside him. They both stared vacantly out the window. Several times Ryan had started to initiate a discussion about what they'd all do and where they'd live but stopped himself each time. Every thought that came into his mind seemed so trite and unimportant next to the loss of Willy, so he stayed silent. There would be enough time later to try and figure out the rest of their lives.

Just before landing the pilot came over the intercom and announced that Boston was 31 degrees, overcast and wet with sleet and snow. Ryan had forgotten that winter was almost upon New England. The plane turned final at 7:20 p.m. and rolled up to the gate at 7:27. As the engines spun down and the seat belt light came off, he turned to Tory.

"How're you doing."

"I'm OK, mostly just tired," she replied trying to sound normal.

He slid his arm around her. "We don't have any coats and it's cold as hell out there."

Tory just shrugged and he wasn't even sure whether she'd processed his remark. They waited till last to disembark because of Ryan's cast and crutches and he made his way awkwardly up the aisle in a sideways crab. Once outside the plane he got into a wheelchair the airline provided and was pushed up the ramp to the terminal by an agent. The short trip up the gangway seemed to take forever and when they finally emerged behind the slow-moving line, they found out why. Someone had tipped the press and they were besieged by the media as they entered the terminal. While their story had understandably been front-page news in Bermuda for days previous, they had no idea that it had also become front-page news in the U.S.

Bill and Stephanie shouldered their way through the hungry reporters and came to their side. "Sorry about this guys. If we'd had any idea that this was going to happen, we'd have let you know before you left," Bill apologized.

The reporters pressed in with their disregard for anyone.

"Ms. McCane, Ms. McCane!" one reporter interrupted. "Do you have any idea why you were kidnapped by this man." And another. "Any leads yet?" And another. "Do you have any comment on the Attorney General's call for an increased crackdown on smugglers?"

All the reporters kept pushing and interrupting one another in their frenzy to be on their own camera with an exclusive looking interview that the questioning didn't stop, even as Tory fainted and slid to the floor.

Jan immediately started screaming, "Leave her alone, leave her alone!" And fell to her knees next to her mother. Instead of backing off the news people pressed in tighter sensing a great shot.

"Please, just leave us alone!" Jan plaintively wailed.

Ryan lost it and began swinging one of his crutches down on top of the cameramen and their cameras. So intent were most of them on staring through their viewfinders and catching Tory's pain and Jan's anguish for the late edition news that he was able to successfully clock three or four before the others realized what was happening and they backed off several feet.

"Christ, can't you people leave us the fuck alone!" Ryan shouted. "Bill, see that electric cart over there?" He pointed to one of the electric airline courtesy carts. "Get it so we can get the hell away from these people!" Bill nodded and broke through the reporters to talk with the driver.

Ryan looked over the assembled group of faces looking for a friendly one and found it in a state trooper standing off to the side.

"Please sir, can you give us a hand here? These animals are smothering her."

The trooper pushed his way through the reporters to clear a path so that Bill could get nearer with the courtesy cart. Tory was starting to come around and the trooper helped her to her feet and then got her into the cart. Ryan, Stephanie and Jan quickly followed. Ryan was certain that the reporters would also have tried to jump in if it hadn't been for the young trooper running interference at their rear. He was the last to jump aboard on the bumper.

Ryan turned to Tory. "You OK?"

"Yeah, I guess so, just get us out of here."

As they drove through the concourse towards the arrivals area Ryan tapped the trooper on the shoulder. "We only have one checked bag and can probably get the airlines to send it later. Can you just help us get out of here?"

The trooper felt guilty that the situation had gotten so out of hand back at the gate and nodded his head and reached for the mike button on his chest mike. "Central, this is Trooper Barrett, would you please have a unit meet me at the Delta arrivals level to transport five?" He turned back to Ryan. "Do you folks have a car?"

Bill answered, "Yes, it's in the short-term lot on the lower level."

Trooper Barrett keyed his mike again. "That will be to transport five to the short-term parking lot."

"Affirmative on that. Do you require assistance?" Central inquired back.

"Negative, I'm just trying to help that family off the Bermuda flight get away from the reporters."

"Understood."

Trooper Barrett turned to Ryan. "I'm sorry that whole thing got so out of hand, I should have stepped in sooner. One of our units will meet us at the terminal door and take you folks to your car."

"Thanks."

"If you give me your baggage check I'll make sure that the airlines send it along," he offered.

Ryan nodded and after asking to borrow his pen quickly wrote Bill and Stephanie's address on the back of his ticket folder and handed it to him. "The claim check's inside." And after looking at the officer's name tag added, "Trooper Barrett. Thanks for your help. We had no idea that all this was coming and I'm afraid the whole thing kinda took us by surprise."

"I understand. Now if we can just keep the ones you hit with your crutch from suing you, you'll be fine." He smiled an approval at Ryan.

"Can they really do that? I mean they were the ones assaulting us!"

"I'm afraid so, the public's right to know and all that. Not only can they, but they probably will."

"Great, that's just what we need on top of everything else," Ryan mused.

Trooper Barrett stuck out his hand. "My name's Chris, Chris Barrett. You've been pretty big news here in the States. There are a great many people that are real sorry about what happened to the little boy and your boat."

"Thanks Chris. I really appreciate you taking care of the bag. Tory and Jan have been through enough in the last few days.'

"No sweat," Chris replied as the electric cart pulled up at the terminal exit doors.

As they got out of the courtesy cart one of Chris's fellow officers stood by the automatic door and motioned them to the cruiser at curbside. "It will be kinda tight, but I think we can get everyone in if the little girl sits on someone's lap."

"We'll fit," Bill answered. "Just get us out of here."

"No problem sir," the trooper replied.

Bill, Stephanie, Tory and Jan sat in the back. Ryan sat in the front, unrolled his window and stuck his hand out to Chris. "Thanks again for your help."

"You're entirely welcome. Take care of yourselves."

As the cruiser accelerated off Chris turned to the herd of reporters spilling out through the doors.

"I'm afraid you folks just missed them."

"Do you know where they're heading?"

"Not exactly," Chris started. "But they said something about a relative in New Hampshire."

All the reporters immediately rushed off to their satellite trucks and Chris smiled to himself as he walked towards baggage claim. It wasn't much, but it might buy Ryan and Tory a day or two of peace and quiet before the media got back on their scent.

Ryan filled Bill and Stephanie in with a lot of the details of what had happened to them in Bermuda as they drove from Logan Airport back to Sippican; details that hadn't been reported in the media. Ryan had been a drug user himself at one time and always believed in an individual's right to choose. As drugs like meth and crack had flooded the market, his opinion had changed. The new drugs being pushed were so addictive that choice no longer seemed part of the equation.

"I don't know Bill. On the one hand I'm glad for the increased focus on the whole industry because maybe it will somehow hurt the man who hurt us, but I don't really think it will make any difference. We've never had the balls as a country or a society to do what really needs to be done to end the whole thing. I mean it can be done. Look at what the Ayatollah Khomeini in Iran did after they got rid of the Shah."

"What did he do?" Bill asked.

"He hung 12 heroin dealers in one day in the main square of Tehran. That sent a very clear message. End of drug problem. True zero tolerance," Ryan replied.

"Do you think that's what we should do?"

"I don't know anymore. The problem is where do you start and stop. Three quarters of the dealers I ever knew were people just like me. I mean do we start hanging the kid next door who sells a couple of joints to his friends or just heroin dealers who carry a gun?" It was quiet in the car for a while and then Ryan continued.

"I do know one thing. None of the people I ever knew would kill for drugs or purposely try and screw up another person's life. We just wanted to have a good time. This guy Edward is truly evil and needs to be put down. And I don't want to hear stuff like, 'he had a dysfunctional childhood' or 'one of his chromosomes isn't quite right.' Shit, half the people I know had screwed up childhoods. This guy is different. He needs to be eradicated like a contagious disease. This is the first time in my life that I actually feel like I could kill another human being. I don't mean in the heat of the moment; I could have done that easily if I'd had the chance out at sea. I mean with malice and forethought."

The drive to Sippican took about an hour and Jan and Tory slept most of the way. After they pulled into the driveway Ryan gently shook them awake and the three of them went inside where Stephanie showed them to their bedrooms. It was only 9 p.m., but both Tory and Jan decided that they were going to bed. After they were done in the bathroom Ryan went in to check on each of them and say goodnight. He was still too wound up to go to sleep himself and went into Jan's room first, adjusted the covers as best he could, balanced on one crutch, and then smoothed the hair off her forehead.

"Goodnight kiddo," he whispered and then moved to his and Tory's room down the hall. She was seated on the edge of the bed with her back to him and he watched as she tipped several Valium into her hand out of a large prescription bottle and swallowed them with water from a glass on the bedside table. Still without turning towards the door, she clicked off the light, lay down, and pulled the covers up around her. Ryan came into the room and sat down awkwardly on the edge of the bed next to her. He put his hand to her brow as he had with Jan. She didn't say anything to him and instead just pulled his hand into the fold of her neck and assumed a fetal-like position turned away from him. Ryan sat silently feeling the warm pulse in her neck. There would be enough time later when things settled down to talk with her about the

Valium. For now, it was enough that she and Jan were alive and safe. Eventually he got up and hobbled as best he could out of the room and down the hall to the kitchen where Bill and Stephanie sat drinking coffee. They had been whispering something to one another and looked up almost guiltily when he entered the room. Stephanie finally thought of something to fill the silence and held up her coffee mug.

"Want a cup?"

"No thanks, I'm too wound up as it is."

"It's decaf."

Ryan hated decaf but he smiled and nodded his head, "Sure, I'll have a cup." He sat down at the kitchen table with his broken leg sticking out into the middle of the floor.

" I can't wait to get this damn cast off."

"How long?" Bill asked.

"Believe it or not, just another week. They put a titanium rod in and screwed all the pieces together sort of eliminating the normal healing time. I have to go back some day and have the rod taken out, but for now I'm happy with the prospect of getting out of the cast quickly."

Both Bill and Stephanie nodded their understanding and were silent again and the three of them alternatively took sips of their coffee and fidgeted with items on the table amidst the quiet. All of them were uncomfortable. In the brief time he'd known Tory his contact with Bill and Stephanie had been limited to mostly superficial exchanges. He was acutely aware of the fact that the interim living situation to which they had agreed implied an intimacy that he did not yet share with them. He also had the feeling that they probably blamed him in some way for what had happened to Willy, Tory and Jan.

Ryan blinked first. "I'm not really sure where to start. So much has changed since we left here five weeks ago. First, I want to sincerely thank you for taking all three of us in. I know this is disrupting your life in a lot of ways. I also know you must have some second thoughts about me in light of what's happened..."

"No, really, we're happy to have all of you," both Bill and Stephanie interjected simultaneously.

"I appreciate that, but let me finish," Ryan continued. "What I was starting to say is that since we left, my relationship with Tory has expanded into something very special; despite what has happened. Both of us have struggled personally in many ways for a lot of years and I believe we've found in each other something that makes us whole. In many ways we both feel as though our lives started over since we met each other. Don't get me wrong. Right now, everything is in shambles. Willy's death has been devastating to all of us and we have a long road ahead of us, but I think we can make it if we stick together. It's going to be toughest on Tory. She really does blame herself. When Edward pumped that shit back into her body, it brought back every bad feeling and insecurity she ever had. As you both know, I had my own share of problems with drugs and alcohol years ago, so maybe I'm better able to understand and explain what's happening with her now."

"How can she blame herself; she was forced into taking drugs again?" Stephanie asked in outrage.

"When Edward released her, he left her with a bag of coke, a "little present" was how he phrased it, I believe. I learned this from the crewman who was in the raft. Apparently, it was this crewman Manuel who found out Tory was an addict by following her to an NA meeting one day. Edward's intention was not to simply kidnap and terrorize her. He wanted, no, he knew, that all he had to do was get her started again, and then the addict in her would take over. What that scumbag wanted was to reintroduce her addiction back into our whole family. That way he could hurt all of us and best get to me. Anyway, he partially succeeded. Tory didn't tell me about the whole thing right away because she was so ashamed that the stuff was back in her body in the first place."

"But it wasn't her fault!" Bill yelled.

"Of course, it wasn't. But she was starting to come down off the stuff and hadn't told me yet. The addict whispered to her that maybe the whole thing could just be avoided and forgotten if she had a couple more lines. Believe me, I understand. I went through that whole thing so many times back in the days when I still drank and used. You know the deal, "Tomorrow I'll stop." you say to yourself, and you really mean it, but when tomorrow comes it's just too painful to deal with your reality, and the circle goes round and round," Ryan paused then continued. "We have an interesting expression in AA. It says that, 'one is too many, and a thousand's not enough.' Does that make sense to you?"

They both nodded, but Ryan knew they probably didn't really get it.

"What it means is that if an alcoholic or drug addict has any alcohol or drugs it sets off a physical compulsion in them to have more. That's why as long as they stay away from the first one, they can stay sober. If they do have just one, then that compulsion gets reignited and once that happens then a thousand's not enough. Their cravings know no limit. I certainly don't blame her, but she blames herself."

Ryan thought for a moment then continued. "Unfortunately, the doctors in Bermuda put her on Valium since the accident to combat her depression and shock."

Bill and Stephanie nodded again as though this had been a reasonable thing to do. Ryan looked at them realizing that they still didn't really understand.

"What that means is that they are continuing the cycle that Edward started. Tory's still on drugs. She has no freedom of choice and won't, until she's weaned off that crap too. Tory has a lot of healing to do regarding Willy's death, we all do. But in addition to that, and maybe in spite of it, Tory also has to deal with her addiction again like she did 14 months ago. I just wish that the two weren't so intertwined, it's going to make dealing with either one more difficult for her."

"What can we do?" Stephanie asked.

"I'm not sure yet, although I think you're doing it. I can't tell you how much it means to all of us to be able to move into a stable home right now. Everything in our lives is upside down. Listen, I know you two hardly know me and I suspect that you probably blame me a little bit for everything that's happened,"

"Ryan," Bill interrupted. "Don't be ridiculous."

"I know you don't think I willingly exposed them to danger, but I also know that you guys looked a little askance on our whole trip. That's OK, but it's really important to me that you know how much I care for the two of them. Tory's like a missing link to me, someone I've been looking for all my life. And Jan, well you both know her, she's incredible. I'll do anything to make things better for them again. I know you both feel the same way and I hope that maybe you and I can build some kind of relationship based on our common interest."

Stephanie spoke next. "It makes me feel a lot better to hear you say all that. I know you're also very special to her. Over the years I've seen her go through a world of shit and quite a few losers. She's always deserved more. I mean, of all the possible people this could have happened to. When I first learned that Willy had been killed, I just stumbled around for days. I was very sad for him, he was a wonderful little boy, but the implications of that loss to Tory left me bereft! I felt like going down to the church and banging on the door and yelling, 'Hello, is anyone up there still minding the fucking store?' Pardon my French, but really, give me a break."

Ryan smiled at her allusion. "Yeah, I know what you mean. This whole thing has really shaken my faith too."

Bill spoke again. "I just want you to know that you're welcome here with us. You were right about my reservations about your whole trip, but I don't doubt the sincerity of your intentions. Just let us know how we can help. You know how much we love the two of them."

"I do. Going forward I really think all of us need to pay particular attention to Jan. She's the quiet one, too quiet, and because of that and because she never wants to stir the pot or call attention to herself, I think everyone including me has underestimated how this thing might be affecting her. I got to know her pretty well over the last few weeks and she confided a lot to me about her life when Tory was still using. I'm worried that she has emoted so little since Willy's death because inside I know she's really scarred. She's incredibly strong, even by adult standards, but she's still just a kid and should be worrying about stuff like boys and what to wear to school. Instead she's taken on the responsibility of her whole family and everything that happens to them. She could easily disappear inside herself or blow up with rage or hurt herself. She has some tough times ahead of her. I think the most important thing right now is for the four of us to just love her and try to give her as much stability as possible."

Bill and Stephanie nodded in agreement. "Maybe we should see if we can get her some counseling? I have a good friend who specializes in adolescent psychology. I'll talk with her tomorrow."

"That's a great idea Stephanie," Ryan agreed. The three sat around the table for a few more minutes absently pushing their coffee cups around but more comfortable about their relationship. Ryan finally got up.

"I don't know if I can sleep yet, but I'm going to give it a shot. I've got a feeling the next few days are going to be long ones."

Bill and Stephanie got up at the same time and Stephanie came around to Ryan's side of the table and gave him a kiss on the cheek.

"I'm glad we got a chance to talk some alone. I feel a little more comfortable about..."

"Me, right?" Ryan finished for her.

She smiled back warmly. "Yes, with you."

Bill reached out and put his arm somewhat awkwardly around Ryan's shoulders. "That goes for me too."

"Thanks, I appreciate it." Ryan got up, put his empty cup in the sink, said goodnight, and moved towards the guest bath on his crutches. Several minutes later he got into bed alongside Tory and after propping his head up on one wrist, lay silently next to her, listening to her breathe and watching her in the faint moonlight that came in through their window. She was still curled in the same fetal position he'd left her an hour earlier and he lay staring at her, amazed at her existence in his life. He wished that he could remove all of her pain; past, present, and future. In spite of the challenges he knew lay ahead of them, he made a silent vow to stand by her and Jan, unconditionally. When his wrist finally started to fall asleep, he laid his head on the pillow and spooned his body around her flank so that her buttocks nestled into his pelvic area and cupped one of her warm, little breasts in his hand. She briefly stirred at his closeness and then squirmed backwards reflexively to seal any small gaps between them.

He awoke at seven the next morning feeling rested and better physically than he had since breaking his leg. Tory was still asleep, and he decided to let her sleep as long as she could. He'd awoken just once during the night when he heard the sounds of her taking another pill in the dark and decided that today he would raise the issue of her Valium use. He knew she'd eventually develop a physical dependence if she kept it up and thought back to the Valium withdrawals he'd witnessed

115

10 years ago in others. They were frequently more difficult than alcohol and he knew she would have enough trouble getting over her psychological dependence without the added challenge that a physical withdrawal would entail.

He slipped from beneath the covers and hobbled into the bathroom on one crutch resolved to the fact that he'd speak with her later in the morning. The pin in his leg was working well and with the swelling finally down he found himself able to put some weight on his bad leg for the first time since leaving the hospital and decided to try for a bit more than the sponge bath he'd been settling for since they put the cast on. After filling the tub halfway, he lowered himself carefully in with the casted leg supported on the edge of the tub and the rest of his body in the warm water. "Jesus that feels good." He said out loud and let the warmth soak into his tired bones for a few minutes, washed his hair the way he once had as a child by rinsing it in the tub water and then began to soap his body.

"Anyone in there?" a voice asked.

"Who is it?" he asked.

"It's me, Tory. Can I come in? I have to pee real bad. I won't be a second."

"Yeah, sure."

Tory came in looking half asleep and barely looked at him as she sat down on the toilet.

"Good sleep?" Ryan asked.

"I guess, how are you?" She looked over at him through puffy eyes. "That's a pretty good arrangement you've got there." Referring to his casted leg on the tub edge. She reached for some toilet paper and as she did, looked down at him in the tub noticing his wet, naked body and smiled. It was her first smile and acknowledgment of him as someone special to her since the hospital and *the day*. That was how he now thought of their lives together now. Everything was dated and started from *the day* of Willy's death and the sinking of Parthenia.

He smiled back and watched her as she stood. As she did so the back of her T-shirt hung briefly on the curve of her slender flank before falling back into place over her buttocks and vagina, and in that one brief instant he suddenly wanted her very much, to be deep inside her, feeling her move beneath him with need and warmth, giving and receiving. He wanted to reestablish and renew their commitment to one another. He looked into her eyes and for an instant saw the same longing. And then, as if a curtain fell between them, it was replaced by the glazed, distant, expression that she'd borne since *the day* and the smile faded from her face.

"Would you like to climb into the tub with me? There's plenty of room for two."

Tory hesitated. "No, thanks. I really have too much to do today and, well, I'm just not sure I'm ready yet."

Ryan felt guilty immediately. "I'm sorry babe. I understand and didn't mean to pressure you. I just thought that maybe it would be good for us to be close. We've been so far apart and I miss you is all."

"I miss you too, maybe in a few more days after I adjust to being back and we start to get our lives together again."

"Yeah, sure. Whatever, whenever, I'm here for you. Don't stress about it, OK?"

"OK. See you in the kitchen for coffee?" she asked.

"Yup. Just let me shave and change and I'll be right in."

Fifteen minutes later he entered the kitchen and just before he sat there was a knock on the kitchen door. Ryan turned around to the sound as did Tory and Stephanie and saw a man in a flannel shirt holding one hand up to shield his eyes from the sun, standing in the doorway.

"I wonder who that is? Do either of you recognize him?" Stephanie asked.

Although there was something vaguely familiar about the man Ryan couldn't place him and shook his head. "I'll see what he wants." Ryan volunteered and turned and opened the door.

"Can I help you?" he asked, and then it dawned on him and he recognized the man as the state trooper who had helped them at the airport the night before.

"Come in, come in. I didn't recognize you out of your uniform."

"Thanks, and it's Chris, Chris Barrett."

Ryan held the door for him. He was carrying their checked bag from their flight home that they'd left at the airport.

"Of course, that's great, you have our bag I see! Please, come in," Ryan said feeling sort of stupid and at a loss for words.

"I hope I'm not intruding?" Chris asked.

"No, not at all, it's just a surprise. I didn't know you guys do delivery service too."

"Well, you know our motto, *to protect and serve*. This is the service part."

Ryan laughed. "Yes, I guess I've heard that before. Come on in and join us for a cup of coffee.

"Thanks, I will," Chris replied and sat down at the small kitchen table with Stephanie and Tory, unzipping his jacket as he did so.

"Cream, sugar?" Ryan asked as he poured.

"Both would be good, thanks."

"I didn't even think about the bag until it was time to shave this morning." Ryan tilted his head back to expose his neck showing several small cuts. "Ended up using a guest razor." Ryan raised his eyebrows to Chris in an expression meant to convey the disdain all men feel for women's well-worn blades.

Chris laughed as did Tory and Stephanie, more to cover their slight unease than in amusement. Despite his lack of uniform, Ryan, Tory, and Stephanie were all children of the '70s and Chris' short flat-top crew cut and erect posture continued to betray his true profession despite his friendly bearing. Chris was nervous too, as many police are when they are amongst civilians. All of them knew what was going on and disliked themselves for it. Ryan, truly grateful for his gesture, broke the impasse by making a joke out of it.

"All right, what did we do?" he asked with a straight face.

Stephanie was the first to get it and choked on her coffee as she started to laugh. Tory and Chris quickly got it and started laughing too.

"Good, now that's over with, we can start communicating like real people. God, what is there about police that makes us civilians so nervous?" Ryan asked.

"I don't know, but the same thing goes for cops. You'd think we'd be more comfortable around the people we work for. I guess we just see so much of the negative side of society that we tend to look at all non-police through suspicious eyes. Believe me, I hate it sometimes."

"Well, let me open the negotiations by saying how much I appreciate you bringing our bag by. How come you didn't just let the airlines do it?" Ryan asked.

"Well, when I went down to baggage to ask them to send it along it occurred to me that some of the reporters might have the idea of tracing you through your bag and I just figured I would be less corruptible than one of the airline delivery people. They're all pretty hot on this story and would love to know where to find you. I only live about 15 miles from here and had the day off anyway, so I figured, 'what the hey?'" Chris paused for a moment. "Actually, since we're trying to communicate here, I might as well tell you I'm also a frustrated sailor and really curious about what happened to you guys."

"Really, what kind of sailing have you done?" Ryan asked.

Stephanie interrupted. "You three will have to excuse me. I can already see where this conversation is heading, and I have to go to work. Tory, what are your plans? Can I do anything for you today?"

"Thanks, but I don't think so. Jan and I are going to go by the middle school this morning to re-enroll her and other than that we don't have any plans," Tory replied.

"OK, well you've got my cell phone number. Just give me a call if you need anything." Stephanie turned to Chris. "Good to meet you again, and thanks again for last night. You really saved us."

"My pleasure. Hope to see you again some time," he replied.

Stephanie cocked her head a little to one side. "Well, perhaps you can join us for a meal sometime. Are you married?"

Chris smiled. "No, but I'm not against the institution."

Stephanie had a little glint in her eye. "Well, I may know just the person you should meet. Got a steady girl?"

Chris blushed and Ryan interrupted. "Christ, Stephanie, cut the man some slack. It's early in the morning yet," he jokingly chided her.

Stephanie maintained her steady look at Chris. "Get his phone number before he leaves Ryan, I think I have just the right person in mind for him. Do you like kids Chris?"

Chris was really blushing now, and Tory chimed in. "Stephanie, really! We've only known Chris for about 20 minutes. I mean for all we know he's gay. No offense, Chris."

Stephanie dismissed her comment. "Just get his number, OK? I'm serious. And all of you have a good day. I'm off."

"Good to meet you Stephanie. And thanks, I think," Chris said as she gathered her keys and departed the kitchen door with a quick backward wave. Ryan and Tory were both a little embarrassed after the door closed and kept their gazes focused on their coffee cups. Chris spoke first. "Don't worry about it. I'm flattered."

Tory was the next to get up. "I've got to get Jan up and get ready to go myself, so I'll leave you guys to your sailing talk. As you might guess I'm not real big on sailing right now anyway. I hope you do join us some night Chris, maybe when things get a little more back to normal around here." There was a pregnant pause after her comment and suddenly things felt awkward again. She hurried from the room with tears welling up at the allusion to normalcy. How could things ever be normal again?

Ryan knew what was going on right away and got up to follow her. Chris stood up too, feeling guilty and responsible for her sadness.

"I'm sorry Ryan. I guess now isn't a real good time to talk about sailing. How about I give you call a few days from now?"

"No, please don't go. I really feel like talking with someone. Let me just go and check on her."

"You sure?" Chris asked.

"Yeah, I'm sure. Just hang out for a few minutes and help yourself to another cup of coffee. I'll be right back." Ryan followed Tory. When he got to her room, she was sitting on the edge of the bed crying softly and he stood in the doorway for a second feeling her pain before easing himself down on the bed next to her and putting his arm around her.

"It'll be alright babe," he said in a comforting voice.

"Will it Ryan? Will it ever again? When I said to Chris, 'When things get back to normal' this black cloud washed over me. How can anything ever be right again? " Ryan continued to hold her. "You know, I think what bothers me as much as anything is that the guy who's responsible for killing Willy and tearing up our whole life is still walking around out there. I mean what else has that man done and what might he still be capable of doing? It's just not right!"

"I know, I know," Ryan soothed. He did know too. How could they ever have any real closure on the whole thing with the knowledge that Edward was still out there?

Tory wiped her tears after a few more minutes and kissed him on the cheek. "I've got to get going. Is Chris still here?"

"I think so. I told him to hang out."

"Do me a favor and apologize would you? He seems like a nice guy. And get his number like Stephanie asked. It would be fun to have him over some night."

Ryan smiled at her. "OK, I will." And he eased back out of the room.

"She OK?" Chris asked as he returned to the kitchen.

"Yeah, I think so," Ryan replied. Then he hit the table with his fist a few seconds later.

"No, damn it, she's not OK! Who the hell am I kidding? She just had one of her kids murdered for no fucking reason at all and I feel helpless to do anything about it! God, I'm angry! She and her two kids are like the three best things that ever happened to me and there wasn't anything I could do to stop this whole thing. It all just happened so fast and for no damn reason. I mean how is it that guys like this can exist and move around. I mean don't half the law enforcement agencies in the world know about him and what his group is up to?" Ryan asked.

Instead of answering his question Chris had a suggestion. "Ryan, what're you doing today?"

Ryan shook his head and held up his hands. "I don't have a clue. Shit, I don't have a home, a job or a boat any longer. Maybe I'll go out and do something about one of those things. Why, you got a suggestion?"

"Like I said earlier, I only live about 15 minutes away, on a farm in Westport to be exact, and when I'm feeling frustrated like you sometimes it helps to tear up a few cans."

"What do you mean?" Ryan asked.

121

"Well, I have a shooting range set up out there. It's a hobby of mine. As a matter of fact, I'm the top shot on our SWAT team. What do you say? It's a great way to let off steam."

"I don't know. There are a hundred things I should be doing today. Besides, I haven't really shot in years and my only guns went down with my boat."

"So what? Guns I got plenty of and with you in this mood you won't get much done anyway except maybe get into a fight with someone. What do say?" Chris paused for a second and then added in a conspiratorial tone, "It's still pumpkin season."

Ryan smiled at the last. "Alright, you convinced me. Can I draw faces on the pumpkin?"

"Whatever makes you happy," Chris replied.

Half an hour later they turned off the paved road and onto a dirt lane that bordered a large cornfield. The corn had been harvested two months before and all that remained were the stubs where the combine had cut them off. The field reminded Ryan of Chris's haircut and he snickered out loud.

"What?" Chris asked.

"Oh nothing."

"Come on, what?"

"I was just thinking how much this corn field looks like the top of a certain person's head."

"Very funny. You know I didn't always look like this. There was a time in my younger years..." and Chris went on to tell him about his teenage years which were very similar to Ryan's own. Although they were about five years apart, their backgrounds and experiences were amazingly close, and an easy comradery seemed to be developing between them that Ryan had not found in another male for years. As they continued along the edge of the field, they passed a small, dilapidated machinery shed with an old rusted tractor beneath a sagging eve and Ryan chuckled again.

"What is it now?" Chris asked.

"I'm just laughing at your tractor. What is there, a state law that all New England farms have to have one of those and an old bathtub in the front yard?"

"I'll have you know that particular unit is a classic and someday I intend to restore it."

"I'm sure," Ryan quipped back. They continued to joke back and forth as they paralleled the field and at the end of it they crested a small rise. Beneath, there was an old, but well-maintained farmhouse in the middle of a hay field that overlooked the Tiverton River and beyond, the shores of Rhode Island.

"Wow," Ryan said out loud. "This is quite a spread. Don't tell me you bought this on a trooper's salary."

"No, I won't. It's been in my family for about 125 years. When my folks died, I got it because I was the only child."

"Have they been gone long?" Ryan asked.

"About three years now."

They pulled up in front of the house and a Golden Retriever, a black Lab and a Jack Russell terrier bounded off the porch to greet them. Ryan was suddenly very glad he'd come. Amidst the larger concerns of Jan and Tory he'd given little thought to the loss of Clifton and seeing the three dogs leap off the porch in clear ecstasy at the return of their owner warmed a part of him that had been left cold by Clifton's death.

"You didn't tell me you had dogs!" Ryan said with the enthusiasm of a little kid.

Chris could tell from his tone and expression that this was really a big deal to him and kept silent as the car came to a halt. Ryan had the door open immediately and all three dogs immediately raced around to his side of the car with the realization that there was someone in the car with Chris.

"Watch out for the black Lab, she just had puppies and she's still a little skittish around strangers!"

"Not around me," Ryan laughed. "What're their names?"

"The Golden is Oro, the Lab is Raven, and the little guy is Short Stuff.

To Chris's surprise and amazement all three dogs were immediately and simultaneously right next to Ryan vying for his attention, yapping and licking him as if he were their long-lost owner. Ryan started to pet all of them at once and began laughing as they returned his affection with wet, sloppy licks across his face. "Christ, Ryan, did you come by in the middle of the night and give them a steak dinner or what? I've never seen them act that way with a total stranger, especially Raven!"

"No, they just know that I love them and that I miss my Clifton. Maybe he talked to them." Ryan replied.

Although he tried to keep his head averted as Ryan answered, Chris noticed a few tears on the side of Ryan's face. He didn't know what it all meant but decided to let it pass without comment and opened his own door.

"Let me show you around," he said as they got out.

Raven jumped into the spot Ryan vacated on the seat and pawed the air in glee. Ryan reached back in and scratched her belly which belied her recent litter.

"Stop pampering my dogs Ryan. You'll ruin 300 years of breeding and hundreds of hours of training."

"Yeah, yeah, yeah," Ryan replied. "I can see these bowsers have had nothing but a firm hand on their behinds. I'll bet you're worse than I am."

Chris laughed because it was true. He spoiled his dogs rotten right down to letting all three of them sleep on his bed.

Ryan eventually detached himself from the dogs, leaned over his crutches and followed Chris for the short walk into his house. As they approached the front porch Raven separated herself from the pack and led the way into the house through a dog-door alongside the front door.

"Now she remembers she's a mother," Chris noted.

"How old are the pups?"

"Six weeks."

Chris unlocked the front door and held it for Ryan. Just inside was a mudroom. Raven had climbed over the makeshift board enclosure and was busily nosing her five pudgy offspring.

"They're beautiful," was all Ryan said.

At the sound of his voice all of them started mewing and yapping all at once and climbing on top of one another as if they were trying to form a small pyramid and affect escape.

Ryan stroked Raven's head for a moment to reassure her and then after putting both crutches under one arm reached down slowly towards one of the pups, but came up a few inches short, having trouble balancing.

"Here, let me help." Chris reached in and plucked a fat puppy off the top of the pile. "How's this one?"

Ryan straightened, put the crutches back beneath their respective arms and gratefully accepted the proffered pup. His expression answered Chris's question and after tucking the small dog safely to his chest breathed in deeply, savoring the puppy smells of newspaper, urine, mother's milk and new life.

Ryan placed one of his hands on the soft, immature, grey/white belly. "I think you should name this one Clam Belly."

"That one's already spoken for, but I'll suggest it to the new owner."

"Are they all taken?" Ryan asked, although he couldn't even consider a new dog with their lives in such turmoil.

"Yeah, I'm afraid so although I'm going to keep one for myself. Like I need another dog!"

They both smiled and Ryan brought the dog's small cold nose to his own before handing it back to Chris.

"It's nice to see new life."

Chris led him straight through a front hallway to a very large, atypical living room. "Make yourself at home. I'm going to check my messages and feed these canines. Come on guys." The three followed obediently.

"Sure," Ryan replied distracted by the room he found himself in.

Almost shaker in its simplicity and furnishings, the few items in it reflected a culture and taste Ryan had not expected to encounter. A Steinway Baby Grand stood in one corner with sheet music scattered about reflecting recent activity, and an open, leather-bound Faulkner rested on a small, round, tiger maple table alongside an overstuffed chair next to the fireplace. On the other side of the room, polished Georgian silver candlesticks graced a large antique dining table surrounded by matching Windsor chairs, and a pair of ancient Ming Dynasty porcelain vases with a matching bowl about three feet in diameter stood on a sideboard. In the middle of the room, a large, comfortable corduroy couch faced glass sliders and the back deck. It was flanked on the ends by two beautiful mahogany end tables with lamps made from Ming vases matched the ones on the sideboard, and in front of it squatted a small coffee table with hand carved ball-in-claw type legs. The only other furnishings in the room were a large collection of books that bordered both sides of the fireplace and a number of framed photographs on the mantel. Ryan immediately headed towards those, fascinated with his new friend.

Several of them were obviously of his parents. Most of them, however, were of one woman. And an interesting woman she must be, Ryan thought to himself. In one she was helmeted in a kayak on the edge of a wild looking mountain river, in another she was in parachute harness next to the doorway of an old DC3, in still another she was on horseback in jumper get-up. What captured Ryan's imagination more than any of her obviously active and eclectic interests were her eyes. They seemed alive, even on the photographic paper her passion for life clearly showed through.

"You want a coffee?" Chris yelled from the kitchen.

"Yeah, sure," Ryan yelled back distractedly. "Cream and sugar."

When Chris reentered the room several minutes later Ryan was still standing at the fireplace, hunched over his crutches, and holding one of the smaller photographs of the woman so that he could see it better.

"Who is she?" he asked as Chris came up behind him.

"My wife," was all he replied.

"But I thought you were single?"

"I am. She died a few years ago," Chris replied in a flat tone.

Ryan looked after him as he crossed to the coffee table in front of the couch and put down their cups.

"I'm really sorry to hear that man. She looks like she was an incredibly special woman."

"She was, I still miss her very much."

The two sat silently on the couch for the next few minutes sipping their coffees and looking down on the pastoral scene that fell away to the river. Ryan was curious to know more about the woman in the photos but figured Chris would share with him what he was comfortable with, in his own time. "You ready?" Chris finally asked.

"To....?"

"Go shoot some bad guys."

"Oh, yeah I guess so," Ryan replied, having forgotten for the moment why he'd come.

"Follow me and I'll show you the rest of the house and we'll get our pieces."

"Pieces? Oh, like in gats."

"Exactly," Chris replied and led Ryan off through the kitchen door where he was greeted again by the dogs.

"Let's leave them in," Chris suggested and led Ryan into another wing of the house and into what was obviously his bedroom. As they entered Ryan was immediately stricken once again by the number of photos of Chris's wife. There were several framed enlargements of the two of them and even a small oil portrait of her on one wall. Ryan said nothing and followed Chris across the spacious room to a tall Browning gun safe that stood in the corner. Chris bent down slightly to the electronic keypad and pressed several buttons before turning the arm that opened it and swinging the door open.

"Boy," Ryan said in awe. "You do have a whole lot of pieces!" In addition to three shelves of handguns and ammunition on the bottom of the unit, there were at least eight rifles of varying sizes and calibers that stood in a rack in the top section.

Chris laughed. "I guess I do. Like I said earlier, it's a hobby of mine. A lot of the rifles are from when I was a competition shooter in college. Two of them are custom sniper type rifles like the one I carry in the trunk of my cruiser." He handed one of the holstered handguns to Ryan. That's a Berretta 92FS 9mm with a five-inch barrel. Why don't you run your belt through the holster; that will be yours."

The only automatic Ryan had ever handled had been his father's old Colt 45 1911 of military issue and he felt clumsy as he un-holstered the more modern weapon and pulled the slide back to check that it was empty before sliding the hip holster through his belt.

"I've only fired an automatic once before and that was years ago. It was my father's old *1911*; You're going to have to check me out."

"Don't worry I will," Chris replied as he continued to pull boxes of ammo off the shelf and put them in a small knapsack at his feet. He also put a Leupold spotting scope with a small tripod into the knapsack. Then he selected another 9mm for himself and clipped that holster to his belt before reaching back in again and also taking two rifles out of the rack. They both had longer barrels than Ryan had ever seen on a rifle and were equipped with scopes.

"Christ, we could start a war with all this," Ryan muttered.

Chris handed the knapsack to Ryan and then picked up a rifle in each hand. "Can you get the door?" He motioned with his head to the glass slider that opened onto the deck. "My range is right here in the back yard."

Ryan slid back the door and let Chris out ahead of himself. Off to their left was a small copse of trees and after sliding the door closed behind them Ryan followed Chris to a small shooter's stand beneath a lean-to type of roof, feeling self-conscious, although quite empowered with the Berretta on his hip. The area they entered was cleared and showed recent use as evidenced by the litter of shiny shell casings that lay atop the pine needles. Chris immediately sat down at a small bench that stood in front of a shooter's table and started to empty the contents of the knapsack on the table after placing the two rifles in a rack at the side. His movements were smooth and practiced as he began to fill several of the clips with rounds. Lastly, he set up the small spotting scope on the collapsible tripod.

As Chris loaded, Ryan looked downrange at a number of plywood stands set at different yardages. The first one was relatively close to their table with the farthest one being about 300 yards out.

"Pretty cool set-up."

"Yeah, I know. I use it quite a bit."

Chris finished loading and stood up and withdrew a stapler and several rolled up targets from a box behind them. "I'm going to put a few of these up. Do me a favor and wait till I get back before you load."

"No problem." Ryan answered.

Chris walked downrange and stapled one of the life size human silhouette targets to stands at 10, 30, 100 and 300 yards. He had one target left in his hand and continued walking away down towards the river. Along the way he stopped alongside a small, fenced, vegetable garden that had gone mostly to seed, and after rummaging through the undergrowth, held a medium size pumpkin aloft in a triumphant sort of gesture, tucked it under his arm like a football player, and with a quick backward smile continued down the field several hundred more yards. When he finally stopped, Ryan estimated him to be out almost 600 yards and used the spotting scope for a better view. Chris raised another plywood stand that had been lying on the ground, stapled a silhouette to it, and then placed the pumpkin on a nearby stump before jogging most of the way back.

"We'll save the long stuff for last, after we warm up," he said to Ryan.

"I can't even see it!"

"Don't worry about it. Sometimes I shoot at half that distance again with pretty good effect. Now, hand me your pistol. I want to familiarize you with it, so you don't shoot me by mistake."

Withdrawing the Berretta from the holster at his side and careful to keep the barrel pointed towards the ground, Ryan handed it to him butt first.

"That's good. I also noticed that you checked it earlier to see whether or not it was loaded."

Chris picked up a clip off the table and smacked it into the butt of the Berretta. "One of the nicest things about all of the new 9's is that most of them have up to a 16-round capacity; one up the snout and 15 in the clip. That's actually twice as much as the old 1911s that held eight rounds. The larger capacity obviously gives shooters a great advantage over traditional revolvers." He held the gun up so Ryan could see what he was about to do next. "Watch as I engage and disengage the safety." Chris flipped the safety on and off several times using his thumb to illustrate how it worked. Then he fingered the safety "on" and handed the gun to Ryan.

Chris continued. "When you fire your last round the reciprocating slide will lock open on the load stroke which lets you know you're empty. Got it?" Chris reached into his coat pocket and handed Ryan two green ear plugs. "If we don't use these, we'll regret it later."

Ryan inserted the two ear plugs. "Which target should I shoot at?" Ryan asked as he assumed what he thought was a proper two-handed shooter stance, although he was canted at a slightly odd angle as he continued to support a lot of his weight on his left crutch.

"Start with the closest-in one and fire your first clip into the head area."

The first target was just 10 yards out. Ryan tightened his grip and extended his arms outwards in the direction of the target. It felt a little odd to be firing at a life size image of another human being.

"Don't worry, you won't feel a thing," Ryan said out loud to the silhouette. He flipped the safety off, took a breath and then slowly pulled the trigger. It bucked lightly as it fired, and he lowered the gun immediately to better see the target and where his first round had gone. "I don't see it."

"Off target to the right. Don't even think about it. It's cocked now, in automatic mode. Keep shooting."

Ryan nodded, reassumed his stance, and tried to get the center sight to settle down between the rear sights. The Berretta was lighter than the six-shot revolver he'd kept on Parthenia and about the same as his father's old 45. He added a small amount of pressure to the trigger and took a deep breath before taking up the rest of the slack. The pistol jumped in his hand again and when he lowered it slightly to check the shot, he was gratified to see that it was within two inches of the head. Without commenting, he squeezed off three more measured rounds and checked his progress again. All were within the head region. Feeling more confident, he emptied the rest of the clip into the target without stopping. All his shots but one had impacted somewhere in the head area.

"Not bad, eh?" he said in a self-congratulatory tone and lowered the automatic after ejecting the empty clip into his other hand and checking that the chamber was empty.

"Actually, that was pretty good and as long as the bad guys are considerate enough to walk up to within 10 yards of you and stand still, you'll win every time."

"I guess we are kinda close," Ryan admitted.

"It's alright though. Here, let me give you a couple of pointers on your stance. First of all, keep your right arm more rigid. You want that arm to be like a rifle stock and you want it to absorb the recoil straight down its length. I noticed that the gun twisted slightly as each of your rounds left the pistol. Let me show you."

Chris racked a round into his gun, replaced it in his holster, paused briefly and then in a smooth, quick motion that belied his years of competition combat shooting, drew it and fired three rapid rounds. All three went into a small area about an inch-and-a-half across through the heart of the silhouette. He was totally comfortable with the high-power weapon. The gun had looked like a tethered extension of Chris's hand as he'd drawn and fired. Ryan wondered how many thousands of rounds he'd fired to be able to achieve such control.

"You're very good," Ryan said with honest admiration.

"Thanks, I worked pretty hard over the years to get that type of consistency. I used to compete quite a bit. Ready to try it a little farther out at the 30-yard target?"

"Absolutely," Ryan replied.

"OK, same thing as last time but lock your right arm out a bit more and rather than squeezing your trigger all at once, take up half the slack first, steady your aim again, and then take up the rest.

Ryan nodded, took his stance again and fired center mass at the target 30 yards out. It was three times the distance away of the first target. His first two shots missed altogether but the other 13 all hit the paper. There was no grouping of any sort, however.

"Shooting a pistol accurately is lot harder than people think. In reality pistols are strictly close-in weapons and are most frequently used at just 10 to 20 feet. That second target is just under 100 feet out so in reality that's pretty good. You just need to refine your stance a little more and practice."

They each fired several more clips at the two targets closest to them. Ryan was starting to feel more comfortable with the Beretta and was able to smoothly cock it, hold it and change clips without feeling as though it might jump out of his hands of its own volition. But he found his ability to consistently hit any area of the target at the longer range, minimal. Chris's patterns stayed to within about six inches at the longer distance.

"Now that we're warmed up let's do some real shooting."

Ryan holstered his Berretta. "I guess, but don't expect much."

"Relax, you're doing fine. With these next shots we can really take our time. Also, we'll be shooting from a rest position."

Chris swept the spent shell casings into a can off the end of the shooter's table and then stacked two sandbags on top of the table. Then he grabbed one of the long-barreled rifles out of the rack and set it in front of Ryan.

"This is a Parker-Hale Model 85. It fires a standard 7.62 mm NATO round, and it's very accurate up to about nine hundred yards and effective to almost 1,100. It's bolt action but has a 10-round magazine. It's British made and has a muzzle velocity of about 2,820 feet per second if my memory serves me."

Ryan suspected it did.

"The scope is a 1.5-10 power Leica Magnus which has six hand ground lenses, nitrogen filled, adjustable parallax, with an illuminated L-4A reticle; very clean optics. Oh, and one click on both the elevation and windage dials equals 1 cm (1/3 MOA) at 100 meters. I also have 10-inch sound suppressors attached to the end of the barrel, so you won't need to wear ear protection."

"Aren't silencers as illegal as machine guns?"

"Not if you pay a $400 registration tax."

"Can we blow up the pumpkin now?" Ryan asked with a straight face.

Chris stopped and looked at Ryan like he'd just farted loudly during High Mass. "You're impossible. Here I am trying to serve you a gourmet meal, and you want fast food. This is art! I'm giving you details on probably the finest rifle you'll ever fire and all you can think about is the pumpkin? Why don't I just give you a big stick so you can go smash it?"

"OK. OK," Ryan replied. "I'm sorry. It's just that you're so good and know so much about this stuff that it's a bit intimidating. I just wanted to blow off a little steam, not try out for the Olympics."

"You're right. I've been out here in the country a little too long. Let's start over. See that little round metal tube on top of the gun? Look through it, put the cross hairs in the center of the chest area of the silhouette at 100 yards and gently pull the trigger. I'll use the spotting scope and tell you where your shot went."

"Now you're talking."

Ryan looked through the scope. "OK, I've got it but I've got to tell you, even with me resting the gun on the sand bags I can see my crosshairs jumping up and down every time my heart beats."

"That's normal, you have to learn how to shoot between beats."

"I'm surprised you haven't mastered the art of stopping yours," Ryan joked.

Chris just looked at him.

"You mean you can?" Ryan asked incredulously.

"I can't exactly stop it, but I can control it to the point that I can affect the interval."

Ryan shook his head.

"When I went down-field to set up the targets earlier I noticed that we have a crosswind running from left to right at about five miles per hour. That means I expect your first shot will go about 3 to 4 inches wide of what you aim at to the right. That's OK. Don't try and compensate. I'll tell you how to adjust the scope after seeing where your round goes. This rifle has hardly any trigger slack compared to the pistol so expect it to fire with just minimal pressure."

Ryan was already sighting and trying to feel the beats of his heart so that he could time his pull to the interval. When it felt right, he gently squeezed the trigger. The rifle spat and recoiled, the rear end of the scope hitting him in the eye. Chris winced in sympathy.

"Shit, that hurt!"

Chris tried to keep from laughing. "I'm sorry, I was concentrating so hard on the target I wasn't really paying attention to your stance. I guess you were hunched a little close to the scope eh?"

Ryan rubbed his eye socket.

"You're lucky the scope has a rubber eye piece on the end. You actually hit the target; I'm impressed. Your shot went into the target spec data in the lower right-hand corner, about a foot wide and two feet low. Turn the windage knob two clicks clockwise and the elevation knob four clicks clockwise."

Ryan adjusted the elevation and windage knobs on his scope as Chris had suggested, cycled a fresh round into the firing chamber, settled the sights again and tried to think through his previous shot. He centered his crosshairs on the heart but was careful this time not to pull. The rifle cracked again.

"Good, you're on center and about three inches low. Try another," Chris observed.

Once again Ryan settled himself and waited for the right moment to slowly take up on the trigger. This time he focused as best he could on his heart. The scope acted like a visual stethoscope and magnified each beat as the cross hairs rose and fell on the target 300 feet in the distance. As near as Ryan could tell there was no interval between his heartbeats, and he tried to time his shot at the very same instant as his heart finished a contraction.

The rifle cracked again, the crisp sound rolling out in front of them and down the hill to the river.

"An inch high, six right," Chris coached from the side. Ryan kept trying.

"Four left, 10 low; three right, horizontal good; 12 high, two left; off the target to the right."

"Off the target? You're kidding," Ryan asked.

"To be honest with you, I think you're doing great. Most people would have difficulty getting any shots on the paper." Chris reached down to the rack and brought the second rifle up on the table.

"You spot for me. Let's see if I can't do any better."

Ryan reached over and slid the spotting scope in front of him. "Ready when you are." As the last word left his mouth, and Chris' first round was away, leaving a neat hole through the center X in its wake. Before Ryan could speak, his second round was away. It too punched a neat hole within an inch of the first. In all, Chris fired all 10 rounds in his magazine before lowering the rifle. Ryan had stopped even looking through the spotting scope. It was no longer necessary, as a large round of paper about three inches across was gone where the X had once been. He could see the hole with his naked eye and watched Chris' form and concentration instead. Again, the rifle looked like a natural extension of his body and will, as had the pistol.

"Pretty incredible," Ryan finally managed.

"Let's try 10 rounds each now on the 300-yard target and then we'll go for the pumpkin."

"I'm ready."

They went through the exact same process of sighting the scopes in at 300 yards as they had at 100 yards and each fired 10 rounds. Ryan struggled at the longer distance but still managed to put several rounds into the paper.

Chris reached down into the knapsack and pulled out a small plastic box and opened it on the table. "I reload most of my rifle ammo and I have a couple of *special rounds* we can use on the pumpkin."

He pulled six of them out. Ryan took one from his hand and looked it over. Other than one tiny spot of lead on the tip it looked the same as the other cartridges he'd fired.

"What, do you put extra powder in or what?"

"No, that would make their trajectory less predictable. I drill out a small cavity in the base of each slug and drip in a couple of drops of mercury. Then I solder them closed again. When this slug impacts against a target, the mercury slams forward and mushrooms the whole thing. Watch when they hit, you'll see what I mean. Because your target is downrange another 300 yards, you're going to need to add eight clicks each for both windage and elevation."

Ryan simply nodded, adjusted the scope as Chris suggested, loaded the six special cartridges in his internal magazine, and settled into his stance. "These won't like blow up in the gun or anything will they?" he asked.

Chris chuckled. "No, they leave the gun like regular rounds."

The stump Chris had placed the pumpkin on was about three feet tall and Ryan took his sight trying to recall his best shots at the silhouette, how he'd been breathing, his stance, where he'd fired on his heartbeat stroke. When he finally felt ready, he fired a shot and immediately brought his scope back on target to see if he'd hit. Chris started laughing next to him.

"Damn those work good!"

Ryan looked. At first, he couldn't see why Chris was so pleased with the shot. He could see the pumpkin lying on the ground, unscathed.

"What are you talking about, I missed." Ryan said.

"Look at the stump dummy," Chris countered.

Ryan looked through his scope and didn't see it at first. Then he did and was both appalled and impressed simultaneously with the damage the small projectile had done. The neatly trimmed three-foot stump was now two feet tall, the top a jagged mess of splintered wood.

"Jesus," was all Ryan managed.

"Pretty nifty, huh?"

"I don't know as 'nifty' is the first word to come to mind, but yeah, they work real good."

Chris snickered like a little kid. "Try again before the pumpkin gets away."

Ryan fired four more rounds, cratering the earth around it before he finally got the pumpkin with his last shot. When he did it seemed to vaporize in a mist of orange mush. Neither said anything for a few seconds.

"Those are some nasty rounds partner. I sure wouldn't want to be on the other end!" Ryan observed. "Although I do know someone who deserves one."

They both knew who he was referring to and an awkward silence followed his comment.

"Why don't we go up to the house," Chris finally suggested.

Chapter 10

The street in front of Bill and Stephanie's house was mobbed with people when Tory returned with Jan from the junior high school. At first, she wondered if something had happened. Then she noticed national television logos on several trucks on the street, and realized it was the media. They pulled into the driveway as close to the house as possible. All the reporters rushed at them as they exited the car making escape into the house impossible.

"How does it feel to lose a son?" one shouted.

"Do you think your own background with drugs had anything to do with the attack on you?" another shouted.

Jan clung to Tory's side. "Mom, let's get in the house," she cried out nervously.

"Please, just let us through," Tory asked plaintively.

The first reporter asked his question again. "Ms. McCane, tell us, how does it feel to lose your son?"

Tory exploded. "How in the hell do you think it feels, are you simple? Get away from us and let us into our house."

They didn't move an inch except maybe to press in closer. Her hostile comment was good, it meant she might do or say something newsworthy and they all pushed her harder.

"What will you do next?"

"How does your daughter feel?"

"Do you plan on marrying Mr. Cunningham?"

Their questions hit her like machine gun fire, and they pressed in closer. One of their cameras hit her in the back of the head as its operator was pushed forward into her and she started to get frantic.

"Please, leave us alone. We don't have anything to say." With her last comment Tory started to push at the reporters closest to her that were cutting them off from the house. "Let us through!" she yelled.

They continued to block her and fire inane questions. Just when she thought she was going to completely lose it she felt a strong hand on her shoulder and Chris reached around her and pushed three of the reporters aside to give her some space.

"I'm Trooper Barrett, and all of you are trespassing on private property. Anyone still on this lawn or anywhere else on this property in one minute will be arrested for criminal trespass. Any questions?"

The horde went silent. Ryan used the break to limp up behind Jan and Tory on his crutches and ushered them the rest of the way up the walk and into the house.

"C'mon officer, the people have a right to know. This story has captured everyone's attention including lawmakers. Can't you at least tell us whether or not they'll be coming forward at a later time to tell their story?"

His questions emboldened the others and they all started shouting questions at Chris until he held up his hands.

"Listen up! These folks have lived through a terrible tragedy that includes the loss of a small child. Don't any of you have children of your own? For Christ's sake give them a break and a little time to grieve. As to the public's right to know, that applies to individuals that serve the public trust. These people are private citizens and they have at least as powerful a right to their privacy. Give them some space!"

The same reporter who had spoken first repeated his earlier question. "Trooper, will they be coming forward to tell their story?" It was if he hadn't heard a word Chris said.

Chris sighed in exasperation. "Look, I don't know, I'll ask. But in the meantime, I want you all off this property."

"When will you know?" the reporter persisted.

"I'll go ask right now, but I want you off this property in the meantime." Chris leveled his best cop stare on the reporter making it very clear that he would be the first target of Chris's frustration if he didn't move. Reluctantly all of them headed up the driveway to the street.

"Thanks Chris," Ryan offered as he closed the front door behind him. "How long will they keep this up?"

"I don't know. I told them I would ask you if you'll be giving any interviews. I hate to say it, but you might want to consider it. They'll keep bothering you everywhere you go until you do. I know it's unfair but that's the way it is. Whatever you decide I can keep them off your property but there's nothing I can do to keep them away from you on the street."

Ryan thought for a few moments. "Would Tory have to speak to them? I know she can't handle something like that right now."

"No, I don't think so. We can use you as the sacrificial lamb. You'll probably dull their hunger enough so that we can keep her out of it."

"Alright. Tell them I'll speak with one of them on camera, but that they will have to share the tape. I can't deal with the whole lot of them."

Chris smiled. "Good thinking. When do you want to do it?"

"How about 20 minutes? Might as well get it over."

"Alright. I'll tell them. Where do you want to do it?"

"I guess right here. Bring one of them and his camera man to the back door and I'll do it in the kitchen."

"OK, 20 minutes. Sorry you have to deal with this."

"Yeah, me too."

The sound of breaking glass in the bathroom behind them got both of their attention. "What the hell?" Ryan asked out loud and started towards the bathroom door with Chris close behind. When they got to the door Ryan quickly knocked.

"Tory, are you alright in there?"

"It's not Tory, it's me Jan. Yeah, I'm OK. I just knocked a glass off the edge of the sink by mistake," Jan answered back in a sheepish voice.

"Can I come in sweetie?" Ryan asked.

"I guess so."

Ryan opened the door and was startled to see blood trickling down her wrist and onto the floor. Although the cut was not serious, it still panicked him to see her bleeding and he grabbed a hand towel off the rack and dabbed at it. Jan seemed nervous and he tried to soothe her.

"It's OK kiddo, nothing serious. I think a Band-Aid is all you need. Here, why don't you sit down while I clean it and put one on."

When Jan looked up, she was teary eyed. "I'm sorry, I didn't mean to do it."

"Of course, you didn't. It's fine. I'll have you fixed up in a jiffy," Ryan replied.

Chris had been standing behind them and knelt down next to the broken glass and picked up one of the larger pieces and looked at it for several seconds before throwing it into the trash. "That doesn't look too serious, if you've got it under control I'll go out and talk to the vultures," Chris said.

"Yeah, we're fine. Just give me 20 so I can finish here and throw on a different shirt."

As Chris left Ryan looked up into Jan's eyes again. "How did you cut your arm babe?"

"I don't know. I was washing my hands and I guess I hit it," she replied.

It didn't make any sense to Ryan, but he figured no real harm had been done and after applying a Band-Aid tightly across it reached up and wiped the tears off her face. "Well don't worry about it. Why don't you head off to your room? I'm going to talk with one of these reporters so the rest will leave us alone. I think it'd be best if you stay out of sight while they're here, OK?"

Jan nodded and walked down the hall towards her room. Ryan spent a few minutes cleaning up the glass and then went to change and see how Tory was doing. He knocked softly before entering and found her sitting with her back up against the headboard with her arms gripped tightly across her chest. She'd been crying and looked scared and distant. On the bedside table the prescription bottle of Valium sat with the cap off.

"Tory?" Ryan asked softly at first. She didn't respond and he suddenly felt angry at her distance.

"Tory!"

"What?" she snapped back.

Ryan backed off a notch, surprised at the vehemence in her reply. "Look, you and I need to talk. I know how much you're hurting, I really do. I'm hurting too. But we have to keep things together." He paused and gestured with his hand towards the Valium bottle. "I don't think the Valium is helping. We've got to help each other through this, and you'll never get through this if you're not here. I know you know how bad that shit is for you, you've been around the program too long not to and I really think it's time you thought about stopping."

She stared back at him hard, her anger just below the surface.

"I was going to bring this up later when we could take some time to talk it over and I have to go talk to those reporters right now, but I really want you to think about it. Will you do that? Please?"

"Don't tell me..." she started, and then caught herself. It was like Deja vu for her and the guilty addict in her deferred to her intellect. She knew that any drugs that altered her consciousness were bad for her and the prospect of additional conflict was more than she wanted to deal with at that moment. What she desired was the absence of feeling. Fighting with Ryan would only add to what seemed an impossibly heavy load.

"I'm sorry. You're probably right. It's just that everything hurts so much right now, and at least with these I can sleep."

Ryan continued to stare directly at her, hearing the denial in her reply. Once it was out of her mouth, she heard it too.

"You're right, who am I kidding? I hear you and I know you're probably right. Just give me a couple of days to taper off."

"A couple of days, what, two, three, five? You know it'll just be harder the longer you wait."

"Two, just give me two," she replied.

They were interrupted by a knock on the door. "Ryan, you ready? They're in the kitchen." It was Chris.

"Shit," he muttered. "Yeah, I'll be right out," he replied loudly enough for Chris to hear.

Ryan moved over and sat on the edge of the bed. "You know I'm only telling you this for your own good, right?"

"Yes, I know. I mean it too. Just give me two days," Tory replied believing her own words.

"OK. I wish we could talk more about it now, but I agreed to talk with one of the reporters. Chris thinks it might help keep them off our back."

"I don't have to do I?" Tory asked.

"No, that was one of my conditions. They have to leave you and Jan out of it." Ryan got up to change his shirt before heading out to the kitchen.

As soon as he was gone Tory swung her legs off the side of the bed and stared at the Valium bottle for several seconds. Then she tipped half the contents into her hand and looked around the room for a good hiding place for her back-up stash. Ryan was right that it was a good idea to stop. She also believed that he could never understand how painful losing a son was, especially when it was your fault.

Chapter 11

Edward was not in a pleasant mood and despite a liberal dosing of Oxycontin and two well packed nostrils of cocaine, he was still in considerable pain. He was lying in his bedroom in Miami and tenderly touched the bandages that covered most of his face. He'd undergone two separate operations over the previous week to change his appearance and grimaced at his own touch.

"Fucking doctor!" he swore out loud. "Redondo you lazy fucking spic, bring me another scotch. I'm dying in here!"

The man he was yelling at turned down the volume on the TV, sighed, and then reached down for the reclining arm on the Lazy-Boy and lowered the footrest. "Si, Senor Edward, uno momento." Redondo slowly made his way across the room to a large mirrored bar and poured several ounces of single malt scotch whiskey over ice in a 12-ounce glass. Redondo had worked on and off for Edward in the capacity of bodyguard and enforcer for several years. Edward used him when he wanted to put the fear of God into someone. Not a cruel man by nature, as Paulo had been, Redondo relied on his large size to intimidate. He was very lazy, of minimal intelligence and generally unfeeling towards anything but food. The work Edward provided was not very physical despite his job description and suited him well. For the most part he was able to rely on his ugliness and fearsome proportions to intimidate and coerce, and seldom had to do more than show up to get people to comply with Edward's wishes.

Edward turned on the television in his room and started channel surfing as he waited for Redondo and his drink. Right before one of the stations went to commercial, the words "piracy" and "Massachusetts man" caught his attention.

"Senor Edward, I'm going to call for some take-out. Do you want...?" Redondo started as he entered the room.

"Shut-up you moron. It's him!" Edward cut him off.

"Who?" Redondo asked.

"The fucking gringo responsible for everything! Now shut up, I want to hear this." The advertisement ended and the network anchor capsulated the story of Parthenia's sinking off Bermuda before cutting away to a segment of the interview with Ryan.

"So, you still to this day have no idea why you and your girlfriend were targeted by this smuggler?" the interviewer asked.

"No, not a clue. As I said before, I had a brief verbal confrontation with him in a restaurant in New England over his abuse of a waitress but that was it. None of it has ever made any sense. Even the crewmember that was in the raft with us after the sinking had no real idea. He just said that the man was high on drugs all the time and evil by nature," Ryan replied.

This was the first Edward had heard of Manuel being in the raft at all. He had assumed that Manuel had died in the water he and exploded at Redondo. "Fucking Manuel, I should have killed that prick when he first got soft on the woman."

The interviewer continued. "Do you think your girlfriend's prior history with drugs might have had anything to do with it?"

The camera came in tight on Ryan's face as the question was asked and Edward could see the sudden anger that came into his eyes. "No," Ryan answered emphatically. "My girlfriend has been drug-free for some time and she did not recognize the man."

Ryan's anger pleased Edward and he mentally congratulated himself for his whole idea of reintroducing her to drugs.

"Your story is getting a lot of attention by lawmakers and they're calling for increased penalties on a whole range of drug related crimes. How do you feel about this?"

Ryan paused for a moment before answering. "I don't really know what difference they will make. Piracy and murder on the high seas are already capital crimes. As far as I'm concerned, our lawmakers lack the balls, excuse me, resolve to make any real difference. What happened to us is a good example. I've been told that law enforcement people already knew the man who murdered our little boy and sank my boat and that they might even know the men he works for. These men run an ongoing criminal enterprise! So why hasn't something already been done?"

The reporter just stared on silently preferring to let Ryan elaborate. "Like I said before, they don't have the guts. People like Edward seem to move freely in and out of various countries that are either sympathetic or controlled by these men and we fail to treat them like the national threat that they are. What's the cost to our country of these hard drugs in lost productivity, broken families, crime, health care, disease, incarceration costs and overdoses? This year alone there were over 50,000 deaths from opiates which is as many people as we lost during the entire Vietnam War! I mean Christ, what's the difference between these drugs and biological weapons? Do you think we'd sit still if someone was shipping and distributing poison gas into the country?"

"Don't you think there's a difference in that people choose to take these drugs?"

"Well I guess many of them do initially and I'm not an expert on this, but I'd guess that most of them are minors when they started and the problem with these drugs is that they're so addictive that the ability to make a free choice is really an illusion. I've come to believe that they should not be available, period. And that we should be willing to go to any length to interrupt the supply."

"Including breaching the sovereignty of other countries?" the reporter asked with skepticism in his voice.

"Look, I'm not a diplomat, but yes, absolutely. We should be willing to do whatever it takes to protect ourselves. We've certainly proved in the past that we're willing to cross borders to go after people who tried to kill us. Why should drugs be any different?"

Edward continued to listen to the rest of the interview, but his mind was busy assessing how Ryan's comments might affect his already tenuous existence with his employers and suppliers. His employers were reserving final judgment on what to do over his loss of White Lady and the international attention his vendetta had brought on their otherwise out-of-sight operation. His successful delivery of the cocaine despite the search mounted against him had counted heavily in his favor. He wasn't sure how they were going to react to the increased heat that was bound to come out of the publicity that this man was getting. Ultimately, Edward knew he was expendable. This man Ryan needed to be disappeared. Without giving it further thought Edward simply picked up the phone and ordered a hit on Ryan and Tory. He was told that it would take several days to arrange and cost extra due to their notoriety.

"Do it." He was about to hang up the phone when he had another thought. "Wait!"

"Yes?" the party on the other end of the line asked.

"Right before it goes down, I want you to call me on my cell and let me speak with them. That way they'll know it's me who is taking them out."

"I can't promise that, but I'll do my best."

Chapter 12

After the reporter left Ryan turned to Chris. "Well?"

"Well what?"

"How did I do?"

"Well it depends on what you consider success to be." Chris answered. "If you wanted to get the reporters off your ass, I guess you did a pretty good job."

"Yeah, go on."

"But you certainly didn't take yourself out of the limelight. I'm sure all our fearless politicians are running around trying to think of things to say to counter your comments. I would also guess that every drug lord in the world probably has a big hard-on for you now. Did you really mean those things you said about going to any lengths to stop the traffic?"

"Yes, of course I did. Why else would I say them?" Ryan asked back a little perturbed.

"A lot of people talk tough like you just did but they're not willing to back up their talk with action. Take the average guy who says he believes in capital punishment and ask him to come into the prison some time and actually throw the switch. Then see what he says. Or take you for instance. Do you eat beef?"

Ryan nodded.

"Ever slaughtered a cow?"

"No."

"Think you could? I mean is your love for beef so strong that you'd be willing to shoot one in the head, gut him, skin him and butcher him just so you could have a hamburger?" Chris asked leaning forward.

Ryan saw what he was getting at and took a moment to think before answering. "I know what you're asking, and I think the answer is yes, about the drug dealers. The burger, I'm not sure about. Right now, I think I'm angry enough to pull the switch on the man who killed Willy."

"Without all the 'jury-of-his-peers' crap? Because you know, guys like him never go down like that. First they'd have to find him, then they'd have to find a group of 12 individuals who couldn't be bribed or intimidated, then they'd have some ridiculous trial where half the evidence would be excluded for bullshit reasons and then the prosecutor would have to get the jury to vote unanimously for the death penalty. Even if all that happened, he'd just appeal. So, where does that leave you?"

Ryan knew that everything Chris had just said was true and it infuriated him. He was also angry with Chris for shoving it in his face. "How the hell do you think that makes me feel? I know that everything you just said is true. That's why I said all that to the reporter."

"I'll tell you where that leaves you. It leaves you in the exact same position as all those politicians that you just condemned."

"What more do you expect me to do?" Ryan demanded.

"Be willing to go to any lengths, just like you said. Just think about it overnight. We can talk more later. Will you call tomorrow?"

"Yeah, sure," Ryan replied absently.

"Good, talk to you then."

Ryan thought about their conversation after he left. Chris's comments were perplexing coming as they did from someone who was in law enforcement. 'What does he expect anyway?' Ryan asked himself, "that I go off, find Edward, then shoot him?"

Stephanie roused him from his thoughts as she walked in from work several moments later.

"I can't believe all those reporters out on the street. If Chris hadn't been leaving when I drove in, and protected me, I think they would have mobbed me."

"I know. They got the three of us when we all got back and I ended up doing a short on-camera interview in an effort to get them off our back."

"Well they're still here… Hey, guess what?"

"What?"

"I think I found a place for you guys. It's only for a couple of months, but it's free and it will give you some time and space to decide what you're going to do next."

Stephanie's revelation took Ryan by surprise and it showed on his face. He had mixed feelings about leaving the stability of her home so quickly and was already nervous about Tory's condition and his ability to provide the stable kind of environment that Jan needed. He also knew, however, that the three of them had to start getting on with their own lives.

"Of course, you're welcome to stay here as long as you like. We're not trying to hurry you guys out," she added.

"I appreciate that Stephanie, but it's probably a good idea. Where is this place?"

"Just five blocks from here, down near the public beach. It's small but it has a great view of the marsh and the ocean. We'd practically be neighbors and any time you need us for anything we're just down the street. It's up to you. Like I said if you want to stay on here for a while, we really wouldn't mind."

Ryan smiled back his appreciation. "Thanks, but I think it would be good for the three of us to have some mutual goal to work towards and getting settled in a place of our own might be just the thing. When can we see it?"

"We can go look at it right now if you want. Another teacher from the school I work at owns it and she and her husband are both on sabbatical in South America for a year. They hadn't wanted to bother with tenants, but I was talking with her today on the phone and she said if I was willing to vouch for you two, you could have it. They're happy to just have the place heated and looked after without having to worry about crazy tenants. It really would be perfect for you guys and it's furnished right down to the linens. All you have to do is move in."

Ryan liked the idea the more he thought about it. "I'll go see what the girls think of the idea and we can go over and look at it."

Ryan hobbled back upstairs and sat down on the edge of the bed next to Tory after getting Jan.

"Stephanie just told me about a fully furnished house we can move into down near the water if we want. The people who own it are away for six months and wouldn't charge us any rent. What would you two think about us going over there to look at it?"

Both Tory and Jan seemed strangely apathetic to the idea but agreed to go look at it. After looking at it later that afternoon they decided to move in the following day. Between the three of them the only possessions they had were in the duffel bag that they'd bought subsequent to Parthenia going down. Ryan hoped that Tory would emerge from her depression as they all attempted to turn the house into a home. For the few days they had been at Bill and Stephanie's she'd kept pretty much to her bed and only interacted with the rest of the household during mealtimes. Jan was scheduled to start school the next day and he hoped that the routine chores associated with having a place of their own would give Tory some incentive and sense of purpose.

"So, what do you think?" Ryan asked. The three of them were sitting around the kitchen table that overlooked the marsh and outer harbor. The water came right up to the edge of their lawn. "We can live with this right?"

"Yeah, this is nice!" Jan replied with a bit more enthusiasm than the day before.

"What do you think Tory?" Ryan asked.

Tory shrugged her shoulders and continued to look out the window. "It's nice enough I guess."

Her indifference irked Ryan but he held his tongue and continued with the list he'd started for the supermarket. Then, remembering that he'd told Chris he would call him, picked up his cell phone off the table and started to dial the number off the card Chris had given him.

"I'm going to walk down to the public beach. Is that OK?" Jan asked.

Tory continued to stare out the window and Ryan finally answered. "Yeah sure, that's fine." Chris picked up after the fifth ring.

"Hey Chris, Ryan."

"How're you doing?"

"Pretty good. We found a place right near where we've been staying and moved in already."

"You should have called earlier. I would have been glad to help you move," Chris replied.

"Nothing to move, just the duffel bag you brought from the airport. We lost everything, remember?"

"Yeah, sorry."

"Anyway, if you really want to help out, I could use a lift to the supermarket. My truck is a standard shift and I can't drive it with my busted leg. This place is totally empty for food."

"No sweat. I'm not used to having time off and was wondering what I'd do today anyway. I'll be over in a half hour."

Ryan hung up the phone. "You know Tory, there are a lot of things we should talk about."

"Like?"

"Like finances. I've got about $15,000 to my name. The rest went down with the ship and we need to start thinking about what we're going to do next."

Tory sat mutely looking out the window.

"Tory, you have to snap out of it. We've got to make some plans if we're going to get our lives going again."

"Is money all you're worried about? Because if it is, you can stop. I already told you. When my grandfather died, I got a huge chunk of money. Just tell me how much we need for stuff and I'll write you a check. As for everything else, I don't want to talk about it now. I'm too tired."

"Tory, I'm not just talking about money! You need to start participating in your life again. You've still got a daughter."

She glared at him. "Don't tell me what I need!" She stormed out of the room.

Ryan followed her to their room. He was slower, and by the time he reached the room she'd gone into the adjoining bathroom and shut the door behind her.

"Tory, running away isn't going to change things." He heard the water run for a few seconds and knew she was probably taking a pill which maddened him further and he tried to turn the knob. It was locked.

Jan was outside beneath their window pulling one of the bicycles out from under the house and could hear them clearly as they argued.

"I thought you were going to stop taking that shit?" he yelled at the door.

Tory tipped about 20 additional Valium into her hand and put them in her pocket before wrenching the door open and throwing the capped prescription bottle at Ryan.

"I am stopping! You keep them, but it's not going to change how I feel. I can't just turn my feelings on and off like you. You can have the pills but leave me alone!"

"I'm saying these things because I care about you. Jan needs you and I want you back in my life!"

"Well I need more time. Now go!"

Ryan was tempted to argue more but was both surprised and pleased that she'd given him the pills. At least now, she wouldn't be under the influence of anything. He decided to give her the time she wanted.

"All right you win. Take another damn nap, but you're going to have to wake up sometime."

Jan looked away from the window as their argument ended and rode off on the bike she'd found under the house. As usual, she felt responsible.

Ryan heard a knock at the front door ten minutes later. "Shit, what now?" he muttered to himself and wrenched the door open abruptly. He looked into Chris's startled face. "I'm sorry, I forgot you were coming and thought you might be Jehovah's Witnesses or something."

"Glad I'm not!"

"Come on in for a sec while I get my coat."

"Thanks, is it just us or will Tory be coming?"

"No, she's sleeping. We can ask Jan though."

"Don't think so."

"What do you mean?"

"I just saw her riding down the street on a bike."

"Oh." Ryan replied not particularly concerned.

"Shaw's or the A+P?" Chris asked.

"Doesn't matter to me," Ryan replied.

"Well let's go to Shaw's then." They got into Chris's Jeep.

Ryan smiled. "Sorry, things are a little tense around the house and I'm just not sure what to do."

"Want to talk about it?"

"Tory needs to get moving again. All she does is sleep and it's starting to get to me." Ryan stared out the side window as he spoke. "She's also been taking Valium which hasn't been helping matters."

"Maybe she needs something like that for a while," Chris offered.

"No, that shit's like poison to her. I'm sure you've heard of her drug history in the media reports. She really shouldn't take anything stronger than aspirin."

They drove just two blocks before slowing to a stop behind a long line of cars on the quiet street. They could see a blue light ahead and a patrolman routing traffic to a side street. There was some type of accident. As they drew abreast of the activity Ryan looked over towards the ambulance. Several paramedics were lifting someone onto a stretcher. Because their backs were to him, he couldn't see a face but what did catch his attention was the mangled frame of a bicycle beneath the front bumper of the car next to them.

"Pull over!" Ryan yelled in a panicked tone.

"What?"

"Just pull over." Ryan was almost frantic. "What color was the bike that you saw Jan on?"

"I don't know, I wasn't really paying attention."

As soon as they came to a complete stop Ryan had his door open and rushed towards the ambulance as best he could. A small crowd made up mostly of rescue workers temporarily blocked his way, but Ryan pushed through.

"Please let me through, I think it's my little girl!"

It was in fact Jan and she lay moaning on the stretcher as two EMTs worked on her. Her entire front was covered in blood and at first Ryan thought her chest may have been hurt, but as he looked closer, he realized that most of the blood had originated from her mouth. Her left arm was splinted, and her neck was encased in a cervical collar.

"How is she? Will she be all right?

He was ignored for the moment and the EMT tending her head asked, "Do you have that ice yet?"

A policeman rushed up with a bag of ice that he'd purchased in the convenience store down the street. "Where do you want it?"

The EMT dumped the sterile pads out of a plastic container and pointed to the small empty container. "In there."

The policeman poured a measure of ice into the small container and then the EMT reached for a bloody piece of gauze that was lying on the stretcher. He carefully laid it in the ice and then took a few more cubes and covered it.

Ryan quickly realized that there was a piece of Jan wrapped up in the gauze and he looked her over quickly trying to see what was missing. Both her shoes were on, her hands were visible and seemed to be intact. He couldn't figure it out and tried speaking again.

"I'm her father. Would you please tell me how she is?"

Jan turned towards him at the sound of his voice and although she didn't seem to be able to vocalize anything, she spoke to him with her eyes. He could tell she was scared. She also seemed to be saying she was sorry.

"It's OK sweetie," Ryan started in a soothing voice. "You're going to be fine. I'm here and I'll ride with you to the hospital."

She responded back with tears running down both cheeks.

"OK, I'm ready. You guys ready to transport?" the EMT that had asked for the ice asked out loud.

"Ready." Was the reply and for the first time he turned to Ryan. "Can you ride with us?"

"Of course." Ryan replied. "Is she going to be all right?"

"I'll talk to you in the ambulance. OK, on three, one, two, three." Two of them lifted the Stryker stretcher in unison and wheeled it to the back of the ambulance and then up and in. After they got her secured two of the men got out and motioned Ryan in.

"I'll follow you," Chris said.

***

'Why won't everyone just leave me alone?' Tory asked herself. Ryan's demand that she give up the Valium was insulting and demonstrated his lack of understanding of her emotional pain. After all, a doctor had prescribed it, and the more she thought about it the more indignant the addict in her became. Eventually she took two more 10mg tablets from her stash to quell the debate going on inside her head and lay back waiting for the escape of sleep. As the drug took over her anger and indignance faded, but sleep would not come as it had over previous days and was instead replaced by a tremendous sense of guilt. She lay tossing for several minutes until tears of self-pity started. With almost no thought, she got up, went to the liquor cabinet in the kitchen, and poured herself a glass of vodka.

***

Ryan positioned himself in a jump seat that was near Jan's head and watched as the EMT continued to work on her. "Everything's going to be fine Jan. We'll be at the hospital in just a minute." He took her right hand in both of his and then he turned back to the EMT who cleaning some of the blood off Jan's face.

"Please tell me, how is she?"

"All in all, I'd say she's very lucky considering what happened. It looks like her left arm is broken, although I can't be certain until they do an X-ray, she has a concussion, numerous abrasions and although it's not life threatening…" The EMT paused trying to think of a way to phrase it. "Her tongue. She must have just been starting to scream when she was hit, and she bit down hard and severed part of her tongue."

"Jesus!" Ryan let out without meaning to.

"That's what I have on ice. I'm hoping they can reattach the piece she bit off."

Jan started choking on the blood flowing into the back of her throat and the EMT quickly reached for a suction hose and slid it into the corner of her mouth. An ER doctor and several nurses were waiting at the hospital door when they pulled up. Ryan tried to stay at Jan's side but was told to take care of the admission paperwork while they evaluated her. The receptionist quickly figured out that Ryan was not her father or any other relation and informed him that they'd require parental permission for treatment and failing that permission from a close relative. He was also unaware of what if any health insurance Jan might have.

"You mean you won't treat her unless you have a health insurance number?" he asked in anger.

"No sir, I didn't say that. What I said was that we would prefer it if we had the informed consent of one of the parents or a close relative. As to insurance, why yes, we'd like to know that you have some way of paying, but I assure you we won't deny her treatment if there is none."

Chris had been standing behind Ryan the whole time. "I'll tell you what, you stay here with Jan and I'll drive back to the house and get Tory. It won't take more than 15 minutes."

"Would you do that? I'll try and call her in the meantime and let her know what's happened, so it isn't a complete shock." Ryan replied.

"No sweat. Jan's in good hands now and I'm sure things will turn out all right."

Ryan nodded. "I'll call Tory right now."

Chris turned and jogged off down the hall towards the door and then Ryan tried calling Tory's cell phone. He tried to think of the words he would say when she picked up.

***

Tory was sitting at the kitchen table when her cell phone rang. She was finishing her third glass of vodka and feeling no pain from the combination of Valium and alcohol. She looked over at her phone noting that it was Ryan calling, but ignored it. After six rings it stopped and went to voice mail then started ringing again several seconds later. She reached over and turned off the ringer. She knew she was blotto from the combination of alcohol and drugs and consequently had no desire to speak with him and the inevitable guilt trip that he would lay on her. She stumbled into the counter on her way to refill her glass. Several minutes later she heard someone pounding on the front door but ignored them also and instead drained her glass as if it were the only thing protecting her from everything that had happened over the previous two weeks.

Chris figured she might be asleep in her room and finally barged in after receiving no response to his knocks. He was surprised to hear crying sounds coming from the kitchen.

"Tory," he called out tentatively. He didn't want to startle her but was surprised she hadn't answered the door if she was just in the other room. The crying stopped.

"What? Who is it?" she called back in a flat tone.

He entered the room. "It's me, Chris. Are you all right?"

She looked up at him with blurry eyes. "Yeah, I'm fine. What do you want? I'm kind of busy right now."

He looked at the half-empty vodka bottle on the table. "I can see that. Did you talk to Ryan?"

She thought for a second. "Yea, I talk to him all the time."

Chris shook his head assuming correctly she didn't know. "There's been an accident."

She cocked her head and looked up at him with an expression that reflected her diminished capacity and slurred her next words. "What kind of accident?"

"It's Jan. She's been hit by a car. Ryan's at the hospital with her but they want your permission to treat her and also your health insurance if you have any."

Tory continued to stare at him, the words taking much longer than they should have to sink in.

"Jan? What are you saying? Jan's fine!"

He shook his head. "She's not fine. She's been hurt and needs you, if you can break away from what you're doing." Chris was angry.

The reality of what he was saying started to cut through her chemical fog. "Chris, this isn't some kind of sick joke is it? I mean, Ryan's not trying to get even with me or something is he?"

He held her gaze levelly. "No."

She knew he was telling her the truth and for a moment she couldn't breathe. Then she started to sob.

Chris came over to her side, gently helped her up out of the chair then hugged her. "I'm sorry Tory." Chris continued to hold her. He knew better than he cared to remember what she was going through and for a moment revisited a part of his own past as he tried to quiet her.

They rushed through the hospital doors 20 minutes later. Ryan had been pacing nervously awaiting their return and had just finished talking with the surgeon as they appeared. Even from a distance Tory looked shaky and Chris held one of her arms in his as they came down the corridor. Ryan knew she'd been drinking as soon as she opened her mouth but decided that the most important thing to deal with at that moment was Jan.

"She's resting right now. They gave her something for the pain but she's going to have a tough time of it for a few days and that's if everything goes well. She has a concussion, her left arm is broken, and..." Ryan searched for the words as the EMT had. "And she bit part of her tongue off."

Tory winced as Ryan had when he found out about the tongue. "What do you mean she bit off her tongue? Can they fix it? Will she be able to use it again?"

"The surgeon I spoke with is pretty optimistic about that. I guess it's a pretty simple muscle and there are few nerves. Most of her sense of taste is located on the back of it which was unaffected. She bit off about two inches."

"Where is she? I've got to see her."

"Tory, she's really woozy from the pain killer they gave her, and I don't think that's as important as you taking care of the damn paperwork and giving them your health insurance number. The doctor is ready to begin but wants you to sign the consent form before they put her under."

Ryan was clearly in charge and rather than argue she deferred to him as a new wave of guilt washed over her.

"Where do I go?"

Ryan took her by the hand and led her over to the receptionist station and then stepped back to talk with Chris while she filled out the forms.

"She's drunk," he stated flatly.

"Yes, she is," Chris agreed.

"I can't believe with everything that's going on that she's fucking drunk."

"That's what drunks do. They drink when they're happy, they drink when they're sad. They drink period. It's not like she did this to purposefully hurt you or Jan. She's trying to hurt herself."

Ryan knew what he'd just said was absolutely true. He hadn't expected such insight from his new friend.

"How come you know so much about alcoholism?" Ryan queried.

They were interrupted by one of the police officers that had been at the scene. "Excuse me, are you the father of the little girl?" he asked Ryan.

"Technically, no; practically, yes. I mean I'm the resident one."

The cop looked slightly confused but continued anyway. "Sorry to take so long getting here but I had a call on the way over I had to respond to. Anyway, the reason I wanted to speak with you is because the best I can figure it, what happened to your daughter wasn't an accident."

Ryan was stunned. "You mean someone did this on purpose?"

"Yes. I mean no. Look; I spoke at length with the driver and two other people who saw the accident and they all agreed that your daughter rode her bike in front of that car on purpose."

Ryan shook his head. "That's ridiculous; that couldn't be."

"All three of them had the same story. Right before she swerved in front of the car she looked backward over her shoulder. She knew the car was there."

159

An awkward silence fell over the three as Ryan considered the implications of what the policeman had said.

"Have you and your wife been having family problems recently or has your daughter been under any unusual stress?" the officer asked.

Ryan looked him in the eye. "I guess you haven't recognized us yet?"

The policeman looked closer and suddenly his eyes lit up with recognition. "Of course, you guys are the ones that lost your boat and the little boy."

Ryan nodded. "I guess that answers your question about family problems and stress."

"Jesus, I am so sorry about everything that's happened to you guys."

"Yeah, me too. Her mother and I had planned on getting her into some kind of counseling after she started school, but from what you're telling me I guess we need to do something right away."

The policeman nodded and gave Ryan a pat on the shoulder. "Good luck to you, I've got to get back on duty."

"Thanks." Ryan replied and turned his attention to the surgeon who had come out of the ER to talk with Tory.

"I've done this repair several times," he was telling Tory. "And in every case but one, had a good result. In the one that didn't work out, the piece we were attempting to reattach had not been kept on ice and there was too much tissue degeneration for it to grow back together properly. That's not the case with your daughter, however. I don't think you have to worry. As far as the arm goes, we have that stabilized but we'd like to wait until the swelling goes down before we cast it. We'll probably do that first thing in the morning. Any questions?"

"No, I guess not, except will she be able to talk normally after all this?"

"Yes, that shouldn't be a problem. But if you'll excuse me, I'd like to get started right now. It's kind of a race against the clock to get that piece reattached. The operation isn't a complicated one, but it requires a lot of stitches. It will probably take me about two hours. I'll let you know how it went as soon as I'm done."

"Thank you, doctor," both Tory and Ryan replied in unison.

After he left, the three of them went to a small waiting room off the hall to await the outcome of the operation. Late afternoon was a slow time of day for the hospital and they were alone in the waiting room. As soon as they sat down Tory felt compelled to try and explain. She felt horrible inside; not only had she let herself and Jan down, she also felt she'd let Ryan down. She didn't want to lose him and his understanding, if not approval, suddenly seemed very important to her.

"Ryan," she started. "I know you're angry and disappointed in me, but I know I can beat this thing. You just have to have a little faith and give me some time." Her tone was plaintive.

Ryan had been thinking about what to do and say since the moment he'd smelled the alcohol on her breath. Her 'slip' was escalating. His instinct was to reach over and hug her and tell that everything would be OK. She'd been through more in one week than many people go through in a lifetime and he knew he could forgive her. But that wasn't the issue he kept reminding himself. The issue was how best to help her get back into recovery again and he knew it was unlikely that she'd be able to get off the drugs and alcohol on her own. Her will to be better had to exceed her will to be absent and he knew that ultimately that was not something he could give her. It had to come from within and anything he said or did that minimized the seriousness of her behavior would hurt her and her ability to fight her disease. He knew the only way that could happen was for her to get back into some kind of treatment program.

"Tory, I love you very much and it's important that you understand that," he started.

"I know you do, and I love you too, just give me a little time and I'll beat this. I've done it before and know I can again," she interrupted.

"Please, let me finish."

Chris interrupted. "I'm gonna go get a cup of coffee."

Ryan looked up at him as he arose. "Thanks, maybe we'll join you in a few minutes." He looked back at Tory and continued. "If I believed a little time was all you needed, I'd give it to you. I really do care about you. But because I do, I'm not going to let you bullshit yourself. I'm not equipped with the skills to help you get back on track and you should know from before that you can't do it on your own. You need help. If I told you I'd let you try to do it on your own I'd just be enabling you; you'd keep slipping, I'd get more resentful, and Jan would get crushed between us," he paused then continued.

"I wasn't going to say anything right now, but I think I should. I spoke with the policeman who investigated the accident when you were filling out the paperwork. He said that it wasn't an accident. Jan ran her bike in front of the car on purpose."

"Ryan, that's ridiculous. Why would she do that?"

"I'm not really sure. I'm not a child psychologist but I suspect that she's just overwhelmed. She's felt responsible for you and Willy for years and now suddenly Willy is gone and you're falling apart. She feels like a complete failure."

The idea that she was once again hurting Jan made her want to crawl off somewhere and die. It was as if she were spiraling downward into some bottomless black hole as Ryan spoke.

"Oh God, Ryan, what can I do? I love that little girl so much, and all I seem to do is hurt her."

"I think you have to go back into treatment. You need to be detoxed and you need to work through all that's happened in the last week in a supportive environment. If you don't do that I don't know whether you'll ever be able to forgive yourself and be the kind of mother Jan needs."

"I can't do that Ryan. I can't separate myself from her again. She needs me! I know I can beat this on my own, and I will. Besides, I would never let strangers take care of her again."

"I know she needs you! But not as you are now. It will kill you both! You can't be there for her if you're destroying yourself and you can't hide it from her. You know that! As far as who will care for her, I will, if you'll let me, or Bill and Stephanie. I know they'd take her in a second. You can't let her care be the obstacle to you getting help."

Tory shook her head trying to see some easy way out.

He stood up. "I can't force you, but if you don't do it you're going to lose both of us and yourself in the process. Think about it." He put his hand on her shoulder. "I'm going to have a cup of coffee with Chris. Do you want one?"

She just shook her head and stared down at the floor.

"You can do this. I know you can. And we'll both wait for you."

***

In a café across town the waitress asked the taller of the two men. "What can I get you two?"

"Two coffees, black," the man responded.

"Anything else?"

"Nope."

"I'm curious, isn't the guy whose boat got sunk from around here?"

"You must mean Ryan Cunningham. Yeah, he's from around here, lived here most of his life."

"Terrible thing that happened to him."

"You can say that again."

"I'm a sailor myself and might be interested in talking with him. Know where he lives?"

"You don't look like a sailor?"

"Yeah well I left my captain's hat home. I'd still like to talk him." The tall man put a $50 bill next to his coffee cup.

The waitress figured they were probably reporters and smiled at her good fortune. "Well it must be your lucky day. Not too much goes on in this town that everyone doesn't know about and it just so happens he moved into a house about a block and half from me."

"And what address might that be?"

"I'm not sure of the exact street number but it's the Francis place and I'd guess that would be near 66 Water Street."

"Thanks, I might just try and look him up."

"Whatever."

***

Ryan found Chris sitting at a table alone in the rear of the hospital cafeteria.

"Sorry you had to be there for that."

"Nothing I haven't been through myself," Chris replied.

Ryan looked at him quizzically. "What do you mean?"

"Did you think at all about what I asked you yesterday, you know, about going to any lengths?"

"Yeah I thought about it but still don't really understand what it is you think I might be able to do. It almost sounded as though you thought I should hunt down this guy Edward and kill him."

"What if that was what I meant?"

"Come on Chris, don't be ridiculous. What do I know about killing someone?"

"You know he's just going to keep doing what he does don't you? The authorities will never be able to touch him. Didn't Willy mean anything to you? And what about Tory and Jan? Tory's a mess and Jan almost killed herself today. Doesn't that bother you?"

Ryan was furious. "Of course it bothers me! Sometimes I feel like I'm going to explode when I think what that motherfucker did but what gives you the right to talk to me like this? You're the goddamn police, why don't you folks do something about guys like him?"

"We can't. Every time we arrest someone like him, they're out a couple of hours later and they either skip bond and leave the country or hire a fucking dream team and do a two-step with our legal system until they're acquitted on some technicality! The police can't do shit!"

"All right, but that still doesn't explain how you can expect someone like me to take the law into my own hands. Like I said, I wouldn't know the first thing about killing someone and right now I kinda have my hands full trying to keep my family from killing themselves. So, stop talking ragtime at me like I'm some kind of failure! If you're so hot to see justice done, you do it, you're the one in law enforcement!"

Chris was silent for a minute as he waited for Ryan's temper to cool. "I'm sorry, that wasn't really fair, and I owe you an explanation." He took a sip of his coffee and continued. "It's just that I'd hoped you'd have a different frame of mind about this whole thing. I haven't been totally honest with you since we met, and I guess it's time I was. I'm trusting you with a lot, but I can't do what I'm thinking of doing alone, so I have to," Chris paused then continued.

"It wasn't just an accident that I was on duty the other night at the airport. I requested it and had to call in quite a few favors to get it." Chris took a deep breath. "We're more alike than you'd guess. My wife Paula was everything to me. We were friends from early childhood and neither one of us ever wanted anyone else; it was like we were born for each other. When she walked into a room it was like a small miracle was taking place each time. We never tired of one another and did everything together. Anyway, Edward, or some other scumbag just like him was responsible for her death."

"What do you mean?"

"My wife Paula was an addict, just like Tory except she never recovered. She just got worse and worse until one night she died of an overdose. Oh, we tried detoxes and treatment centers, but she just couldn't put any sober time together. That shit she put up her nose and into her arm and in her lungs was more powerful than our love and I can't ever forgive those responsible! As far as I'm concerned, they aren't even life forms. People like you and me need to stand up and take real action. If we don't then they are just going to keep selling their shit to millions of other people."

Ryan tried to digest what Chris had just told him. "Why the charade with me? Why didn't you tell me all this before?"

"I didn't know anything about you. For all I knew you might have been a flake or a junky yourself and what I'm asking you is not the kind of thing you bring up with a stranger."

"I guess I can understand that, but I still don't understand exactly what it is you expect of me? I mean are you suggesting that we go around randomly bumping off drug dealers?" Ryan asked.

"I don't know exactly! I do know that it goes on and on and no one seems able to make any difference. I guess I just figured that at least in your case it was really easy to fix on a target. You know exactly who did this to you and I figured you for a logical ally. You see I wasn't always a cop, that's something I got into after her death. I wanted to take some kind of concrete action and I figured that was the way to do it, you know, go out and catch a few of the people responsible. But it hasn't made a bit of difference, we can't ever seem to get to the people at the top."

Chris had Ryan thinking and it was not as though he hadn't already considered something like he was proposing himself. That had been the main reason he'd spent so much time questioning Manuel in the raft. He'd been thinking about revenge. But faced with the reality of it and what it would entail frightened him. He knew he could have killed trying to defend them in the heat of it all, but what Chris was proposing was entirely different.

"Chris, back on the boat I wouldn't have hesitated for even a second to blow that guy away if I had the chance and I did take a couple of shots at him when he was attacking our boat. I do think about revenge, but when I get honest with myself and actually think about taking a gun into my hands, hunting him down and then shooting him in cold blood, I got to tell you, it goes against everything I've been taught. I'm not sure I could. But hearing you say you want to do the same thing and knowing why you want to do it, I can totally understand. Does that make any sense?"

"I take it that's a no?"

"It is, but I also want you to know and believe that your secret is safe with me. I'm willing to acknowledge your right to seek that kind of retribution, I just don't think that I can be a part of it."

"I'm sorry to hear that." Chris was silent for a few seconds. "I suppose now you think I'm some kind of a nut?"

"Nope, I already knew that. I'd just hate to see you end up in prison and become another casualty of these people," Ryan replied.

"You have to understand, there isn't anything of real importance that hasn't already been taken from me."

"I hope you find something man. I really do for your sake."

They returned to the waiting room and several minutes later the doctor who had worked on Jan walked in. He was smiling.

"Everything went really well. I had to put in about 36 stitches in her tongue which means she won't be eating steak or talking much for a few days, but I'm quite optimistic that she'll have normal use of it again within several weeks. She's in the recovery room now and should be waking up from the anesthesia in about 20 minutes. I'm sure she'd like to see you there when she wakes up. As for tonight I'm going to keep her sedated and on pain medication so after you've seen her you might as well go home. The meds should keep her out all night. In the morning we'll cast her arm and you can take her home. Questions?"

"How long before the stitches can come out?" Ryan asked.

"I think a week will do it. The skin grows really fast in that area."

"Thanks doctor," the three of them replied.

"My pleasure. If you'll follow me, I'll take you to the recovery room."

Tory had yet to see Jan and was a little taken aback at her appearance. Her mouth was quite swollen from all the trauma visited on it and her face was covered with abrasions as were her hands. In addition, they had her broken arm bound snugly to her stomach so she couldn't move it. Tory touched her gently.

"She looks so defenseless." Tory leaned over and her whispered in her ear. "Hi babe. It's me, Tory. I just wanted to let you know that I'm here and everything's going to be fine."

Jan responded to the sound of her voice by groaning softly and an effort to open her eyes. She got them open about halfway and then let them fall shut again. Everything was blurry. "I'm sworry mom," she slurred in a drugged voice. "Thought I could make things better."

Tears came to Tory's eyes as it dawned on her what she meant. "Sweetie don't try and talk now. We'll talk in the morning. I just wanted you to know that everything's going to be fine. They're going to keep you overnight, but we'll be here with you when you wake up in the morning, OK?"

Jan just moaned, "Uh huh." And her breathing became regular again as she fell back asleep.

167

Tory kissed her softly on the forehead and then turned to the nurse. "Is there anything that she'll need like a nightgown or anything?"

"No, she'll be fine overnight. As long as there are no complications with her concussion you can take her home late tomorrow morning after they put on the cast."

"Can I stay with her?" Tory asked.

"Of course, you can, but there's really no point. She'll be sedated all night. People with an injury in their mouth like hers have a tendency to move their tongue around a lot as they regain feeling and the doctor wants to make certain the two pieces have as good a chance as possible to rejoin. That's why he's going to sedate her overnight."

"Tory, the nurse is right. Why don't we all go home? We need a good night's sleep."

Tory was torn but what Ryan said was true and she nodded. "Ok, but you'll take good care of her right?" She asked the nurse. "And call us if anything changes?" she added.

"Absolutely," the nurse replied with a smile.

Chris, Ryan and Tory all kept their thoughts to themselves on the ride home and it wasn't until they were turning into the driveway that Ryan remembered that he'd never made it to the supermarket. "Shit, I forgot. We don't have a thing to eat back at the house. I hate to ask but would you mind terribly if we got a few things at the market Chris?" Ryan looked at his watch. "It's only 8:15, we've still got time. How about you give me a lift and I'll make dinner?"

"That's an invitation, right?" Chris asked.

"Of course."

Chris thought for a few seconds. "Yeah, that would be nice. I just have to make a call and see if the woman next door who cleans my house would mind feeding the dogs."

"Do you mind doing the shopping without me?" Tory asked.

"No, that's fine. You go relax. We'll be back in about 40 minutes," Ryan replied.

Tory got out and used the light from the headlights to go down the walk and then Chris backed his car out onto the street. As he cut the wheel, he noticed a car that hadn't been there earlier across the street from Ryan's driveway. Something bothered him about it, but he couldn't quite put his finger on what it was. The license plate indicated it was a rental but there was nothing odd in that and he continued on without saying anything about it to Ryan.

"So, do my revelations preclude us from a friendship?" he asked a few minutes later.

"Why would they?" Ryan asked.

"You might not want to be associated with someone who is contemplating what I am."

"Just don't tell me any details. That way I can deny any knowledge of your actions if anything ever happens."

"Fair enough. Hey, I meant to ask you something back there as we left the house. It's probably a little paranoid but I was just wondering if you knew anything about the people who live across the street from you?"

"No, why?"

"There was a car parked across the street from your house that I noticed as we left that wasn't there this afternoon and you only have that one neighbor right across the street that's really at all close to your house."

"So?"

"There weren't any lights on in that house. And if the people driving the car live there, how come they didn't park in the driveway?"

"I don't know, maybe they have some house guests and they all went out for dinner."

Chris thought for a few seconds. "You're probably right but it might be one of those damn reporters who's sniffed out your new address. I'll look around the property when we get back. Don't mind me, just being a cop."

Tory let herself into the dark house and started turning on lights. She was feeling depressed and hungover from the alcohol she'd consumed earlier and headed up to the bedroom for a Valium from her stash. After pouring a glass of water in the upstairs bath she thought back to the confrontation she had with Ryan and looked at herself in the mirror. He was right and she knew it. Once she was into a cycle like the one she was in, she couldn't stop on her own. The timing never seemed convenient and there was always an excuse for just one more. The pill she held in her hand was a perfect example. In and of itself it was harmless and would help ease the depression she was feeling. But once it wore off she'd just feel more guilty and more depressed and her body would cry out for more. One always led to more, always. She took the pill and continued to stare into the mirror looking into her own eyes as if they might reveal some overlooked truth about her addiction. They stared mutely back and her cell phone rang in the next room. While she was tempted to ignore it she figured it might be the hospital and answered.

"Hello."

"Hi Tory, it's me, Stephanie. How're you doing?"

"Hi Steph, it's been a long afternoon. Jan had a bicycle accident and we've all been at the hospital. She's going to be alright but it just never seems to end."

"Oh no! What happened?"

"She got hit by a car and broke her arm and bit off a piece of her tongue. Don't panic, they sewed it back together and she'll be out by tomorrow."

"Can we go see her?"

"Not tonight, there's no point. That's why we're home now. They're going to keep her under sedation all night."

Tory heard a knock on the door. "Listen don't worry, I think she'll be fine. I've got to run right now. Someone's at the door."

"Ok, talk with you tomorrow."

"Love you."

"Same here." The knocking started again at the front door and Tory hung up.

"Coming!" she yelled and turned the knob. She didn't bother asking who it was.

The car parked outside Tory and Ryan's house kept niggling Chris as they shopped and when they returned 30 minutes later, he decided to act on his suspicions and pulled his own car to the side of the road before he got to Ryan and Tory's driveway. The strange car was still outside their house on the street.

"What are you doing?" Ryan asked.

"That car still bothers me. I want to have a look around. If one of those reporters is outside your house taking pictures or something, I want to catch him. Leave me off here and I'll have a look around. You pull the car into the driveway and just go in like nothing's up."

"You really think someone's spying on us?"

"I 'm not sure." Chris reached across Ryan for the glove box and withdrew a flashlight and an automatic pistol.

"Christ, you've got guns everywhere!"

"Actually, I'm required to have one with me even off duty."

Chris opened his door, stepped out into the night, and disappeared around the back of the Cherokee. Ryan shook his head once, slid across the seat, put the Jeep back into drive and turned into the driveway.

"Here he comes!" the short one named Peter whispered loudly. Peter hated his name and had always associated it with queers and mommy's boys. His dear, sweet, mother 'the cunt' (as he affectionately referred to her) had named him after Saint Peter hoping, he supposed, that some of the good name would rub off on him. It hadn't and had instead had the opposite influence over his behavior. Peter was one of those rare human beings who enjoyed hurting other people for absolutely no reason. He never felt the slightest trace of remorse after a job and was really looking forward to tonight's assignment. Maybe he'd fuck the woman in front of the man before cutting her throat? They'd just have to see.

"I told you this would be easy. Just don't kill him or the girl yet; that crazy fuck Edward wants to reach out and touch him on the phone, so the guy knows who's doing him and his girlfriend. You gotta love that guy's sense of humor, who's he think he is anyway, AT and fucking T?" Emilio laughed at his little joke and pressed the blade he was holding to Tory's throat a little harder. She was cuffed and gagged and sitting on the floor between his legs, but he wanted to make sure she didn't do anything to spook the hit as he came in the door.

Ryan's feet crunched the gravel underfoot as he came up the walk and he struggled some trying to use his crutches and grip the two plastic grocery bags he held. All the lights were on and he hoped Tory would still be up as he pushed the front door open with his foot.

"Tory, I'm home," he yelled. "Jesus it's cold out there."

The door slammed shut behind him and he turned to find the barrel of a silenced Glock 9mm three inches from his forehead. The gun was so close that his eyes crossed as they tried to focus.

"What the hell...?"

"Not yet, but soon," Peter replied with a smile.

"What do you want?"

With one quick movement Peter rolled his wrist to the side and cracked Ryan across the bridge of his nose with the Glock. Ryan dropped his crutches and slumped to the floor bringing his hand to his head as he did so.

The blow startled Tory also and she started squirming on the floor. The other thug found this amusing and with his free hand grabbed a handful of her hair and shook her head back and forth until he had her full attention again. Ryan noticed Tory across the room for the first time since entering the house and started to drag himself towards her.

"Christ, you two are pathetic. Can't you have a little dignity?" Peter asked out loud and after one quick skip and a hop, dropkicked Ryan in the chest. The air whooshed out of his lungs and he lay still on the floor.

"OK, before we go any further let's get the rules straight! First, if either of you move again without my permission, we shoot you. Second, if either of you cries out, we shoot you. And third, well there is no third, but I'll shoot you anyway, so don't do it," he laughed.

"We don't have anything to steal. What do you want with us?" Ryan asked in a pained voice from the floor.

"I personally want nothing, but there is a certain man in Florida who has a real hard-on for you two. He's very angry and sent us up here to have a little chat with you. Can you guess who it might be? Can you think of anyone you might have pissed off just a teensy little bit in the recent past?"

"Edward." Ryan stated more than asked.

"Bingo my friend. Now, before we go any further, where's your daughter?"

Ryan said nothing.

"You don't have to worry about her, he only cares about you two, but I don't want any unexpected surprises so tell me?"

"She's at a friend's, no one will be coming by," Ryan almost spat out.

"That's good, very good. Emilio, get a pair of bracelets on Mr. Cunningham here and we can get started."

As Emilio got up he pulled his knife away from Tory's throat and dropped her head none to gently on the floor. Then he pulled a second set of cuffs out of his sport coat pocket and approached Ryan from behind. Peter kept his pistol pointed squarely into Ryan's face leaving no doubt as to what would happen if he resisted.

Chris was on the back porch looking in through one of the French doors that faced the ocean. Watching what was happening inside without taking any action was one of the hardest things he'd ever had to do. But he knew if he barged in right now the most he could possibly achieve would be a standoff and more than likely either Ryan or Tory or both would be shot or cut in the process. He'd have to wait and see if the two assailants let down their guard after they finished restraining Ryan. He tried to guess at the motivation of the two. From the calm, determined way that they had subdued Ryan and the handcuffs they were using to restrain both of them he knew they weren't amateurs. A burglar would have been nervous, and these men clearly weren't. Additionally, the Rhode Island tag on their rental car suggested premeditation. What concerned him the most, however, was the silencer attached to the Glock in the shorter one's hand and the lack of masks. Clearly, they weren't worried about being identified later. He was suddenly certain of their purpose.

"Let's all get comfortable." Peter went back over to Tory and grabbed her roughly by the arm and jerked her to her feet. "Aren't you the sweet thing," he stated in a lecherous tone and after tucking his gun into his waistband, grabbed her by the hair, pulled her head back, and ran his tongue over her neck. Tory recoiled in disgust and struggled against his grip. He answered by pawing at one of her breasts and crudely squeezing it, then laughed.

"Darlin, I can't wait to fuck you, and by the time I'm done you'll think you died and went to heaven."

Tory squirmed against his grip, so frightened that she was hyperventilating and having trouble breathing through her gag. In desperation she kicked out at him. He turned sideways to deflect the kick, then punched her once in the face. She stopped struggling immediately, dazed, and two lines of blood started trickling down over her upper lip.

"No!" Ryan cried out as Peter punched her. There was nothing he could do though. Between the handcuffs, his broken leg, and the knife being pressed to his throat he was helpless. Then he remembered. Chris was out there and sure to come to their aid any second. He'd just have to roll with things long enough for Chris to save them.

Peter threw Tory down on the couch then pointed at Ryan. "Hold him in that chair over there and keep the knife at his throat. I want him to watch this."

Peter reached down and brutally tore Tory's blouse off. One sleeve was left when he finished, and Tory stared up at him in abject terror with her chest heaving as she struggled to breath. He reached down again and grabbed her brassiere in its center with one of his fists and yanked at it. The material didn't give way as easily as he thought it would and Tory came with it and up off the couch on his first jerk. On the second try he held her down by the throat and pulled again. This time it came free and he leered down at her and started to undo his pants.

Ryan couldn't move and tears of frustration welled in his eyes. Where the hell was Chris?

Chris was almost as frantic as Ryan as he looked in through the window. But he also was powerless to help as long as one of them had a knife to Ryan's throat and the other had an automatic within close reach. He reached to the doorknob in front of him and silently checked its freedom of movement. It was unlocked and he hunched down waiting for his opportunity.

"Do her Peter! Give it to her good!" Emilio encouraged from across the room. He was struggling with Tory's pants. She wouldn't give up easily, however, and kept lashing out with her feet until he finally punched her in the face again in frustration. She stopped moving long enough for him to pull her pants off her ankles and then he knelt down between her legs and reached to tear her panties off. Tory, whether from fear or design, chose that moment to void her bladder.

Peter leapt back in disgust and stood up. "Fucking bitch pissed on me!" he screamed and awkwardly pulled his pants back up with one hand. "Oh, you'll fucking pay for that, I promise you. I'd pop you right now, you slut, if I didn't have to keep you alive for a stupid phone call. Goddamn, I can't believe you did that!"

Emilio was doing his best not to laugh at his partner across the room but couldn't keep a smile off his face as Peter turned toward him.

"Don't you even think about it!" Peter yelled at him. "Where's the cell phone? I want to make this stupid call and get the fuck out of here."

Emilio continued to keep the knife near Ryan's throat, reached into his sport coat pocket with his other hand, and held out a small burner phone. Peter grabbed it, still muttering under his breath and dialed Edward's number in Miami from memory.

***

"Yeah?" Redondo answered on the other end.

"Give me Edward, it's Peter."

Redondo sighed at the prospect of hauling his bulk into the next room. "One sec., he replied in a bored tone and dropped the leg rest of his Lazy-Boy and shuffled into Edward's bedroom.

He held out the phone to him. "It's Peter."

Edward grabbed it. "You got 'em?"

"Yea, they're both here in front of me."

"Put it on speaker so they can hear me."

Peter hit the speaker button on the phone and held it up. At about the same time Emilio shifted the knife to his other hand and let it fall to his side.

"Mr. Cunningham, can you hear me OK?"

Ryan responded, "I hear you."

"It's really quite incredible that you're still alive."

Ryan was filled with conflicting emotions and tried to think of what to say to the man who had done so much damage to their lives. For whatever reason, it didn't appear that Chris was going to show up in time to save him and Tory and he was resigned to the fact that they were about to die. He wanted to know why their lives were about to end on one hand but as he looked over at Tory mostly naked and trembling on the couch all the bitterness and pain he was feeling came to the surface and he exploded.

"You scumbag! I only wish you had the balls to face me like a man."

Edward laughed into the phone. "That would take the fun out of it Mr. Cunningham. It's the raw obscenity of the things that I do that provide the thrill. I'm calling to let you know that I'm taking your life and that I win. Now I want you to say goodbye and be sure to give my best to your woman. Ta ta!"

"You fuck!" Ryan started, but was interrupted as Chris came through the door.

Chris achieved total surprise as he came through the French doors and focused his fire on Emilio first. He'd decided that he had to be immobilized first due to the knife he still held in his left hand and his close proximity to Ryan. Chris snapped off three quick rounds in under a second directly into Emilio's upper chest which threw him backwards across the room and clear of Ryan. There was no need to check the rounds for effect, he knew all three were killing shots and instead of watching as Emilio fell to the carpet he immediately spun on his axis and brought his sights to bear on Peter, ready to let go an equal number of rounds at him.

Peter had been slow to react to the unexpected threat and hesitated a half second too long before he dove for his gun which was still at the bottom of the couch six feet away. Chris couldn't fire immediately for fear of hitting Tory who was directly behind him and had to wait an extra nanosecond for him to start his rise back up to a standing position. Instinctively, Peter kept sideways to Chris as he started up and began to swing his own gun around. He wanted to present as small a target as possible.

Chris was only 14 feet away, however, and the shot was a simple one for him. He let go one round at precisely the right moment that tore through the ball of Peter's shoulder shattering bone as it went. The gun fell harmlessly to the floor as Peter spun from the impact and presented Chris with a full-frontal shot.

Chris started to take up the slack on the trigger to finish him but pulled the gun up into the air just prior to firing. If he killed them both they'd have no way of knowing if these two were solely responsible for the assault and he already suspected from the odd business of the cell phone call that they weren't acting alone. He wanted to question him first and took four quick steps across the room to kick the man's gun across the floor. "Sit!" he barked.

When his shoulder shattered, so too had all of his arrogance. Peter was not used to being on the receiving end of violence and he started blubbering.

"Oh my God, I'm shot! I can't fucking believe it," he continued to stand reeling in circles. "My shoulder! You destroyed my shoulder!"

Chris closed the rest of distance between them and brought the pistol down hard on his collarbone. Peter shrieked out, "No, please don't hurt me!" as he fell to the floor.

"Shut up!" Chris yelled back. "Where are the keys to the handcuffs?" Peter didn't answer, and just sat where he'd fallen, crying and mumbling to himself.

"Where?" Chris demanded again and slapped him with his free hand to get his attention.

Peter cowered beneath him. "In Emilio's pocket, over there." He pointed to Emilio's body.

"Don't move a goddamn muscle. I'd love to shoot you, you piece of shit, and I will if you do. Understand?"

Peter nodded back and Chris backed across the room to Emilio's fallen form and searched through his pockets till he found the small silver key that would open the cuffs. He went to Ryan first. "You OK?"

"I guess so but what took you so long?" Ryan asked.

"I couldn't get a clear shot without risking one of you till that moment. There was either a gun or a knife on one of you the whole time!"

After Chris got one of the cuffs free Ryan brought his hands around front and undid the second one himself. "I really thought that was it. Jesus I was scared!" As soon as the cuffs were off Ryan hopped across the room on one leg to Tory, reached down and pulled the gag out of her mouth. She had a crazy look in her eyes and started taking in huge lungfuls of air as though she'd been trapped under water. Ryan reached out to gently touch her face and she shook his hand off.

"Get these off me!" she hissed through clenched teeth and rolled onto her side so Ryan could access the cuffs on her wrists. She got up immediately, pulled her pants on, and then with no warning started kicking, punching, scratching and finally stomping on Peter's chest with her heel. Finally, a real person to vent all her anger and pain on and if Chris hadn't finally grabbed her arms, she would have stomped him to death.

"Enough Tory, enough!" Chris yelled as he yanked her back. "We need to find out who's responsible for this."

"We already know!" she hissed back. "It's still fucking Edward!"

After saying the words, she burst into tears. She was red faced with shame at her partial nudity and the fact that she'd urinated on the couch and ran from the room and up the stairs to shower and try and wash the humiliation away.

Chris looked towards Ryan who nodded back. "It's true, that was him they had me talking to on the phone." Ryan reached down and picked the small instrument up off the floor and put it up to his ear. He was surprised when he realized that the line was still open.

"Edward?" he yelled. "Are you still there you gutless prick?"

"Oh, I'm still here. It would seem that things didn't go quite as I'd planned. It's so difficult to find good help these days. Don't you agree? Oh well, next time I guess."

Ryan's earlier fears and impotence were suddenly gone, replaced with a hard, determined rage. He realized that they'd never be able to get on with their lives until this man was dead.

"Save yourself the trip, there won't be a next time!" Ryan replied back in a voice that belied his new resolve. "I'm coming for you!"

"Really? Awfully big talk for a family man!" Edward laughed and hung up.

Ryan stood staring at the dead phone for several seconds.

"He just said he'd try again. He's not going to leave us alone is he?"

Chris looked him in the eye and just shook his head, wondering if Ryan had meant what he'd said. He knew well the conflict going on inside him about right and wrong and also the very real possibility of going to prison if they were caught. He was fighting a lifetime of conditioning that the police and courts took care of things like these and in spite of the provocation it was not an easy decision to reconcile oneself to taking up arms against another human being, hunting them down, then killing them. The heat of passion was one thing, but with malice and forethought?

"Were you serious about coming for him?" Chris asked.

Ryan hesitated and took a deep breath before answering. "Yes."

After picking up the handcuffs that had been on Tory Chris grabbed Peter by his good arm and dragged him roughly across the carpet to one of the sliding glass doors. He put one of the handcuffs on Peter's good arm and attached the other end of the handcuffs to the door handle. "Where are the keys to your car?" he asked Peter.

"In my right front pocket," he responded.

Chris fished them out and turned back to Ryan. You and I need to talk; let's go in the other room. They walked into the dining room out of earshot of Peter.

"I think we should let that one go."

"What, after what he did?" Ryan asked incredulously.

"He's nothing, and if we report all this we're going to be tied up here for months with more paperwork and court time than you can imagine. It will make all of us easy targets. I think we should let him go and use him to our advantage. I can't think of an easier way to get rid of the other guys body. We'll throw the other one in the trunk of the car and let this one deal with it. What's he going to do anyway, go to the police and say he and his buddy were shot as they tried to rape and kill someone? I don't think so." Ryan thought about it for a few seconds and agreed.

"And as soon as we can get things in order here and get our shit together, we'll go after this guy Edward."

"Chris, listen. I agree with you in principle that we should go after him. He's a sociopath and God knows I've got reason to go after him, but the reality of the situation is I've also got a woman who is a total basket case and a little girl in the hospital who just tried to kill herself. I can't just run off like this is some kind of a fucking western and kill the bad guy. I've got people here right now who need me. Somebody's got to pull things together for them because Tory certainly can't."

"What other choice do you have? If you stay here and do nothing you might as well kill yourselves."

"I know that, but what am I supposed to do with them? I might be able to talk Bill and Stephanie into taking Jan for a while, but what about Tory? She's a mess!"

"You know as well as I do that there's nothing you can do for Tory until she's ready to help herself. You can't just sit around all day watching while she drinks and drugs herself into a coma. She belongs in a treatment center!"

"I know that and I already brought that up with her earlier at the hospital. I just don't know if I can talk her into it."

They were both startled to hear her voice behind them. "If I went to a treatment center, would you two go after him? Is that what this is about?"

"Shit," Chris said, uncomfortable with the fact that anyone else would know what they were planning.

"Is it?" Tory asked again.

Ryan and Chris both looked at each other and then nodded their heads.

"I'll go then. God knows I might deny ever having said this tomorrow morning but right now I'd agree to anything that would end that man's life. And although I don't much like admitting it, I know I need help."

"What about Jan, Tory?" Ryan asked.

"I know it's not fair but I'm killing her anyway the way I am now. I think if she knows I'm getting help she'll hang in there. I'll talk with her and Bill and Stephanie first thing in the morning. I'm sure they'll agree." With that Tory turned on her heel towards the kitchen and several seconds later Ryan heard the sounds of ice, and then liquid being poured into a glass. He wasn't about to say anything to her after what she'd been through.

Chris and Ryan went back into the living room and rolled Emilio's body up in the carpet and then dragged him down the front steps and across the street. Made rigid by the rolled-up carpet the body did not fit easily into the trunk and they had to struggle with it and bend things that didn't want to be bent to get it in. Ryan felt like he was going to get sick as they forced the body in.

"Is there anything else you want to ask the other one before we go back in, like where to find Edward?"

Ryan thought for a second before answering. "Let's not, that will only tip Edward for certain that we're coming for him. I already have a pretty good idea of where he might be from my conversations with the crew that died in the raft."

"I've got an idea. Where's that cell phone that they had."

"I guess it's still in on the table, why?" Ryan asked.

"Most phones have a redial function so you can re-call the most recent number. If we can get that number, we can do a reverse lookup and get his address. When we go back into the room bring a towel or something to stop that guy's bleeding and put your body between the two of us. I'll get that number without him noticing. We could just keep the phone, but this guy Edward is smart, and he might figure out that we could locate him that way so I think it's better to let him leave with his phone."

"Got it. I'll get the towel."

They returned to the living room and Ryan started wrapping a towel around Peter's upper arm. Chris took the cell phone off the table and copied down the last number dialed on it. Then he unlocked the cuffs that held Peter to the sliding door, slipped both the car keys and the handcuff keys into his front pocket. Then he took Peter's wallet out of his rear pocket and pulled his license from it before shoving the wallet back into his pocket.

"You know you're lucky to still be alive, don't you?" Chris asked him.

Peter said nothing and Chris slapped him. "Don't you?"

Peter nodded.

"We're going to let you go. We put your friend in the trunk of your car. Now listen, there's very little I can do to influence the scumbag you work for, but I want you to be very clear on how dead I will make you if I ever set eyes on you again." Chris pulled out his badge and held it up for him to see.

"When you talk with Edward let him know that these people are under my personal protection, and any further attempts on their lives will bring down the righteous wrath of every law enforcement person in this country on him. You see, for him to get to them, someone has to go through me, and cops don't like it when other cops get shot at. Understand shit head?"

Peter nodded again.

"Am I being crystal clear?"

"Yes," Peter mumbled, barely audible.

"What?" Chris screamed at him.

"Yes!"

"Good."

Chris held up Peter's license. "I'm going to hang on to this. If anything happens to me, or to them, I'll make sure my brothers in blue know to look you up. You hearing me?"

"Yes," Peter said.

"You may leave."

Peter turned for the door.

"Don't forget this." Chris held out his cell phone and Peter quickly stuffed it into his pocket before hobbling through the door.

Ryan and Chris stood in the doorway and followed the rental car with their eyes until the taillights disappeared around the corner. Chris put his arm around Ryan's shoulders and helped him back into the house. He was trembling. "You look like shit."

"I'll be all right I guess; I'm just not used to dead people in the living room," Ryan replied with a casualness he didn't feel. In point of fact, it was the first violent death he'd ever witnessed.

"Jesus Christ, Chris, what the hell are we doing?" Ryan had never done anything outside of the law before and while he was sure a jury would have no problem with their acts of self-defense, the premeditation and cover-up that they were now engaged in was something else entirely.

Chris turned and put both his hands on Ryan's shoulders. "Don't be fooled by my John Wayne attitude. Inside I feel sick, just like you. If I didn't, I'd be no different than those two who came here to kill you and Tory. Just remember that they want to kill you. If you don't fight back, they'll succeed."

Ryan choked back a sob. "Christ, when that one was about to rape Tory all I could think about was killing him and I was cursing you for the fact that you hadn't come to help us yet! I don't understand why I'm not happy that you shot them both."

"Because you care, about life and people! Try to keep in mind how many lives this guy has destroyed and how many more will be lost if we don't do something. It's because we care that we'll do what we're planning to do." Chris paused for a second. "Listen, let's get this place cleaned up and then you spend some time with Tory. I know she's in trouble, but you have no idea how lucky you are to still have her. I'd give anything to be able to just crawl in bed with my wife one more time, to hold her and tell her how much I love her. I can't do that, but you still can."

Ryan looked up at him. "Thanks, for everything. I know you're right."

Ryan took the covers off the couch cushions and threw them into the washer and then they both went to work getting all the blood off the hardwood floor and washed and scrubbed it several times. A good forensic team might still have been able to make a case against them by the time they were done, but the average civilian wouldn't notice anything amiss.

"I'm going to leave you my gun."

"You aren't staying?"

"No. No one will be back here tonight, and I have to go back and take care of my dogs. I never did get around to calling my neighbor. You'll be fine. Just lock up after I'm gone. I'll be back first thing in the morning to give you guys a ride to the hospital."

Ryan looked at him quizzically. "What exactly are we going to do Chris? Let's say he's still at the location of that phone number, are we just going to go down there and assassinate him?"

"I don't know, maybe we can come up with something a little bit more elaborate in addition to shooting him. Maybe something that has a broader effect. We'll talk tomorrow, and don't forget what I said about Tory. Love her while you can man, there's no telling when you'll see her again."

"I will, and Chris?"

"What?"

"Thanks for saving our lives."

Ryan went carefully through the house locking every single door and window and then went into their bedroom. The light was still on and she was sitting up in bed staring off into space.

"Hi."

She turned to him. "Hello yourself." There was an empty glass on the bedside table next to her, but she didn't seem to be high. Ryan took off his clothes and climbed under the covers with her after swinging his broken leg up onto the bed.

"We got things cleaned up downstairs. I..."

"Ryan, I don't even want to know. I know that sounds selfish, but I just don't feel like I can cope with any more right now. If I talk or even think about everything that's gone on this evening, I'll fall apart!"

"I understand."

"How's your leg?"

"It's fine. I'm going to see about getting a walking cast tomorrow when we pick up Jan."

"I spoke with the hospital a few minutes ago and the nurse said that Jan's sleeping soundly and there's nothing out of the ordinary."

"Good, I'm glad to hear it."

"You two will make quite a pair with your casts," Tory paused, then continued. "I don't know when we'll have a chance to really talk again but I did want to talk a little about finances. I know you've agreed to be an executor if anything happens to me, but I wanted you to know that I've also named Bill and Stephanie as co-trustees in case anything ever happens to both of us."

"That was smart."

"It's a lot of money."

"How much is a lot?"

"Several million."

Ryan whistled, "Wow."

"Wow is right. The reason I'm bringing it up is we really don't have to worry about money right now. I left most of it in an investment account but transferred $250,000 into an interest-bearing account that I can write checks on. Tomorrow I'd like to make you a signatory on the account."

"That's ridiculous!"

"You don't think I can trust you?"

"Of course you can trust me but it's not my money and in spite of everything that's gone on I think I can take care of myself."

"I'm not suggesting you can't. I just think it would be a good idea for you to have access to funds while I'm away in case anything happens to Jan or in case you need money for tracking Edward down. I want to participate in some way. That man has taken away two of the most important things in my life; Willy and my sobriety. I want to support you in any way I can. As far as I'm concerned you have carte blanche. If you need more, call me and I'll have the funds transferred."

Ryan was silent for a minute as he thought about what she said. He hadn't really thought through how he was going to survive over the next few weeks and he was bound to need money.

"I won't argue with you. I hadn't really thought about it before but obviously I'll need money no matter what Chris and I do. I respect your right to be as full of rage as I am. I'm not going to tell you how to spend your money. As a matter of fact, if it were mine I'd spend it the same way."

"Good, I'm glad you understand."

A long silence followed as both avoided discussing what had happened only an hour before in the living room. Despite the alcohol and Valium, he knew were flowing through her blood stream he was still able to see through to the person that he'd fallen in love with. He knew all those qualities were still there, as was his love.

"Tory, the person I'm looking at right now is wonderful, warm and strong. She's also a good person, although she may not believe that. Just remember that whatever happens in the future, that I believe that, even if you don't."

She wiped at her eyes with the back of her hand. "I hope you're right Ryan. I used to believe it and I want to feel that way again. All I can promise is that I'll try."

"I know you will." Ryan reached over and pulled her gently into his arms and they both fell into a deep sleep.

Chapter 13

Ryan awoke after Tory at about 7:30 and found her on the phone when he came out to the kitchen. "That's right, McCane, em, cee, cee, aye, en, ee." He poured a cup of coffee as she continued to talk.

"I can be there tomorrow morning. No, not tonight. No thanks, my boyfriend will give me a ride. No, I'll pay in cash. Right. See you then." She hung up the phone.

"Who was that?"

"A treatment center North of Boston in New Hampshire. Do you think you can give me lift?"

"Of course. What kind of a program is it?"

Tory rolled her eyes. "You know the one with the TV ads that talks about dignity and restoring a sense of self-worth? That's the one," she laughed.

"Why are you laughing?"

"It's such a crock. You forget, I'm kind of an expert on treatment centers. They all work the same way."

"And how's that?"

"They all beat the shit out of you before they try to rebuild you. It's all right though, I'll get through it."

"Come here, you."

Tory crossed into his arms and he gave her a long, soft, kiss. "I love you."

"Yeah, I know." Tory nuzzled his neck. "Let's try and call Jan."

"OK."

Tory found the number of the hospital and dialed it. "What time is Chris coming?"

"I'm not sure, but he said early."

Tory held up her finger. "Hi, could I have the third-floor nurses station please? Thanks. Good morning, this is Tory McCane, I was wondering if my daughter was awake yet? Yes, room 310. How is she? That's wonderful, do you know what time they plan to put the cast on her? OK, would you please tell her that Mr. Cunningham and I will be there shortly? Great.

"They said she's doing really well although she can't talk because of the stitches. She should like her diet for the next week though, nothing but ice cream sodas."

"How're you feeling this morning?" Ryan asked.

"I'm doing pretty good."

"Second thoughts?"

"A lot, it's not easy to admit you failed again."

"You didn't fail. The only way you can fail is if you give up now."

"But if Jan ever needed me, it's now."

"Jan needs you alive, and well."

"I know that intellectually, but the mother in me is saying something else."

They sipped their coffee in silence for a few seconds. "Do you want to tell me what you and Chris are planning?"

"Not really. It's probably best you don't know, and we haven't really decided yet anyway. There are a couple of things I've learned about Chris that are important. Apparently, he was married. His wife was an addict who died from an overdose."

Tory raised her eyebrows. "I'm sorry to hear that although it might explain his interest in us and what you two are about to do. It would have been nice if he'd shared that with us earlier."

"Someone has to put a stop to this guy."

"And you think you're the one to do that?"

"I don't know. I do know I'm not going to sit here waiting for him to try and kill us again."

"Do you think we can trust Chris?"

Ryan tilted his head quizzically. "What do you mean?"

"Just be careful and watch out for yourself. Don't you find this whole thing is just a little bit unreal? I mean here you are contemplating murder with a state trooper who lost his wife to drugs. Don't get me wrong, I think Edward should be dead and if you could magically put him in this room right now, I'd pull the trigger. I just want you to watch out for yourself. Your life means far more to me than Edward's death. Keep things in perspective." Tory hugged him again and gave him a long kiss.

"I will," Ryan promised.

After they let go of each other Tory got on the phone again, this time to Stephanie. While she was talking Chris arrived and 15 minutes later the three of them left for the hospital. Ryan grabbed his own X-rays and medical history before heading out the door hoping he could get his cast off at the same time as Jan had hers put on.

"How did it go with Stephanie?" Ryan asked in the car.

"All I've told her so far is that I'm going back into treatment and asked if she could take Jan while I was there. I told her we'd bring her by tomorrow and fill her in on the details then."

"Where did you say I'd be while all this was going on?"

"I said you expected to be doing a lot of traveling over the next few weeks trying to get your finances together and trying to get the insurance claim settled on Parthenia, blah, blah, blah. I was very vague, I just suggested that we both thought it would be more stable for Jan if she were in a real home for a while."

Ryan and Chris both looked at her skeptically.

"Don't panic, I was really vague."

"Do you think she believed you?"

"I don't know but they won't pry. I also told her you'd be keeping in close touch with Jan to make the whole thing sound more believable. No one will guess what you're doing; it's too outrageous."

Tory paused then continued. "Ryan, I'm scared to stay at our place tonight, but I'm also hesitant to stay at their place in case he tries something again. Chris, do you think the three of us could stay at your place?"

"Absolutely, I've got three extra rooms."

They arrived at the hospital several minutes later and after checking in with the receptionist they went straight up to Jan's room. They were greeted by a very swollen faced, little girl who tried to smile as they came in.

"No don't!" Tory almost laughed. "You'll hurt yourself. Oh baby, I'm so glad to see you." She hugged Jan as hard as she dared. "I'm sorry we weren't here when you woke up, are you OK? We've been so worried about you."

Ryan sat down on the other side of the bed and Chris looked on from the side. Jan nodded a sheepish "yes" to Tory's question.

"I spoke to the nurse before I came in and we're going to go downstairs in a few minutes and get a cast on your arm. And then we can get you the heck out of here. Are you ready?"

"Aomm weady," Jan managed, speaking like she had a mouth full of marbles.

Tory and Ryan exchanged surprised glances. "She speaks!" Ryan laughed.

Twenty minutes later they were in an anteroom off the ER with the orthopedic man. He palpated Jan's arm tenderly although he was thorough. "The swelling's gone down nicely and judging from these X-rays it's a nice clean break. You should be out of your cast in three to four weeks if everything goes well." He looked over at Ryan's leg. "What is it with your family Mr. Cunningham. Are you all accident prone?"

"I hope not, although I'm beginning to wonder. Do you think you could have a look at my leg after you finish with her? I'd like to switch this clunker of a cast out for a walking cast. It would be great if you could do it while I'm here."

"I can do that. You can give me your history while I wrap Jan's arm."

Ryan passed him his folder and before he started to wrap the warm plaster around Jan's arm, he snapped Ryan's X-rays into the viewer in front of him to familiarize himself with Ryan's injury as he wrapped Jan's arm. After finishing her cast and making sure she was comfortable, he turned his attention to Ryan.

"Are you able to put weight on your injured leg without discomfort?"

Ryan leaned his crutches up against the examination table and evenly distributed his weight on both feet.

"That's excellent. Sit up here on the examination table." The doctor cut Ryan's plaster cast off and then put a large fiberglass boot around Ryan's lower leg and did up the three Velcro straps. "Try this one."

Ryan slid off the table, tentatively put weight on his broken leg and then took several small steps.

"That feels good."

"You might want to use a cane for a few days as you get used to it. Obviously, don't do anything too strenuous for another couple of weeks."

"Thanks Doctor, I won't."

They stopped at the local bank next, where Tory instructed the bank that her new checking account would be a joint one and the banker had Ryan sign a signature card and issued him a temporary debit card. Fifteen minutes later they got back in Chris's Jeep and headed out on the main highway away from Sippican.

"Wear wee hedded?" Jan mumbled.

All three adults looked at each other anxiously, not having yet discussed how much to tell Jan. Tory answered.

"We had some new problems last night while you were in the hospital and Chris is going to put us up at his house tonight," Tory answered.

Jan looked confused. "Whaa kind of pobwems?"

"It had to do with the man off the boat again."

Tory could see her expression change from one of curiosity to one of fear.

"Everything's so messed up Jan. I'll explain it all to you when we get to Chris's house but please, don't be scared. Chris is a policeman and we'll be safe there," Tory had said the words, but she didn't know whether even she believed them. No one spoke again until they approached Chris's house and they were greeted by his dogs. Tory was gratified to see the funereal look on Jan's face disappear as the dogs leapt off the porch and surrounded the Jeep in obvious glee.

"Look Mom, thwee dogs, and one of them is almost as big as Quifton!"

191

Tory hadn't thought of Clifton in days and before Chris had the car to a complete stop Jan had her door cracked, much as Ryan had at his first meeting with the dogs.

"Be careful of your arm sweetie, they're pretty excited," Tory cautioned, but Jan's obvious delight touched her and she said nothing more as all three dogs started nuzzling her and flipping her good arm in the air with their heads, all vying for her affection at once.

"Noaims Chris?" Jan asked.

"Oro's the Golden, Raven's the Lab, and the little one is Short Stuff. He's a Jack Russell."

Jan immediately focused her attention on Raven because she reminded her so much of Clifton in size and as Jan alternately scratched her ears and ran her hand over her big broad head, she leaned down and allowed her to lick her with her rough, wet tongue. The somber mood was broken.

"I guess you like dogs Jan, huh?" Chris asked with a Cheshire Cat grin as they walked towards the front porch.

She nodded without looking up, continuing to pet Raven.

"Well behold!" Chris opened the front door in an exaggerated gesture and swept his arm towards the pen of puppies. "A whole nest of nippers for your petting pleasure!"

Ryan had purposefully restrained himself from telling Jan about the litter, preferring to give Chris the pleasure and stood to the side with his arm around Tory and watched Jan's face light up. For a few moments it was as if someone had thrown the switch on a giant Christmas tree. Jan was careful at first and reached in to take one out after looking towards Chris for permission but within seconds she was laying on the floor, eyes scrunched shut, as all five clumsily licked and pawed at her face and neck. Chris finally broke up the melee.

"More dogs later. First let's get you all settled, and you, young lady get first pick of rooms. One looks down towards the river from the second story and the other is on the first floor next to the pool. Which would you prefer?"

"Wan won wif dogs," she struggled past her swollen tongue.

Chris laughed. "Well, none of the rooms have dogs but you're welcome to spend as much time as you like with these characters."

Jan looked towards Tory with a look that conveyed she would like to be with or next to her. Chris picked up on it immediately.

"How about the room next to your Mom? That would be the second story one."

Jan nodded.

"That answers my next question because there are only two rooms on the second floor. So why don't you all get settled and I'll see if I can't rustle up something to eat in the kitchen."

Tory reached out and touched Chris gently on the shoulder. "Thank you, she really needed something like this."

Chris prepared a soup and sandwich lunch for the three adults and a black and white frappe for Jan. They ate hungrily. After, a silence fell over the table. There was much that needed to be discussed but no one really knew where to start. The things that needed to be discussed, planned and resolved shared some overlap but Ryan and Chris were about to embark on a course that excluded Jan and Tory and the two women had their own issues that were better discussed in private.

"Jan, there's a lot I want to talk with you about. How about the two of us going upstairs?"

Jan simply nodded, got up, and the two of them left the table. Tory looked back over her shoulder. "See you guys later."

The silence continued at the table for almost a minute before Chris finally spoke. "You seem to have cooled some since last night. Are you still willing to go after him with me or would you rather wait for him to come after you again?" It was the wrong tact and Ryan bristled at the inference.

"Chris, this is a little more complicated than a question of machismo! I'm not afraid of this man! I just want to be around when the smoke clears to be with my new family! It's also about right and wrong and I'm not quite as cavalier about hunting down another human being and killing him as you are. We both know he's guilty of committing any number of capital crimes but don't try and bully me like some simpleton into something that I haven't thought through! Especially something like this! By taking the law into our own hands we're also jeopardizing our own futures and freedom. You may not care anymore because

193

you've lost your wife and feel like you have nothing else to lose, but I do. I'm still very much in, but I want whatever we do to be considered."

Both were quiet again realizing they'd gotten off to a bad start.

"I'm sorry, I didn't mean to insult you. How many years have we been 'waging war on drugs?' Give me a break! Shit we haven't even had a real skirmish yet. If we were serious, we'd fight it like a real war and interrupt lines of supply, bomb factories, blockade coastlines, seize assets and send fucking troops in to go after the people that matter. That's not happening, and you know it as well as I do"

"And you think killing one drug dealer will make a difference?"

"Why are you defending this guy. He *killed* Tory's son, tried to rape her and her daughter and left you homeless! What other justification do you need?"

Chris was right and on a very basic level he did, personally, want to kill Edward. Better still he wanted to hear him beg for mercy first. Ryan forced himself to think things through for several moments before responding. Oro was lying alongside his chair and he reached down and stroked her head gently while he thought.

"I agree we have to go after Edward. I don't have the slightest hesitation in agreeing that we must put a stop to him, I'm just not sure at this point what that means. Yes, you're right, I do want to kill him and killing him may be the only answer. If it comes to that I think I can do it. But I also want to be able to face myself in the mirror each morning and I think we should keep our eyes and our options open as we go into this. I like your idea from last night about doing something that would make a real difference."

Chris realized that this was as much of an agreement as he was likely to get out of Ryan at that point and decided not to push the killing aspect any further that evening. He hoped Ryan would come around eventually but even if he didn't, they'd be that much closer to their quarry and Chris knew that he could easily pull the trigger if the opportunity presented itself. "You agree then that we'll at least hunt down this man?"

"Absolutely."

"OK, tell me everything you know about him."

Tory sat down next to Jan on the bed in her room and hugged her. She realized it was the first time since Willy's death that she'd really given any of herself to her daughter. She'd been so selfishly involved in her own grief and self-recrimination that once again; she'd effectively deserted her. The feel of her daughter's cheek on her own triggered a very maternal nerve.

"I don't really know where to start babe. You've listened to a lifetime's worth of 'sorrys' and probably don't want to hear another one, so I'll skip that, but first off, I want you to know that you are the single most important thing in my otherwise screwed up life."

"I know you wov me mom."

"Good." Tory smiled and after wiping the tears from her own face brushed a loose strand of hair back behind Jan's ear.

"I'll spare you the bullshit. I'm in trouble again, I've been drinking and using drugs for the last few days and although I can give you a lot of very good sounding reasons, you know as well as I do that there are none. I can't use anything, ever. When I do, I lose myself and I'm not there for you or anyone else."

Jan was looking away as Tory spoke and responded shyly past her still swollen tongue.

"Maybe ou ave too many wesponsibilities."

Tory couldn't speak for a second and then turned Jan's face to her own.

"Don't ever think that! You're not some burden I have to bear. You are my joy, my love, my very life!"

"I don't understand. If ahm so important to ou, wy ou keep wusing dwugs and alcohol, cawnt ou just stwop?"

Tory sobbed out loud. "Because I'm sick! I have a disease. I didn't ask for it and I don't want it." She suddenly stopped herself. "Forget that. Those are just more words and there've been enough excuses and empty promises. What I need you to know and believe is that I love you, you are not a burden of any kind and that I'm going to get sober again and stay that way. Do you believe in me?"

"I gwuess." Jan's eyes were downcast again.

"No baby, that's not good enough. Look me in the eye when you say it so that I know it's true."

Jan slowly raised her eyes and looked deeply into Tory's. "Yes, I buweave you."

"Good, now here's what I'm going to do. I'm leaving tomorrow for a treatment center. I know it means leaving you again, but I think it's the only way I can stop. I can't make any promises yet, but I think it will only be for a month. While I'm gone, I want you to stay with Bill and Stephanie. Will you do that for me?"

"Caan't I stay wid Wyan?"

"No, Ryan will be away for a while and also, I think you'll be safer with them."

"Am safe with Wyan." Jan was confused.

"Oh I don't mean it that way, of course you're safe with him, but the problem is the man on the yacht, Edward and his men. He's still after Ryan and anyone who hangs around Ryan is probably in danger."

The mere mention of Edward and his men terrified Jan but she feared for Ryan as much as herself. "Cwis is a policeman, caant he dwoo tometing?"

"We'll talk about that in a second, first I want you to tell me that you'll stay with Bill and Stephanie. I need to know that you're safe."

"I will."

"And you have to promise me something else."

"Waat?"

Tory searched for the words for a moment. "That you won't do anything else to hurt yourself. You're so important to me, if anything happened to you, I wouldn't be able to go on. Please promise me."

It was the first inkling that Jan had that people knew her accident the day before had been purposeful and she felt ashamed and looked down at the floor before replying.

"I fought thwings would be easier for ou if ou didn't aav to worry bout me."

Tory's heart ached and she grabbed Jan firmly by both arms. "Don't ever think that Jan. You don't have anything to do with my addictions. You're my reason for living, not using! So please, don't blame yourself and promise me."

"I pwomise."

"Whaa about Wyan, what will he do?"

Tory rolled over onto her back and looked up at the ceiling. She didn't want to tell Jan too much for fear it would endanger Ryan and Chris, but she also felt that Jan had earned the right to know something. She'd been through as much as any of them.

"Truthfully I don't know and it's important that we don't discuss this with anyone. That includes Bill and Stephanie, but basically I think he and Chris are going to make sure that this man Edward can never hurt us again."

"Are they gwoing to kill him?"

"I'm not really sure but they have to do something, or this man will continue to come after Ryan and to hurt other people."

"I hope they do kwill him. He kwilled Wiwwy and Cwifton."

Tory stroked her head. "I know sweetie, I know."

"Manuel told you he has houses in Antigua and Miami, right?"

Ryan nodded.

"Well the area code and number on the cell phone were in South Florida so it would seem that's where he is. Do you remember the address, or should I run the number through a reverse lookup database?"

"I remember it. What kind of surveillance equipment can you gain access to?"

"Pretty much anything, directional laser mikes that pick up voices right through glass, tape recorders, infinity bugs, phone bugs, locator bugs, NVGs, cameras, you name it. I can't guarantee I won't get in some trouble when the stuff shows up missing and they track it to me, but I'm willing to take that chance. Probably the worst that will happen is that they'll fire me. I can live with that. I can also lift an extra set of body armor for you out of the SWAT equipment."

"Body armor?"

"You know, a bullet-proof vest?"

"And what are NVGs?"

"Night vision goggles."

"Right, I guess that's a good idea. I already know you have plenty of guns but that raises the issue of getting all this stuff south. We can't just hop on the next commercial flight with suitcases full of weapons and surveillance gear."

"True, that means we either have to buy new stuff once we get down there or drive. I'd suggest driving because neither one of us knows anyone down there and we don't want to draw any unnecessary attention to ourselves once we get there. I know Miami's a jungle and you can buy anything you want there, but I think we'd be smart to bring stuff we're familiar with."

"I agree."

"It's going to take a day or two for me to get all the things we want from work. Maybe you can use that time to work a little more on your shooting."

"I'm going to take Tory to the treatment center in New Hampshire tomorrow, but I should be back by late afternoon. After I leave Jan at Bill and Stephanie's I'm yours to mold as you will," Ryan replied with a smile. "Think you can turn me into a crack shot like you in a couple of days?"

"I'll try. Consider it self-preservation. I may have to rely on you at some point to save my ass."

"I hear you," Ryan paused. "You know, I was serious earlier when I talked about doing something that would make a real difference. From what Manuel told me in the life raft these people are into moving big weights of product. I know that killing Edward would solve my immediate problem, but it won't really have any impact on the bigger picture. I'd be quite happy knowing that he was spending the rest of his life in a tiny cell if we could somehow get to the people he works for. That would make Willy and your wife's death actually mean something."

"A noble goal but do you really think we can do something that all the resources of the DEA, Coast Guard, and every other state and federal organizations have failed at?" Chris asked skeptically.

"I don't know, but let's keep our minds open to that."

Chris held his stare for a moment longer and then went back to the list he'd been working on without commenting further.

"I'm going to go up and check on Tory and Jan," Ryan announced several minutes later.

Chris nodded without looking up.

As Ryan approached the door to Tory and his room, he could hear giggles coming from the other side and smiled before easing the door open. Both Jan and Tory were on the floor with one of the puppies and were rolling a tennis ball for the small black retriever. The ball was as large as his head and as he bounded after it, he would as often as not trip and sprawl over it in his enthusiasm to retrieve it.

Tory looked up. "Look at this silly little creature Ryan, he actually thinks he can retrieve!"

"You guys have been puppy-napping!"

Jan laughed. "Ou won't twell, I know ou wov them as much as I dwoo."

Ryan eased himself to the floor and extended his hurt leg carefully out in front of him. "Would you pass me one of the pillows off the bed Tory?"

Tory reached up on the bed and instead of passing him the pillow, threw it aggressively at his head. "There you go!"

The puppy caught the movement of the large white object as it flew through the air and stopped mauling the wet tennis ball long enough to see if something more interesting were occurring. Tory caught Ryan by surprise and instead of throwing it back at her he reached out and quickly snagged the small puppy bringing it to his chest. "I'll get you guys where it hurts."

Tory and Jan looked at each other in mock horror and simultaneously started whining. "Oh no, not the puppy. Anything you want, but don't take our puppy!" They both leapt on him and smothered him and the small dog with their affection. It was the first normalcy the three had shared since Willy's death. Ryan ended up in the middle with their heads on either of his shoulders and the puppy curled up on his chest.

"Boy I've missed you two. And this little guy is adorable."

Neither of the women spoke and instead answered by snuggling closer.

"I know everything is up in the air and seems like shit right now but if I have any say in things, somehow we're going to come through this. Right?"

"Wight," Jan echoed.

Tory didn't speak and instead nodded her head.

"Mom, Wyan, wha would ou two tink about us maybe gettin a puppy? Ou know, won that wooks like this wittle guy here, ou know, a new Quifton."

Tory thought for a moment before replying. She didn't want to let Jan down.

"Maybe when we get settled sweetie. Right now, we don't even have a place of our own to live."

Ryan looked down at the small puppy now asleep on his chest. He was different from the rest of the litter in that he had a tiny white star on his chest. It was not a sign of impure breading but rather a normal anomaly that sometimes happened when yellow Labs were bred with black Labs. It gave him a distinction over his brothers and sisters that Ryan liked.

"I think it's a great idea Jan, but your mother's right, we don't even have a place of our own to live right now. Chris also told me that all of the puppies in this litter are already spoken for although I have to admit this is a handsome little devil. He's feisty and independent like Clifton was when he was a puppy."

Jan was disappointed but didn't want to ruin the mood by pushing. If all the puppies were already all promised, then there seemed little point in pressing the issue.

"Well wet's get a place thoon because I think it's a good idea."

Ryan ruffled her hair. "I agree."

The three continued to lay on the floor for another half hour and Ryan finally stirred when the puppy hopped off his chest and started sniffing an area of the carpet near the door.

"Jan. Jan."

"Waat?" She answered sleepily.

"I think your little friend needs to go and you better get him outside or down to the mudroom before he does, or we won't be very popular with Chris."

"OK."

"How're you doing?" Ryan directed at Tory.

"Actually, I'm pretty chilly. What do you say we go down to the living room and light a fire?"

"That's a great idea. Help me up, would you?"

"I'll talk to Chris and see what he has planned for dinner. Maybe I can make myself useful."

When they reached the bottom of the stairs several minutes later, they were drawn to the sliding glass doors that overlooked the field and river below. The house was quiet save for the crackling of a fire that Chris had already lit, and they watched as the last remnants of the sun cast long shadows through the bare corn stalks of the rear field that sloped down to the river. The shadows resembled bent old men and were projected atop a fresh dusting of powdery snow that had fallen over the last hour. They embraced against the late afternoon chill and watched as the snow twirled pirouettes on the bare brick of the patio.

"I guess Chris beat us to it."

"You mean the fire?"

"Uh huh."

"God, I wish this was our place and we could freeze things right now, just as they are." Ryan mused.

Before Tory could reply they heard the mudroom door slam and the sounds of Chris and Jan returning. As they turned, the inner door opened, and Jan and Chris were proceeded into the room by all eight dogs who were snorting and trying to shake the snow out of their coats. The puppy with the white star on his chest hung back some and Ryan laughed as he tried to shake the packed snow from between the toes of one of his paws.

Jan's cheeks were flushed from the chill air and she bent over in an exaggerated caricature of an exhausted person on noticing Tory and Ryan.

"Ou should ave seen them Mom, it's their firth snowfall. They all walked like this!" And Jan tried to imitate them, pausing between each step to shake the make-believe snow off her raised foot. Ryan and Tory laughed with her again, grateful for anything that could bring about a change in Jan's otherwise withdrawn demeanor.

"Ou know the won with the star on his chest that we pwayed with earlier? Well that's the one that Cwis ith keeping and he sais we can visit him anytime we want."

"That's great babe. Chris, do you have any plan for dinner? I'd be glad to help out if you point me in the right direction." Tory offered.

"Why don't you come out to the kitchen with me and we'll see what's there."

While she cooked Tory helped herself to white wine that was in the refrigerator figuring she'd be in the detox the next day but felt no compulsion to drink to the point of intoxication nor did she make any attempt to hide it from the others. She'd also taken several Valium during the course of the day but again had limited her dosage to a maintenance level. Ninety minutes later she and Chris called everyone to the table where they sat down to a meal of twice baked stuffed potatoes, steak and broccoli. She set the plates full of food in front of everyone but Jan.

"Wears mine?" Jan mumbled.

"Don't worry babe, I didn't forget you." And Tory reemerged a minute later from the kitchen with another tall black and white frappe.

"What time do you plan on leaving in the morning?" Chris asked.

Ryan looked at Tory. "Early, I guess. I told them I'd be up there by late morning. That reminds me, what are we going to do for a car, rent one?" Tory asked Ryan.

"You can take mine if you want. I don't have to do anything first thing," Chris offered.

"Can I cwom?" Jan asked.

Again, Tory and Ryan looked at each other. "I don't see why not, you've seen most of the other places I've been rehabilitated in," Tory replied in a slightly sarcastic tone. Chris raised an eyebrow in Ryan's direction, no stranger to the detox and treatment center scene. It made him think of the years with his wife and the uncertainty he felt each time he would drop her off at one of the facilities; always expensive, seldom effective, but still you hoped and prayed each time that this time, it would work. He didn't envy Ryan.

"Cwool," Jan replied.

Ryan was the first to head off to bed several hours later and lingered in a hot tub for half an hour trying to leach some of the tension from his body. Because the cast he'd gotten that morning was removable he was able to immerse his whole body. He lay there reviewing all of the events that had transpired over the previous weeks. One self-observation he made was that all of his reactions over the previous few weeks had been defensive. Edward was used to people responding in a very predictable manner to his terror and intimidation. "How would he fare if the roles were reversed?" Ryan wondered and steeled himself to the concept that if they were to come out on top, he'd have to shelve his live and let live, laissez-faire attitude and be willing to act proactively. He wondered if Edward had ever been on the receiving end of the type of terror and intimidation he was obviously used to dishing out?

"What're you thinking?" Tory asked after walking into the bathroom.

"Is Jan asleep?"

"Almost. A penny for your thoughts."

"I was just wondering when the last time was that Edward felt the same type of fear that he put all of us through. I also realized that if I'm going to be successful at eliminating him from our lives, I'm going to have to be willing to go to any lengths, just like Chris said. I guess I'm wondering if I have that killer instinct. I mean did you see the way Chris handled himself last night against those two men at the house. His actions were incredibly controlled and focused; it was like he was born to it. I don't think I have that in me."

"I'm glad you don't."

"I'm glad too but that leaves me in one of only two possible modes. I'm either completely docile, or blind with rage. My gut tells me that unless I take on a whole different attitude, he'll continue to hold the advantage."

Tory spoke after a few moments of reflection. "I know that I talked pretty tough last night myself, but now, when I think of what you might be going to do, I don't feel so tough. I don't want to lose you. Can't we just disappear somewhere after I get out of the treatment center?"

"I guess we probably could. But what about Willy and Clifton and all the other people's lives that this guy's going to ruin?"

"There's a lot of evil in the world."

"I know it's not my job, but I don't know if I can live with myself if we ran knowing what he took from us."

"Just don't do this because you feel you have to for me. I wouldn't ask that of you. I want you to know though, no matter what you decide, I'll be behind you."

"Help me up, would you?"

Tory helped him out of the tub and then helped dry him as he supported himself against the vanity.

"Why don't you slip into bed? I'll join you in a minute." Tory emerged from the bathroom several minutes later and undressed at the side of the bed pulling her sweater over her head and then shrugging free of her brassiere.

"You are seriously lovely."

Tory looked down between her breasts and traced the smooth curve of her tummy with her hand before unfastening the metal snap on her jeans. It quietly gave way and the sound her zipper made in the aftermath sounded loud and sensual. Ryan smiled.

"Why're you smiling?"

"That's an incredibly sexual sound to me."

"What, the zipper?"

"I guess it takes me back to my high school days and those sessions of heavy petting that seemed to go on for hours. Whenever I heard that sound it usually meant I was about to get some."

"Get *some*! I swear, you men have an entire vocabulary that the female race is ignorant of. But in this case, you're not wrong. You are going to get some." Tory pulled her jeans the rest of the way off, then stepped out of her panties, and slid alongside him in the bed covering as much of him as possible with herself.

"I'm going to miss you." Ryan started.

Tory placed her finger over his lips and slid down his body entwining her body with his and took him into her warm, wet, mouth. Ryan sucked in a breath and ran a hand through her hair. She was in no hurry and lay there with her head on his belly moving only her tongue until he became fully enlarged. Eventually she brought her head back up towards his chest, flipped her hair back and looked deeply into his eyes all the while continuing to knead and softly stroke him.

"Please make love to me?" she asked almost shyly. Ryan knew what she meant and gently rolled her onto her back and kissed her tenderly. He felt the same way, it was more about love than sex, and kissed her on the neck, ears, throat, chin and lips. He touched her at the same time with his hand, although each caress was more suggestion than reality and often, she wasn't sure whether he'd touched her. Slowly a delicious passion built, and she spread her arms across the width of the bed enjoying the warmth of the room, the clean cotton sheets on her back and Ryan's gentle touch. She felt his breath on the inside of her thighs. She groaned, tucked her free leg up with the knee bent, and then let her thigh fall outwards exposing herself to him. Ryan ignored the implicit invitation to enter her, however, and instead brought his mouth to her open wet lips. Tory had a powerful orgasm and almost crushed his head with her thighs as she came. Then she lifted herself on one elbow and took his thick, corded, length in her hand. "Please Ryan, now. Make love to me now."

Ryan held her eyes for a moment and then after gently kissing her swollen, little clitoris a final time, knelt between her legs and partially penetrated her. Then, still maintaining eye contact, he slid one arm beneath her shoulders, the other under her ass and finally plowed into her in one powerful, complete motion, drawing her hips to his own completely penetrating her. He stretched her tightly as he entered but that was what Tory wanted. She wanted to feel completely connected and as he achieved full penetration, she wrapped her legs around his back and drew him in even further. Tory matched the strength she felt in the arms that surrounded her with her own and moved her hips to meet his as he drove into her with long powerful strokes. From the outset both knew that there would be no changes of position, subtle physical games or laughter; instead their bodies moved in perfect, harmonic unison towards a simultaneous, shared release in which conscious thought and technique played no role. It was both instinctual and perfect as a result, and as the first waves of her second orgasm started to undulate through her, so too did they through Ryan. In spite of his almost violent thrusts, her muscle contractions were so powerful that they overwhelmed his hardness, moving as they did in determined waves up and down his shaft. Her excitement and complete release made him gather her to him all the more tightly, and as he let go, he cried out, almost crushing her in his embrace. Tory didn't care though and buried her own cries in his neck as the orgasm continued to wash over her. Her vaginal muscles contracted over and over and over in miasmic spasms of pleasure, milking what felt like the very life from him.

Neither said anything for a long time and instead listened, in the sudden stillness of the room, to each other's bodies as they returned ever so gradually to stasis.

"I love you Tory," Ryan finally managed. As the words came out, they neither frightened him nor sounded hollow and he pressed his cheek to her forehead and gathered her tightly against his chest again. She felt small and vulnerable and he swore silently to himself that he would do whatever it took to protect her and Jan and keep them in his life.

Tory hugged him back, feeling the same things as he, but said nothing, wondering if she would ever be worthy of the love he professed and the two fell deeply asleep with Ryan still hard inside her.

Chapter 14

Chris was up before first light. Most mornings he found himself tossing and turning by 4 or 5 a.m., his mind full of memories and guilt. He had enough knowledge of the recovery process to know that he'd done everything humanly possible to help Anne through her addictions and attempted recoveries, shy of throwing her out, but he'd drawn the line at that in spite of the fact that it was the one thing that many experts had suggested. Having Tory in the house stirred all those memories afresh and after putting on a robe and turning the heat up a few degrees against the morning chill, he fixed a pot of coffee and sat down at the kitchen table with one of the many photo albums he had of his years with Anne and pored through it.

Reviewing his life with Anne was something Chris did on a nearly daily basis. Some mornings he'd just move from room to room in the still dark house touching things they'd shared and musing. There were so many things they'd talked about doing and plans they'd made. Chief among them was the family they'd hoped for. Anne would periodically stop taking birth control during sober periods, but she never got pregnant during those times. In retrospect he believed that there had been some sort of silent guardian angel or maternal coding within her that prevented her from becoming pregnant. He fantasized that a child might have been able to provide the grounding and senses of worth and purpose that were somehow lacking in her, but deep down he knew that there had been some fundamental flaw in her ability to love herself and that a child might have just provided one more area that she saw herself as inadequate and a failure. As he looked through an album he would pause periodically to dwell on a pleasant memory, but that was seldom his real purpose. He was looking for some clue, some shadow, anything, that would help him to understand why. He'd stop most frequently to look at those photos that featured her full face and he'd stare for minutes at a time into her eyes hoping that they might betray something of the inner side of her that he'd been unable to touch and understand. While he did this, he absently played with one of her old hair "scrunchies" that she'd used to tie her hair back. In spite of the many hours he'd spent sliding it on and off his wrist and smelling it over the months since her death, it was still redolent with her scent because each day he would carefully put it back in the top draw where she'd kept her lingerie and let it renew its bouquet like a sachet. "Sachet of Anne," he thought to himself and drew a breath with the hair tie pressed to his nose. Through it he could smell her hair, her perfume, and her skin and for the briefest of moments if he closed his eyes tight enough, she was almost there. As he did, he thought to himself that he would give anything, anything at all to have just one more moment with her to tell her how much he loved her. It was important to him because she must not have known or at least had doubts. How else could she have done what she did to herself? And why hadn't he been able to protect her and prevent it? He knew he was right on the edge of insanity during moments like these, but he needed to keep his memories of her fresh. He was terrified of slowly forgetting little things about her over time as his memories faded and the photo albums and the hair scrunchy were his way of guarding against this. Somehow the people that trafficked in the garbage that had poisoned her, would pay. Keeping that goal fresh was frequently the only way he was able to get out of bed in the mornings and face another day. As he saw what was happening to Ryan, Tory and Jan as a result of the same poison, his resolve was renewed and steeled. His sadness over Anne's death was profound, but before he simply gave up and checked out at his own hand, he was determined to strike back.

At six he heard someone making their way down the stairs and after putting away the photo album and tucking the hair tie into his bathrobe pocket he walked out into to the living room to see who else was up. He could hear Jan's voice and the sound of the puppies mewing from the mudroom and quietly made his way to the doorway and stood watching as she talked and played with them. He noticed that she payed particular attention to the one with the small star on his chest that he'd picked out for himself.

"You really like him, don't you?"

Jan started at the sound of his voice, but quickly recovered and continued to pet the small pup who had rolled over onto his back with legs splayed. "Yes, he reminds me of Quifton."

"Clifton was Ryan's dog, right?"

Jan nodded. "O, ou don't know about him do ou?"

"Not really. I gather he was pretty big."

"Yes, he was very big," Jan agreed solemnly. "But he was also funny and playful. Most of all, though, he was very brave. He saved my mother's life and mine. Did ou know that?"

"No, how'd he do that?" Chris asked curiously.

Jan paused for a second wondering how to tell the rest of the story. She felt shy because of what had almost happened to her at the hands of Paulo.

"Well wight before Parthenia sank twou of the men came to the boat. Wyan couldn't help because he'd been knocked out and my mother and I didn't know what to do. The boat had holes in it from the gunfire, there was water inside and both Wiwwy and Quifton had been shot. Anyway, one of the men from the boat that had been chasing us came below with a knife and tied my mother's hands and then tore off most of my clothes," Jan colored in embarrassment then continued.

"I think he was planning on raping me. I know he planned on kwilling us both. But even though Quifton had been shot and could hardly move, he jumped across the cabin and attacked the man."

"That was very brave..."

"Bwut that wasn't all; even as he did that, the man stabbed him, over and over! But Quifton never gave up, not until he tore the man's throat out." Chris was stunned thinking of all the implications of Jan's story and tried to envision the terror she must have felt and the long-term effects to her of witnessing such a brutal death. The matter of fact way she related the gruesome story frightened him also. It was as if it were simply a story; something that had happened to somebody else and he wondered at the effect her experience would have on her in the coming years. That one experience alone would screw up most kids and he knew that Jan must have dealt with a lot more living with her mother when she was actively taking drugs. It shouldn't have been a surprise to anyone that she'd driven her bike in front of a car the way she had. He thought back to when she'd cut herself in the bathroom too. He hadn't said anything at the time but when he'd looked at the broken glass on the floor and listened to her story, it hadn't made sense, and one of the larger pieces of glass had her bloody fingerprints on it as though she'd picked it up after she'd cut herself. He wondered what she might have done with it if she'd been alone in the house at the time. He made a sudden decision.

"Jan?"

"Yes."

"Would you like that puppy?"

She stopped petting him, smiled, and then just as quickly sighed and got a wayward look in her eyes.

"Oh yes, I'd wuv this puppy very much but Tory and Wyan said I won't be able to get a dog until we get settled again and have a place of our own. But thank ou for offering."

"I think you need this little guy right now in your life and I can't think of a better parent for him. I'm going to talk to your mother and Ryan. I think we can work something out, even if we have to keep him here for awhile."

Jan started to tear up. "Ou weally mean it?"

"Yes, I really do. This will be your dog. Do I have to ask what you'll name him?"

Jan gathered the puppy to her chest, hugged him tightly, looked up at Chris and simply shook her head.

"I'll bring it up with them. Until then let's keep this between us, OK?"

"OK, thwank you Chris."

Chris left the room feeling better about his gift to Jan than anything that had occurred in his life for a long time and went out to the kitchen to begin breakfast for the four of them.

Ryan hobbled down about 20 minutes later. "Smells good."

"Help yourself," Chris offered and looked up from his paper. "Tory up?"

"Yes, she'll be right down. She wants to get going as soon as possible. She's afraid she's going to lose her courage."

"Ryan, I know I shouldn't have done this without talking with the two of you first, but I gave Jan one of the puppies."

Ryan stopped pouring his coffee in midstream and looked over towards him. Chris continued before he could object.

"We got talking this morning and she told me the story of what your dog Clifton did on the boat and then I started thinking how much she's been through and how lonely it's going to be for her in the coming weeks, and well, I couldn't help myself. She really needs a friend right now." Ryan started to speak again but Chris continued.

"I told her she could keep it here with my dogs until you guys get settled."

Ryan finished pouring his coffee and sat down at the kitchen table. "You've thought of everything haven't you?"

"I tried."

"Oh shit, I'm not even going to pretend I'm mad. With everything else that's going on, a puppy is small potatoes, and you're right, she really does need a friend right now and something full of life. We've just got to square it with Bill and Stephanie, but something tells me that won't be a problem."

"What won't be a problem?" Tory had walked in while they were talking.

Chris and Ryan exchanged looks. "Chris gave Jan one of the puppies. Do you think Bill and Stephanie would mind taking on two boarders? Chris said she could keep it here if there's a problem, you know, until we get settled."

Tory didn't have to think long either before answering. "All we can do is ask. I was going to call them right now anyway and let them know what time you'll be bringing Jan by. Let's find out."

Tory poured a coffee for herself before going over to the phone. Ryan noticed the tremor in her hand. "How're you doing?" he asked.

"I'm alright, but I'll be glad once we get there. I want to get this whole thing started so it can be over." As she reached for the phone Jan walked in with the puppy in her arms and stood silently to the side petting him.

"Hey Steph, Tory. Pretty good, probably around midafternoon. Is that a problem? No, good. Listen, there's one other thing I've got to ask you and please just say no if it's a problem because we can make other arrangements, but I was wondering, how would you feel if Jan brought a puppy with her? She's absolutely fallen in love with one of Chris' litter and he offered it to her, but he also offered to keep it here until we get settled if it's a problem." Tory listened for several seconds with no expression on her face. "Uh huh, I understand. OK, they'll be by around three. I love you too. Bye." Tory hung up the phone and before saying anything, casually reached for her coffee cup.

"Well?" the other three asked simultaneously.

Tory took a long sip then placed the cup slowly back on the counter and finally looked up and broke into a big smile. "They said it wouldn't be a problem."

"Yes!" Jan sighed and hugged Tory with the puppy jammed between them.

Forty minutes later Tory zipped her bag closed thinking that she should have made some time to do some clothes shopping. The small, soft bag contained only four changes of clothes, two of which she'd borrowed from Stephanie. The last thing she did before heading downstairs was to remove her Valium stash from one of the side pockets of the bag. She knew they'd search everything thoroughly for drugs and alcohol when she was admitted. Even mouthwash would be confiscated because of the alcohol it contained. She stood there for a long time debating as to what to do with the rest. While she debated, she tipped two into her hand and quickly swallowed them. She was loathe to throw the rest away. Despite her confident front with Ryan and Jan she wasn't at all sure that she possessed the inner strength and resources to face her own weaknesses and shortcomings in the coming weeks. Yes, she would go to treatment and give it another try, but deep down, she despised herself and had almost no confidence in the outcome. She paced the room for several minutes doing the mental gymnastics of an addict headed for rehab and finally arrived at a compromise and opened her bag again looking for a yellow legal pad she'd packed. After finding it she tipped ten of the Valium into her hand and using the blunt end of a pen pushed them one by one up into the spine at the top of the pad where the sheets tore off. When she finished, she turned to the mirror above the dresser.

'Why did you just do that?' But she knew the question was academic and whispered the reply. "Because I'm a goddamn addict, and addicts leave themselves an out, that's why." Two minutes later she was in the kitchen projecting an enthusiasm she didn't feel. "You guys ready?"

Jan and Ryan looked at each other, then Ryan answered.

"I guess so."

Chris got up also. "I'll carry your bag out."

They said their goodbyes outside before getting into Chris' Jeep. Tory reached up and took his face in her hands and looked him squarely in the eyes. "Thank you for everything."

He put his hands on her shoulders. "You're welcome. Be gentle with yourself."

His simple statement touched her. That was, after all, why she was going to the treatment center. "Thanks, I'll try. You be careful too and take care of that guy." She nodded her head in Ryan's direction. "He's very special to me."

"I will."

"I mean it." Tory held his stare longer than necessary to emphasize the point.

"OK."

She kissed him quickly on the cheek. "OK guys, let's go."

Ryan shook his hand next. "Thanks, we'll stop back for the puppy on our way back and then I'll run Jan over to Bill and Steph's."

"No hurry. See you in a month Tory!" Chris yelled to the departing car.

The treatment center Tory had chosen was in a rural setting in central New Hampshire and housed almost 150 patients in a modern, sprawling, two-story complex tucked into the pines. It abutted a picturesque, partially frozen lake. Their standard program was 30 days of inpatient treatment (for those who could afford it) followed by weekly outpatient

213

sessions at satellite centers for two additional months after release. For patients who suffered from chronic relapses they frequently kept them longer and referred many of them to halfway houses at the conclusion of their stay. Tory knew all this because she'd been through the system before. As they got north of Boston a light snow began to fall and Jan dozed off in the back seat lulled by the sound of the tires on the road and the warmth of the heater.

"Nervous?" Ryan asked.

Tory was alternately crossing and uncrossing her legs and worrying a strand of hair. She sighed and nodded her head in reply without looking at him.

"It's been 10 years for me, but you know, I've made this trip myself. I know what's going on in your head." Ryan looked over towards her as he spoke and reached over to put a hand on the back of her head. "It's gonna work out."

She nodded again not really believing him and tried to hold herself together. She felt like she was going to explode.

"You're worth it," he added.

Tory's eyes filled at his last comment and she buried her head in her hands and quietly cried for a few minutes. He continued to stroke her hair.

"You're doing the best you can."

"Just leave it Ryan," she whispered.

And he did for the next hour, both of them lost in their own thoughts, mesmerized by the drone of their tires on the road and the snow hurtling towards the windshield. He turned off I-95 onto their exit ramp and Jan stirred in the back seat and stretched. "Ow much farther Wyan?" she asked in a sleepy voice.

"Another 20 to 30 minutes I think," Ryan replied. "Anyone want to stop to use the bathroom or anything?"

They were approaching a small intersection that had a gas station on one corner and a nondescript rural roadhouse that offered everything from breakfast in the morning to line dancing in the evening. There was a semi on the side and several beat up pickups in the front.

"Turn in here." Tory ordered without looking at him.

Ryan was skeptical of the quality of the food they were likely to find inside but said nothing and did as instructed. He suspected there would probably be several motorcycles outside if it weren't snowing. As they rolled to a halt Tory exited without a word to either of them. Ryan turned off the key and exchanged looks with Jan in the sudden silence.

"Wats amatter with her?" Jan asked.

"I don't know, nervous, upset, pissed off. A lot, I guess. Let's just go with the flow, we're almost there and it's going to be awhile before she sees us again. Things are moving pretty fast and she probably wants a little time to collect her thoughts."

They took a minute to put on their coats against the cold snow that swirled outside the car and entered the dark restaurant a minute later. Ryan let his eyes adjust for a few seconds and saw Tory at a rear table. She was staring at a drink. Ryan sat down next to her without commenting on the iceless clear liquid that sat in a martini glass in front of her. Jan took the seat on the other side of the small booth. Tory continued staring at the drink as if neither of them were there and finally tossed the liquid back in one smooth gulp before signaling the waitress across the room for another.

"Don't you two have any comment?" she asked, clearly ready for a confrontation.

"I don't." Ryan replied and looked over at Jan. "You Jan?"

She shook her head and Ryan turned back to Tory.

"Do you want to eat something also, or is this just a beverage stop? I don't imagine the food's very good here."

She looked at him for several seconds confused that neither one of them wanted to challenge her. "What, no moralizing, or advice, or concern from either one of you?"

Ryan shook his head and put his arm around her. "You're doing enough of that for all of us. And besides I think I did the same thing myself 10 years ago."

The waitress set the fresh glass in front of Tory. "You guys gonna eat?"

Tory was raising the second drink to her lips as the waitress spoke and put it back down before drinking.

"Oh fuck it! This isn't going to work. Let's just go."

Ryan looked up. "I guess we'll just take a check."

Forty minutes later they turned into an as yet unplowed parking lot and after fishtailing several times finally crunched to a halt in front of the main building of The Birches treatment center and sat for several seconds listening as the now quiet engine began to tick its way to the cooler temperature of the outside air. After bundling back into their coats, they trekked through the powdery snow up to the front door. Ryan carried the single bag that contained all of Tory's clothing.

"When you come up to visit you have to bring me some new clothes. There isn't much in there."

"I'll get you a nice ski parka too. Christ, it's cold."

Ryan held open the first of two sets of glass doors at the entrance and the three of them stomped and scraped the snow off their feet through grates built into the floor. An overhead heater blew down on them and quickly melted the snow on the tops of their heads. Ryan reached around Tory and opened the second set of double glass doors that led into a waiting area filled with comfortable furniture and professionally maintained plants. After looking around, the three of them stood self-consciously in front of a glassed-in receptionist who looked up from her keyboard as they entered. She slid open the glass with what seemed an overly friendly smile on her face. "Can I help you?"

"Yes. I'm Tory McCane, and I'm here for a cleaning and my six-month check-up," Tory offered with a straight face.

"I'm sorry?" The receptionist asked, clearly confused.

Ryan and Jan exchanged looks and then burst out laughing, glad for a break in the tension that they all felt.

"She's here to check in for her chronic drug and alcohol use." Ryan finally managed. "And you!" pointing to Tory, "Be good or you're going to get thrown out before you get in."

"I'm sorry, I know I've got to be here, but shit! How did I end up in a place like this again?" Tory's eyes filled and she banged her forehead several times softly on Ryan's shoulder in mock frustration. Jan reached out and put her arm around her.

"You know Jan, you're almost as tall as me? Shit, my whole life is passing before me and I'm missing it."

216

The receptionist passed a clipboard through the window. "When you're ready just fill all this out. After you're done, I'll take you through into the detox. What are you in for Mrs. McCane?"

"Alcohol, cocaine and Valium although it's been a week since I had any coke."

"How much Valium and alcohol have you been doing?"

Tory averted her eyes from Jan and Ryan. "I guess 80 to 100 milligrams a day and not much alcohol. I only slipped about five days ago."

"Well, your detoxification shouldn't take more than two days at that level. We'll have you in the residence section in no time. How'll you be paying?"

"Check."

"You're aware that our full 30-day inpatient program runs $25,000?"

Tory nodded.

"And that we require full payment, in advance?"

"Yes." Tory reached into the soft bag at her feet and took out her checkbook. Twenty minutes later she'd finished all the requisite paperwork and stood uncomfortably before Ryan and Jan shifting her weight from foot to foot.

"I guess there's not much more to say. I'll miss you guys."

Jan hugged her tightly. "I'll miss ou too Mom. And don't wowy about me and Quifton. We'll be fine with Bill and Stephanie."

"I won't sweetie. You're the sane one in this family."

Jan kissed her on the cheek and hugged her again before turning to Ryan. "Why don't ou give me the keys and I'll wait for you in the car Wyan?"

They both watched as Jan exited the anteroom and put her shoulder to the outer door. The fury of what was now a full blizzard whistled briefly through the gap in the doors closest to them as Jan exited and they turned to each other.

"My girl is so mature. she's not a little kid anymore. Make sure you and Stephanie get her set up with some sort of counseling before you take off if you can. She's got a lot of crap to work through mostly thanks to her mom. Have you decided what exactly you're going to do yet?" she asked.

Ryan shook his head.

She took his chin in her hand and tipped his head down till their foreheads were touching. "Don't forget, as much as I hate this man Edward, I love you more. I don't want to lose you as a result. I don't believe I'll make it without knowing you're going to be there for me when I get out. So, don't get yourself killed and don't worry about money. Use whatever you have to out of the account. If whatever you decide looks too dangerous, then walk away." Tory paused for a second. "I know what I'm saying is a mixed message, but I love you Ryan and getting even won't be worth anything if you aren't around to rebuild a life with after."

"I know."

Ryan embraced her noting how much weight she'd lost since Willy's death. In spite of her almost frail feel, she was warm in his arms and he tried to drink in her heat and savor it. "I'll come see you as soon as they'll let me."

"I'm not sure I want you to come up until I'm better. I mean I want to see you, shit, I don't want you to leave even now. But once I start this thing the only way I can make it work is if I shift all my focus onto me, and I want to get better for us. Does that make sense?"

"Yeah, it does, but I still want to see you. We'll work it out. Call me when you can. Chris said we won't be taking our cell phones with us because he doesn't want to leave a digital track of where we might go, but you can always leave a message with Bill and Stephanie. I'll check in with them regularly. We may be out of town for a week or more anyway depending on what we decide to do about Edward."

They kissed a last time and Tory stood with her nose pressed against the glass and watched as Ryan made his way through the snow to Chris's Cherokee. She continued watching as he and Jan exited the parking lot in a cloud of powdery snow. Only when the taillights disappeared around the corner did she turn from the door and officially enter the treatment facility as a patient; the first order of business being the mandatory search of her clothing and belongings before she changed into paper slippers and a hospital jammy. She was so depressed and detached as they processed her that she didn't even notice as the nurse passed over the yellow legal pad.

End of Part II

PREVIEW of PART III

Chapter 1

Edward was disappointed that the hit on Ryan had not come off as planned but he also took a perverse satisfaction in the knowledge that at least he'd terrified them again. He was particularly pleased with the attempted rape of the woman and when he spoke with Peter over the phone several hours after, had him describe the rape scene several times over and agreed to pay the second half of his fee despite their failure to actually kill them. He loved the image of Ryan being held at knifepoint, helpless and forced to watch as his woman was degraded. He realized that there really wasn't any justification for his obsession with the couple, but it was something to do and left him with an illusion of power and control that he was steadily losing to the drugs. Ryan's threat to come after him seemed laughable and after dismissing the possibility outright decided to leave the couple alone for the time being. His future with Mr. Slade and the organization was tenuous at best and he knew they would put a contract out on his life if they felt he was jeopardizing them. The money he'd deposited around the world would do him little good if the people Slade worked for decided his usefulness was over. He resigned himself to laying low for the time being. Later, if an opportunity presented itself, he would finish the couple.

Rip Converse

Chapter 2

Edward's fate and the people deciding it were closer than he knew. One hundred and sixty miles south on a small private island 12 miles west of Key West, two unlikely individuals were debating his future. To all outward appearances they resembled two aging remnants of the '60s caught in a time warp. Basel and Walter would have been computer nerds if they'd been born 20 years later, but they hadn't and had instead spent their formative years smoking pot and attending rock concerts. Between them they had spent more than 12 years at various colleges, but neither had ever graduated with a degree. That was not to say that their education was totally wasted. What they had walked away with after their decade-plus-two of higher learning, were fat bank accounts totaling tens of millions of dollars and an equally valuable list of contacts around the world. They were not a part of any known cartel. They were independents who had set up distribution and sales in eight countries. They operated below everyone's radar and simply pretended to be agents of a cartel when it suited their needs. When increased state and federal interdiction knocked the stuffing out of the U.S.-grown marijuana market, they were well positioned to take a major role in the cocaine trade that replaced it. After that they branched out into crack and methamphetamine and ultimately fentanyl as the markets and demands changed. Neither used hard drugs but both had continued to smoke marijuana heavily over the years and the paranoia that resulted had served them well. They had no permanent home, changed their names regularly and were never present at the transaction level, preferring instead to manipulate things from a distance.

"So, just how lucky do we feel Basel old buddy?" Walter asked, purposefully mispronouncing his name so that it sounded like the herb rather than the town in northern Switzerland that his parents had thoughtlessly named him after. He passed a large, billowing, Jamaican spliff to his business partner of almost 40 years.

"Why're you trying to piss me off today?"

Walter snickered at his own joke despite the fact that he'd used it thousands of times over the years.

"I mean what were your parents thinking when they picked that beauty?"

"Are you completely dense? How many million times do I have to tell you. That's where my Mom thought I was conceived. With a name like Walter I wouldn't talk."

"Fuck you. Your dear sweet mother probably wiped her mouth and then itched her cunt after blowing the entire Swiss Army."

"Jesus you're disgusting. I mean how do you think up things like that? Were you born this way or did the retardation set in slowly?"

Walter took the joint back from him.

"So, shall we have Edward eliminated, or not?" Basel asked.

Walter wrinkled his brow disappointed that Basel had turned the conversation back to business just when he was getting on a roll.

"Shit, I don't know. Despite all the problems Slade reported, the guy did save the load."

"But he cost us a $12-million ship!"

"Nobody's perfect."

Basel shook his head knowing further discussion would be pointless. Walter was too stoned to care. Both sat silently for the next few minutes enjoying the sunset.

"We'll need a ballsy driver for the "Big Banana." We may want to use him for that." Walter mused out loud. "You got to admit, the guy's got huge stones. After, then maybe we'll retire him to spic heaven."

"Why do you insist on using that stupid name Big Banana?"

"Because amigo this will be the monster Chiquita of all our capers, $200 million in pure fentanyl. John Holmes is going to roll over in his grave when he sees the size of this thing."

Rip Converse

Chapter 3

Ryan dropped Jan and Clifton at Bill and Stephanie's later that afternoon. They'd stopped at a pet supply store on the way and gotten a crate, a bed, bowls and several dog toys. Ryan decided on the drive back that the more truth he mixed into his lies about his upcoming plans and whereabouts in his explanation to Bill and Stephanie, the better.

After introducing them to Clifton and setting up an area for the puppy in the back hall he sat down with Bill and Stephanie at their kitchen table and he explained that he and Chris planned on driving to Florida together in three days' time.

"Why are you going to Florida? Why can't you just file the claim from here?" Bill asked.

"It's not an issue of filing. If that's all it was, I could. The problem is that they're contesting the claim due to the unusual circumstances and I feel I'll have a better chance of a settlement if I'm there in person."

"Don't they have an office up here?"

"Yes, but maritime claims are arbitrated in Fort Lauderdale."

"It doesn't make much sense to me. I mean if we had a loss on our house I can't imagine having to go out of state to get the case settled or heard."

Ryan had shrugged and raised his eyebrows. "I guess boats are different," he'd replied lamely. He knew they weren't completely buying his story and it wasn't just because of the insurance claim. Although they didn't come right out and say it he knew they were also wondering why he would choose such a time to leave Jan on her own, and that hurt. "You're just going to have to trust me. It's important that I do this. I don't expect to be gone more than a week or 10 days at the outside."

Chris had decided they'd leave in three days. Even though it was perfectly legal to transport the guns they were taking with them on a commercial flight, they'd have to declare them as checked baggage and that left a paper trail. That left driving as the only alternative and they decided to drive straight through with only one motel stop. After Ryan dropped Jan off he returned to Chris' farm and over the next few days he practiced with both rifle and pistol until his accuracy and level of comfort with the weapons improved dramatically. On the third day Chris returned from his barracks with the surveillance equipment he'd talked about "borrowing." There was a lot of it and it all looked expensive.

"Didn't you have to sign all that stuff out or something? They can't just leave expensive gear like that lying around."

"They don't, but it's not a big deal."

Ryan hadn't thought much about it at the time when Chris had said he could get access to everything they'd need, but seeing it all on the kitchen table in individual cases made him think again. There was no way the gear Chris spread out in front of him would not be missed and the idea of Chris burning all his "real world" bridges behind him was unsettling.

Ryan opened the case nearest to him. Inside was what looked like a ray gun from outer space.

"What in the hell is this."

"It's a laser microphone. If there are two people having a conversation in a house that you want to hear, you turn it on and point it at the nearest window. It picks up the vibration of their voices off the glass. It's like two tin cans with a string attached although the string in this case is the laser beam." "This is some serious shit."

Ryan opened another one.

"And what are these?"

"Infinity bugs. You can put them anywhere in a house or in the phones and they broadcast on several bands to this multiplex receiver which, by the way, must be located within a few hundred yards of the house."

"And these?"

"Tracking devices for cars, boats, people, whatever. They're good for a couple of miles if you have the proper receiver."

"And we do of course?"

Chris nodded.

"And this thing?"

"That's a Stingray. It's similar to a cell phone scanner but more. It simulates a cell phone tower and harvests the phone numbers of any cell phones in the immediate area that interrogate it."

"Shit Chris, there's no way you can take all this stuff and not have it missed."

Chris shrugged his shoulders. Ryan had agreed to go along with his offer to get the equipment because it would save them time, trouble and money when they got to Miami, but in light of the volume and sophistication of the equipment he'd brought, Chris's cavalier attitude concerned him. A lot. He seemed too willing to leave his present life behind. Tory's earlier concerns about trusting him echoed loudly in his mind.

"I'm getting a bad feeling here Chris."

"Why?"

"Besides stopping Edward, I thought one of our goals was to be able to pick up our lives again after it's over. When you *told* your lieutenant that you were taking some time off, that was one thing. But if they connect you with stolen police property you can just forget ever going back to your job. Doesn't that mean anything to you?" Chris didn't say anything.

"Shit. I was afraid of this. Listen, I'm not going on some suicide mission. Is that what this is to you?"

"Of course not!"

"I hear the words but I'm not sure I believe you."

"I told you, I don't need the job for the money and my earlier idealism is over. It was a noble idea when I started but I realize now it's bullshit. I don't plan on returning to the job, no matter what happens."

"Job or not that's no reason to ask for trouble. If this equipment is available through legitimate private sources anyway let's just do it that way. Money's not an issue."

"We already have it! Case closed!"

Ryan paced around in front of him for a few seconds and finally let out a deep breath acquiescing. "I guess there's no point in fighting about it. You're right, it's already done. I'm just thinking about you; I don't want this to be some one-way street you go down." Ryan put his arm around his shoulders in a conciliatory gesture.

Chris relaxed some. "I'm sorry. I didn't mean to blow up. It's just that I've been thinking about doing something like this for so long and feeling so helpless that now that we're close I just want to get on with it!"

He sounded sincere but Ryan wondered if the words were heartfelt or for his benefit. He couldn't shake the feeling that this trip was something that Chris had no intention of coming back from. Regardless, he felt as though his own choices were limited. If he backed out now and did nothing, Tory, Jan, and his own life would remain in jeopardy. And whenever he thought back to Willy, Clifton and his Parthenia his heart would start to pound again and he saw black. No, he was in it now and determined. He just hoped that he could control Chris's more self-destructive impulses.

"Listen, while you finish packing can I use your car again for a couple of hours? I told Jan I'd take her out for dinner tonight before we leave. I'm also going to see if I can't get through to Tory tonight on the phone and see how she's making out."

"I think it's a good sign that we haven't heard from her," Chris offered.

"I know. They usually bail in the first week if they're going to." Ryan was referring to the fact that many patients who go into treatment find the first few days so uncomfortable that they think of a million excuses why they don't need to be there and often petition their families to let them come home.

"Anne did that a few times and I would fall for it. She always sounded like she was in so much pain and I would drive to whatever place she was in at that time and pick her up. I knew it was wrong but I just couldn't stand to hear her in pain. Of course, she'd usually feel so guilty about leaving that she'd use again by the next day."

Ryan nodded his understanding and after showering and changing left for Bill and Stephanie's to pick up Jan.

***

In truth, Tory had yet to begin the hard part. They had given her Librium for the first two days to ease her withdrawal (which had been minimal) and she'd spent most of the time reading and watching TV in the common room set aside for detox patients. She left her Valium hidden in the legal pad and two days after she entered the detox the head nurse, Marge, decided to release Tory into the general population of the treatment center.

"Tory, you're going to be in C wing in room number 24. That's on the second floor in this building. You'll be sharing the room with three others. Your treatment leader's name is Gail Reed who won't be back in the building till tomorrow morning but if you have any questions tonight you can ask Michael Stone who oversees the night staff or one of your roommates. They're about to start dinner now so I'll walk you down to the dining room and we'll see if we can't dig up one or two of your roommates. After dinner there's a half-hour break, and then the mandatory AA meeting. Any questions?"

Tory no longer had the support of any drugs in her system. She hadn't bothered to shower in two days, her hands shook unsupported, and in general she felt as low and vulnerable as a human can. Everything was gone again, her self-respect, her children, a home. She was acutely aware that the only thing that separated her at that moment from a million homeless people across the country was the money her grandfather had left her. She felt like crawling back into bed and pulling the covers over her head. She knew they wouldn't let her do that though. For the next 28 days her every waking moment and the time she slept would be controlled by no-nonsense people like Margaret the nurse in front of her. She shyly nodded her head in ascent.

Like 50 percent of the staff Marge was a past rehab patient herself. She dropped her officious manner long enough to sit down next to Tory and put a comforting arm around her shoulder. "I was here once myself. Surprised?

"I got caught with my hand in the narcotic locker one day at the hospital where I worked. I'd had a habit for years and hidden it pretty well till then. I mean sometimes I'd have to clean up for a while or shift jobs but I was never confronted. But that day, I needed a fix so bad I took a chance I shouldn't have. Oh, they'd suspected someone for a long time, but at a lot of places it's like they don't want to know; the liability issues and all. But you know? I think I wanted to get caught. I was so tired of lying and scamming and calling in sick and feeling guilty all the time. Deep down I was always afraid I'd kill someone through my negligence. Anyway, I ended up in here the same day as a patient. It was either that or be formally charged, which neither the hospital nor I wanted. They had me in the detox unit for two weeks! That's how long it took to get all the shit I was taking out of my system. When my head did finally start to clear and I realized where I was and the implications of everything I'd been doing, they had to put me on suicide watch. I kept thinking of all the patients I'd mistreated; wrong dosages, wrong medications. A couple of times I even stole pain medication from patients for myself. And that was just what was going on at my job. My family is another horror story. So, no matter how bad a person you think you are, I promise you, there are a lot of us in here who were just as bad or worse. It *will* get better if you just put one foot in front of the other and follow directions. We'll do most of your thinking for you in the next few days."

Tory looked up with tears in her eyes. "You don't understand what's happened, what I've done..."

Marge interrupted her. "Honey, believe me. Whatever it was it couldn't be any worse than what I did to end up here. Try to remember. You're not a bad person, you're a sick person trying to get well. Being here is the beginning and it's where every one of us started. Today may be your worst day. Until now you've had your drugs and booze to comfort you. You'll learn some new skills in here and do just fine."

Marge hugged her. "Enough of that. We need to get you down to the cafeteria before they shut the line. You can leave your bag here and pick it up after dinner. Why don't you get out of those paper slippers and hospital gown and throw on some jeans? That way you'll feel less like a hospital patient."

Tory took a deep breath and smiled at her joke before going over to her bag to pull out a pair of pants. As she rummaged through her bag she ran her hand across the legal pad and immediately thought how much better she would feel if she had a couple of the Valium. But Marge continued to stand in front of her making that impossible.

After walking out of the detox unit they walked down a long corridor that led past a common room with a big TV and then past a small auditorium and gift shop that sold magazines, candy, cigarettes, toiletries and a few gift items. Past that on the other side of the hall she could see an Olympic size swimming pool through the glass insert in the door and finally a larger common room that was full of overstuffed chairs and sofas. At the very end of the hall through large swinging glass doors stood the cafeteria. After the relative quiet of the detox unit Tory felt assaulted by the sudden sound of more than a 100 people all trying to talk at once. She stopped, momentarily overwhelmed. "I don't know if I can eat anything. I might get sick," she offered, hoping she might just be able to go on to her room.

Marge put an arm around her shoulders again and steered her gently forward. "You don't have to eat tonight. Just grab a soda, or dessert and coffee if you like, but I do want to introduce you to your roommates."

Knowing the routine from previous treatment centers didn't make it any easier and reluctantly she let herself be led into the busy cafeteria. Marge looked around for several moments before steering her towards a table to the side. At one end sat two women alternately bending towards each other and then rearing back in laughter at some shared joke. A half-finished tray lay to the right of one of them. One was olive skinned with tight black curls and a bad complexion, the other was about 30 pounds overweight and had graying hair in a butch cut. Tory's first thought was that they were probably gay and that both had done prison stints at one time or another. The Latina had the letters S U C K tattooed across her knuckles which looked like it had been done with a safety pin and pen ink and Tory's sense of dread increased threefold at the prospect of sharing a room with these two.

"Where's Amanda?" Marge asked looking around the room.

"You mean Miss Muffy?" the Latina laughed. "I think she's in the can powdering her nose or something."

"I want you both to meet your new roommate. Her name is Victoria McCane."

The heavier one laughed out loud and shook her hand in midair snapping her fingers as she did so in a parody. "Victoria! What, are you royalty or something?"

"Jesus, you two are a pair, why don't you pretend you're humans for one second and make her feel at home. If my memory serves me neither of you two were feeling so chipper a few weeks back when you came through that door. She goes by the name of Tory," she paused long enough for her admonition to sink in.

"Tory, I want you to meet Isabelle, her friends call her Izzy, and Diane, otherwise known as Di. Don't be put off by their tough manner. They're both actually quite nice once you get to know them."

Tory stuck out her hand between them which both low fived in some sort of inner city greeting.

"She's right you know," offered Di. "We aren't nearly as mean as we seem. We're just funnin wid you. Why don't you go get yourself a tray and we'll make some room for you."

"Thanks," Tory replied grateful that the introduction was over and turned to Marge. "I'll be back later to get my bag. Thanks for your help."

"You're welcome, and if you have any problems feel free to come by the detox and talk with me. Especially if it has anything to do with these two," she added pointing to Izzy and Di.

"Di, tell Amanda I want to see her in my office sometime tomorrow."

Di touched her forehead in a mock salute as Marge turned to leave. Tory watched her walk across the room. Marge stopped several times to chat with other patients. The woman's story had touched her, not so much in what she'd done, but what she seemed to be able to do now. She had a sense of dignity and purpose that Tory envied.

After sliding her tray past the cafeteria offerings Tory settled on a piece of apple pie and a cup of decaf coffee and returned to Di and Izzy's table. The seat next to Izzy where the half-finished tray had been before now had someone in front of it and Tory sat where Di had cleared for her next to the overweight woman.

"If she puts her hand on my thigh I'm out of here!" thought Tory as she took her seat.

Tory stiffened as Di did just that.

"Tory, this is Amanda." She bent closer in mock secrecy. "Otherwise known as Missy to her country club friends." Tory looked across the table at the striking young woman across from her. She appeared to be in her mid-20ss and was dressed as though she were heading out to lunch at a small country inn rather than a cafeteria line in a rehab center. She had on tailored wool slacks, turtleneck top and a cashmere sweater tied casually around her neck. Her most striking feature was her breasts which were Mary Tyler Moore-like in appearance beneath the tight-fitting, ribbed, turtleneck and Tory couldn't help wondering if they'd been augmented by a plastic surgeon. She was model thin and that heightened their size relative to her frame. She had fair skin and the kind of royal blue eyes that men fell into. The hair framing her face was fine and almost white blonde. The only thing that marred her beauty was a strange discoloration of her teeth that Tory noticed when she smiled back at her. It was like the enamel had been washed away in places from them.

"Cut the shit, you big ole dyke." She held her hand across the table. "Hi, Amanda Babbitt, and don't listen to anything either of these two say. Watch your privates around Di and your purse around Izzy." She bent closer as Di had in mock secrecy. "You know, Puerto Rican gypsy blood and all, she really can't help herself."

Tory didn't know whether to laugh or cry and suddenly doubted very seriously if she'd be able to spend one night, let alone 30 of them, in a room with these three. Her expression betrayed her.

"I'm sorry. Shit guys, we've scared the heck out of this poor girl. I didn't mean to take it so far. We're not at all like we're making each other out to be. I'd trust these two with my life and I think they'd say the same. We're just play-acting."

Izzy interrupted Amanda. "Seriously, we three are like sisters to each other and now that you be sharing a room with us, we all hope you'll feel the same. We watch out over each other, get in each other's face when needed, laugh together and cry together. Christ, we even pray together."

Di removed her hand from Tory's leg and put it around her shoulders. "That's right. One for all and all for one in our room. Shit, between the three of us we need three brains just to make one decision anyway. Just think of what we'll be capable of with a fourth girl." The three friends started laughing at Di's joke. Tory finally joined in feeling some relief.

After dinner all three went back with her to the detox unit to pick up her bag and then got her settled in their shared room. After, all four walked together to the mandatory AA meeting, stopping once on the way in the common lounge to have a smoke. There were at least 30 people in the room smoking and even though the smoke hurt her eyes and smelled terrible, Tory felt a warm sense of camaraderie in the room. She'd forgotten how comforting it was to be around others who were as sick as she.

After the AA meeting, Tory separated herself from the other three and went up to the room to unpack her few things. After she finished, she lay down on her bed with the yellow legal pad in her lap trying to decide whether to take one of the Valiums. She surprised herself when she decided not and put the pad back in her bedside draw and returned to the common room to sit with the other three and watch TV.

"Might as well save them for when I really need it," she thought to herself and zoned out on the "X Files" like the rest of the people in the room who were tired of thinking after a long day of therapy, group counseling, AA meetings and workshops. It was the time of day when everyone's thoughts turned to their families and lovers and people on the outside.

Tory was the last out of the bathroom after they all returned to the room and was surprised to see all three of them on their knees at the foot of their respective beds praying when she came back in. Feeling awkward she quietly went over to her own bed and got beneath the covers. The other three wrapped up their prayer session with the shortened version of the Serenity Prayer that she knew well from attending AA meetings.

God grant me the serenity to accept the things I cannot change
The courage to change the things that I can
And the wisdom to know the difference.

As soon as they finished, the playful banter started again and they weren't about to let Tory slide off to sleep without a few jibes.

"What's a matter girl, don't you have a higher power?" Di asked Tory.

Tory had hoped that by leaving her eyes closed they might leave her alone. "Not anymore. And leave me alone would you? I'd kinda like to catch a few winks before they start in on me tomorrow."

"And just how do you expect you're gonna stay sober when you get outta here without some kind of God? You obviously haven't done too good on your own," Izzy responded ignoring her request for peace.

"I thought you guys were gonna be my friends. You know, one for all and all for one and all that crap. Can I suggest that this might be a good subject to drop?"

"Honey, we aren't gonna beat you to death with this, but it was all of our best efforts that got us here in the first place. If you gonna be serious about your recovery you best start thinking about passing control to someone other than yourself. And that's all I've got to say on the subject."

"The God I used to pray to isn't worth the effort," Tory mumbled before turning away from the three.

Her roommates all exchanged knowing glances but let the subject drop. Tory slept poorly, as did Izzy and Di. Between the three of them they must have gotten up seven or eight times during the night to use the bathroom or go down to the common lounge for a smoke. Tory concluded that she wasn't the only one with night demons and lay there thinking about Jan and Ryan and wondered how they were doing. Tomorrow she'd speak to one of the counselors about getting phone privileges and see if she couldn't call one or both. Marge had made it clear on the first day that the center wouldn't accept any incoming phone calls for patients unless it involved an emergency. So, getting phone privileges was important if she wanted to have any contact with people outside the center. She also felt slightly sick to her stomach. In what seemed like just minutes from the time she finally got to sleep there was a knock on the door and a loud female voice announced it was time to rise and shine for breakfast in 30 minutes. Izzy and Di showed no sign of movement so Tory asked Amanda if she could jump in the shower.

"Sure, go ahead. Those two usually shower in the evening. Just make sure you shake us all when you come out in case we fall back asleep. If we sleep through breakfast the group will really get on us and 'our commitment to our own recoveries.'" She said the last in a sarcastic singsong tone with air quotes. Tory smiled, liking Amanda for her sarcasm and identifying with her. In spite of her prim and proper look Tory sensed a wild side to her. She probably came from a wealthy family and had gone to good schools. In many ways Tory's life had been similar even though her parents hadn't played a large role in her life. By the time she emerged from the bathroom the other three were up and Amanda used the shower next as Izzy and Di threw on their clothes for the day. As Tory blew her hair dry she noticed that both again got to their knees and prayed again. Feeling guilty for the noise she turned off the blow dryer and listened as they finished.

"Please God, remove the desire in us to use drugs or drink and help us to know what your will is for us today and give us the power to carry that out," Izzy asked.

Di concluded. "Amen to that, and God, I know this is a little off the path but if you could find a way to make sure they serve that chocolate mousse again at dinner we would be forever grateful."

Izzy elbowed her. "You can't ask for shit like that. Don't be makin fun of the man or what we're doing here. This is serious shit."

"Sorry, I just thought I'd throw it in since we already have his attention."

Tory smiled behind their backs and thought to herself how that was one thing the treatment center would never get her to do; pray to a God again that allowed little boys to get shot in their mother's arms and people like Edward to roam the planet freely. She'd go to the meetings, do group therapy and sit through counseling, but they'd never be able to force her to pray again to God.

MAELSTROM

***

Chris purchased several large duffel bags to carry the long guns in for the trip south. Gun cases would attract the wrong attention. So, in addition to the four briefcases of surveillance equipment, they now had three duffels to pack their rifles, pistols, body armor, binoculars and spotting scope. Right before leaving Chris added two 12-gauge pump shotguns. He put stickers that read "Fragile" and "Camera Equipment" on the outside of several of the cases. An outsider looking into the back of the Cherokee would think they were photographers headed south on vacation.

At 8 the next morning the woman who'd agreed to house sit and care for the dogs in his absence arrived.

"We should be back in a week to 10 days' time if anyone calls. We've going on a diving vacation if anyone asks, and I'll call you once or twice to check for messages. Sorry I can't be more explicit about where we're going but we want to try several locations and may even fly over to Nassau for a few days if we can't get the diving we want in Florida or the Keys."

"Sounds good," the young student house sitter replied. "Have a good time and don't worry about the dogs. I'll take good care of them."

END OF PREVIEW
PART III

If you missed Part I and want to order a copy click below:
MAELSTROM PART I

Mailing List

I promise not to abuse your email address or share it with anyone else; period. I will occasionally use it to let you know about new releases, sales and occasional giveaways. If you would like to join my mailing list please send me an email at ripconverse@gmail.com with the word "add" in the subject line.

Reviews

Please leave a review of Maelstrom on Amazon if you enjoyed it. I can't tell you how important reviews are to a new author. They really help other readers find my work and increase my standing. If I can't find readers, I don't make any doe ray me and can't afford to continue writing and improving my work. I loved writing this book and hope to write many more. Thank you for taking the time to read this story. If you have questions or comments, please send me an email at ripconverse@gmail.com. I try to respond to all queries. Your feedback is important to me; both positive and negative. It's how I improve.

I'm looking for 15 readers who have an interest in reading my next work (at no charge and prior to release) who are willing to provide a review in exchange. Please write to me if you would have any interest in this.

About Me

I've been a pilot, a boat builder, a cabinetmaker, an investment banker, a publisher, a management consultant, and an accomplished builder of custom, sculpted, rocking chairs (see parkerconverse.com). Over the past 18 years I've built over 150 chairs out of exquisite figured hardwoods. Each one is unique, and custom made.

Of all the things I've done and do, perhaps my favorite is Captain. I've lived on or near the water my entire life and had my first boat at the age of 9. Over the years I've had the good fortune to have sailed in the Mediterranean, parts of the South Pacific and up and down the East Coast of the U.S. I've also made over 20 offshore passages between New England, Bermuda and the Caribbean and lived aboard a boat in the Caribbean. I worked as a charter captain in the Keys for many years and also worked as a Captain in the oil fields in the Gulf of Mexico. I love the ocean and the skills it takes to be a good Captain and I've accrued over 3,000 incident free days at sea.

Website:
RipConverse.com

Instagram.png

@rip_converse

Facebook.png

@rip.converse.10

Twitter.png

@ConverseRip

Made in the USA
Columbia, SC
10 May 2020